In The Market For Murder

ALSO BY T E KINSEY

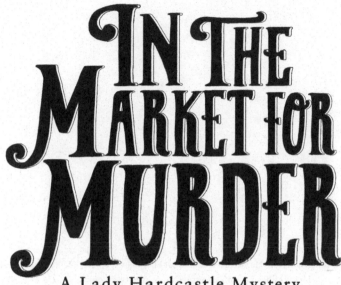

IN THE MARKET FOR MURDER

A Lady Hardcastle Mystery

T E KINSEY

THOMAS & MERCER

Text copyright © 2016 T E Kinsey
All rights reserved.

Published by Thomas & Mercer, Seattle

www.apub.com

Amazon, the Amazon logo, and Thomas & Mercer are trademarks of Amazon.com, Inc., or its affiliates.

ISBN-13: 9781503938298
ISBN-10: 1503938298

Cover design by Lisa Horton

Printed in the United States of America

1

I was pleased as Punch on that glorious spring morning when Lady Hardcastle finally said, 'Come on then, Flo, what about a nice Wednesday walk?'

It had been a difficult winter. She had seemed to recover quickly from the shooting the previous summer, but after another dangerous adventure in the autumn, she had suffered a severe relapse.

This time she had recovered much more slowly. It was only now that the spring of 1909 had arrived that both body and mind had healed sufficiently for her to feel able to recommence our regular walks through the fields, lanes and woods around our Gloucestershire home.

'I should be delighted, my lady,' I said, getting up. 'I shall fetch your coat.'

'And boots, hat, gloves and stick, please, dear,' she called as I went out into the hall. 'And a flask of brandy. And . . .'

I returned with the required items. 'Would you like me to carry you as well, my lady?'

'I say, what a good idea,' she said. 'But if you're doing that, could we pop into the village, too – we could pick up a few things from the shops.'

It was good to have her back.

We settled on the idea of a stroll into the village and set off down the lane towards the green. The trees were already in bud and I was still blissfully incapable of identifying any of them. The sunshine was weak and the temperature was struggling to reach the bearable side of chilly, but there was a definite promise in the air of the summer yet to come.

We walked slowly, with Lady Hardcastle relying rather more on her stick than I thought she would – her wound had been fully healed for quite a while. We had also been doing the gentle exercises we had learned in China to try to return the strength and flexibility that she could so easily have lost for good.

'Might I ask you a personal question, my lady?' I said as we rounded the last bend and the village green came in sight.

'What an odd thing to say,' she said. 'Of course you may.'

'That stick,' I said. 'How much do you really need it?'

'For walking? Hardly at all. Fit as a flea, me, dear thing, fit as a flea.'

'And yet . . . ?' I said.

'Ah, yes. Well. Now. You see, there's the thing. I still sort of feel I need it. For show, you understand.'

'Not entirely, my lady, no. If it's not helping you to walk, what use is it?'

'It's a sort of badge, I suppose you'd call it. People have been so kind and solicitous over the past months that I would feel something of a fraud to go skipping into the village like a schoolgirl. I felt I needed something that might reassure people that their concerns were well founded and that I really was as poorly as they thought.'

'You nearly died. Isn't that poorly enough?' I said indignantly. I could still vividly remember the long bedside vigils I shared with her brother, Harry, while we wondered whether she would ever wake.

'Yes, dear, of course,' she said, patting my arm with her free hand. 'But they didn't see the immediate aftermath, they just heard what had happened. I just feel they need a little visual clue that all was once rather serious but that it's getting slowly better.'

'I'm still not sure I understand, my lady,' I said. 'But if it makes you feel better, then by all means carry on. It makes progress a little slow, but I suppose it will make an excellent cudgel if things cut up rough.'

'That's the spirit. Though I doubt we'll meet any footpads at the butcher's.'

'I don't know, my lady,' I said. 'Them's strange folk in these rural villages. They can turn on strangers.'

She laughed. 'We're still strangers, do you think?'

'Actually, I really don't think we are any more, my lady, no.'

'I don't think so either. But just to be on the safe side, we shall avoid Mr Spratt's butcher's shop and make instead for the pub. I wonder if Old Joe would make us a cup of tea.'

'Tea, my lady? At the pub? What a peculiar notion. If you fancy tea, perhaps we should see if we can rustle up a lift from someone to go to the tea shop in Chipping Bevington?'

'You're probably right, but it's a bit of a trek just for tea. How about some nice fresh buns from Mr Holman and you can make the tea when we get home?'

'Very well, my lady.'

'Splendid. Come then, tiny servant. To the bakery.'

We made our slow progress around the green, which was still too dew-damp to walk across at our slow pace. We were just about to enter Mr Holman's bakery when we were hailed.

'I say, Emily! How wonderful to see you up and about.'

It was Lady Farley-Stroud, the local landowner's wife, whom we had known since we moved to Littleton Cotterell. Strictly speaking, Lady Hardcastle had met her thirty-six years before that – the Farley-Strouds had been friends of her parents – but she had been only four years old so she had no memory of the encounter. Gertrude, Lady Farley-Stroud, gave every appearance of being a formidable old battleaxe, but we knew another side of her. Once you got past her social armour she turned out to be a charming, amiable and ever-so-slightly dotty old lady of the sort that made for a splendid aunt but a thoroughly embarrassing mother.

'Good morning, Gertie,' said Lady Hardcastle with a smile.

'It's a joy to see you, m'dear,' said the older lady, kissing Lady Hardcastle's cheek. 'And you, too, Armstrong. Is she treating you well? Don't forget there's always a job for you up at The Grange if you tire of the dangerous life.'

'Passing well, my lady,' I said. 'She can be cruel and demanding at times, but a maid has to do her duty.'

Lady Farley-Stroud gave her hearty laugh. 'Jolly good. But now that you're back on your feet, m'dear, you really must come for dinner at The Grange. Could do with some company. Hector and I just rattle about the place. Do say you'll come.'

'I should love to, Gertie, really I should.'

'Splendid. I shall consult "the lord of the manor".'

Even I could see the ironic quotation marks hanging in the air as she said it, but there was affection in her voice. There was no doubt who really ran The Grange, but they were a charming old couple and obviously still terribly devoted to each other.

'Thank you, dear,' said Lady Hardcastle warmly. 'I shall look forward to it.'

'Splendid, splendid— I say!' she said abruptly as a thought struck her. 'I've had the most wonderful idea. Have you ever been to a cattle market?'

'A cattle market?' said Lady Hardcastle with no small amount of surprise. 'No, I honestly can't say I ever have.'

'I pop over to Chipping on market day whenever I can. It really is quite the best day out. We're selling a few head tomorrow and I thought I'd make one of my regular appearances, you know? Show the old face, what? Our estate manager will be doing all the real work, of course, but I do so love it. And we have lunch in The Hayrick with all the farmers and cattle brokers. It really is the most fun. And the language! My word, you've never heard the like. Oh, my dear, you really must come.'

Even if pressed, I'm not sure I could come up with a particularly long list of things I'd rather do less than attend a cattle market. Somehow, though, the girlish gleam in Lady Farley-Stroud's blue-grey eyes made me wonder if even I might enjoy a day out at Chipping Bevington (the town's slightly cumbersome full name) on market day.

Lady Hardcastle was clearly similarly affected. 'Well, if you put it like that, Gertie dear, how could I possibly demur?'

'Oh, my dear, how wonderful,' said Lady Farley-Stroud with quite the hugest smile on her plump, lined face. 'Please bring Armstrong, too. She'll be company for Denton. We'll make a day of it. I'll send Bert over with the motor car at eight tomorrow morning. Oh, I'm so excited.' And with another kiss on Lady Hardcastle's cheek, off she went. I watched as she met her own lady's maid, Maude Denton, coming out of Pantry's Grocery. She was obviously telling her the good news, and Maude looked over and gave me a grin.

'It seems,' said Lady Hardcastle, taking my arm and leading the way inside the bakery, 'that I have re-entered the social scene and that the two of us are committed to a day of smells, lowing and impossibly fast chatter.'

'It does rather seem that way, my lady, yes. And a pub lunch. Do you think there will be pies?'

'Oh, rather,' she said. 'I love a good pie.'

'Then you have come to the right place, my lady,' said Septimus Holman, the baker, from behind his counter. 'Welcome back. It's lovely to see you up and about. Now, what can I get you? Pie, was it?'

Market Day dawned with a clap of thunder and the sound of torrential rain clattering against the window panes.

With the car coming at eight, I had been up since before dawn to make sure that we were both dressed and breakfasted in plenty of time. But whereas it was usually the rising sun peeping through the kitchen window that signalled the true start to the day, this morning it was the apocalyptic deluge outside.

Edna and Miss Jones arrived shortly after I got up. Edna had set to work straight away, starting by lighting the fire in the morning room. Miss Jones got breakfast going.

Lady Hardcastle had originally planned to rent 'a lovely little cottage, somewhere like, oh, I don't know, Gloucestershire', perhaps with 'a thatched roof and roses growing round the door'. Instead, she had been lucky enough to secure the tenancy of a newly built house on the outskirts of the village of Littleton Cotterell. One of her old friends had had the place built for himself and his family, but when his business concerns had forced them to remain in India for another few years, he had cheerfully let the house to Lady Hardcastle so that she could look after it for him.

And so we two occupied a house built for a family of six and their household. I never really gave much thought to what advantages there might be in living in a modern house. Indeed, until Lady Hardcastle hired Edna, I had grumbled about how many rooms there were to dust and sweep. But on days like today, with the rain lashing against windows and walls, I was glad to be in something altogether more substantial than a quaint old cottage with straw for a roof. I could very well appreciate the wisdom of the third little pig as the fierce March winds threatened to huff and puff and blow even our house of bricks down.

At precisely eight o'clock, just as we were donning raincoats and galoshes in the hall, there was a ring at the doorbell. I opened it to see a damp and bedraggled Bert, with rain dripping from the peak of his cap.

'Good morning, Miss Armstrong,' he said. 'Car's here.'

'Thank you, Bert,' I said.

Lady Hardcastle poked her head round the door. 'Bert!' she said. 'You're getting drenched. Do come in for a moment, we shan't be long.'

'Very kind, my lady,' he said. 'But would you mind if I waited in the car?'

'Of course not, of course not. We shall be but a few more moments. You get into the dry.'

'Thank you, m'lady,' he said. He beetled back to the safety and comfort of his driver's seat.

'Are we all set then?' asked Lady Hardcastle as she checked her appearance in the glass.

'As we'll ever be,' I said. 'Do you have your vagabond-beating stick? We might need it today to fend off obstreperous cattle.'

'Do you think that might become necessary?'

'Well,' I said hesitantly. 'You know, my lady. Cows. Big beasts. Unruly. Dangerous.'

'Florence Armstrong,' she said gleefully, 'I do believe I've finally found something you're afraid of.'

'Wary of, my lady.'

She laughed delightedly. 'Fear not, tiny servant. I shall protect you with the Cow-Nobbling Stick of Doom.' She brandished her walking cane.

'You may very well mock, my lady,' I said. 'But—'

'May I? Oh, you're so sweet. I shall.'

I gave her my most disapproving stare.

'But come,' she said with a chuckle. 'We must brave Nature's drenching fury and hie us to market.'

We stepped out into the storm. Lady Hardcastle hurried down the path slightly more quickly than she had the day before. Bert leapt out and opened the rear door of the car for her and she bundled herself in to sit beside Lady Farley-Stroud. I wasn't far behind and managed to squeeze into the front seat with Bert and Maude. We were off.

Lady Farley-Stroud was a nervous traveller at the best of times. This meant that with more rain lashing down onto the roads than I'd seen anywhere other than India during the monsoon season, Bert was compelled to drive frustratingly slowly and with exaggerated care. It would ordinarily have sent me insane with impatience were it not for the infectious jollity of Maude Denton, Lady Farley-Stroud's lady's maid.

She and I had met the previous summer. I found her ingenious efforts at avoiding almost all work absolutely infuriating but she was extremely good company.

Maude and I chatted in the front seat, with half an ear on the conversation of our employers in the back of the motor car. The journey passed quickly, with only one near-miss with a milkman's cart to induce shrieks and earnest entreaties for caution from Lady Farley-Stroud in the back and barely suppressed giggles from Lady Hardcastle. We were soon drawing up at the top of the High Street.

Chipping Bevington is one of those little market towns that have been dotted around England since the Middle Ages, serving as the hub of local commerce. They usually have broad high streets or, in this case, a wide area at one end where market stalls magically appear on market days. Lady Farley-Stroud proudly told us that they had been hosting a cattle market on Thursdays since 1473.

There was no way through the High Street on market day so Bert let us out beside one of the small town's seven pubs, where we watched as he reversed the car carefully back up the road in search of a parking place.

The rain hadn't abated and the wind was too fierce for the umbrellas that Maude had taken from the car as we got out. With one last check that our hats were pinned firmly in place, we began to battle our way down the street.

Stallholders and shoppers alike greeted Lady Farley-Stroud with a cheerfully informal warmth. There was deference and respect, but a good deal of affection – she was clearly well liked.

The rain was cold; the wind was harsh. I was keen to have everything over and done with so that we could get indoors out of the weather, even though that would mean being in uncomfortably close proximity to a large collection of beef on the hoof.

We ducked down a small side street which led us to the livestock market. In times gone by this had been held at the bottom end of the High Street around the market cross, but there was now a purpose-built yard with covered pens and a large auction hall.

We finally made it under cover, and Lady Farley-Stroud looked around.

'Can't see Mogg,' she said absently. 'Estate manager. Supposed to be here. Denton, go and see if you can track him down, would you.'

With a bob and a 'Yes, my lady', Maude was off into the growing throng.

'I say, Gertie,' said Lady Hardcastle, 'this is fun. It's like the markets in Shanghai or Calcutta.'

'Much colder, though, m'dear,' said Lady Farley-Stroud. 'I remember when Hector and I were in Madras in the sixties. Oh my word, the heat. There was one day—'

Maude had returned with a middle-aged man in farmer's tweeds.

'Found him, my lady,' said Maude.

'Mornin', m'lady,' said the man.

'Ah, Mr Mogg,' said Lady Farley-Stroud. 'There you are. How goes it?'

'Not bad, m'lady. We got just ten head in today from the dairy herd. Tryin' to sell 'em as one lot. Second up. Shouldn't take long. Got a few folk sniffin' round. Caradine from up Top Farm looks interested. Ackley from over Woodworthy was lookin', too. Should be some biddin'.'

'Wonderful,' said Lady Farley-Stroud. 'Let's hope we make a few bob, eh?'

'Hopin' so, m'lady. Would you 'scuse me, m'lady? Got a few more things to sort.'

'Of course, Mr Mogg. Thank you for all your efforts.'

Mogg knuckled his forehead and disappeared into the still-growing crowd.

I should like to report the details of the auction, which I'm sure were thrilling beyond measure for those in the know, but for me things were a little less clear. Some sheep were led in. A man in a flat cap jabbered incomprehensibly – I could make out numbers here and there – as other men nodded and signalled. Within less than a minute, the sheep were led back out again and a deal had, apparently, been struck.

Before the last of the sheep had left the sawdust-strewn arena, Mogg came in, leading the first of the ten cattle he was selling. The rest obediently followed. After a few words of barely intelligible introduction, the flat-capped man began his sing-song, 'Her-ba-da-dip-dah-dip-dah-her-ba-da-HEY-ba-da-dip-dah-dip-dah . . .' A skinny man who appeared to be in his fifties, with an impressively bushy beard and a slight squint, seemed to be competing with a taller and altogether more solid man on the opposite side of the arena.

Once again, before I had fully worked out what was going on, the auctioneer let out a loud 'Sold!' and the skinny man began making his way towards the cashier's counter.

'Oh, I say, how splendid,' said Lady Farley-Stroud. 'It absolutely couldn't have gone better.'

'It couldn't?' said Lady Hardcastle with a frown. 'How could you tell?'

'What do you mean? Oh, I see. I suppose it is all a little arcane. Just as Mogg predicted, there was a bidding war between the two local rivals, Caradine and Ackley. Caradine won. The splendid thing was that their silly rivalry pushed the price way beyond what we were expecting to achieve. I couldn't be more delighted.'

'Well, that is good news, darling. I'm very pleased for you,' said Lady Hardcastle.

'Thank you, m'dear. Luncheon, I should say, is on me.'

'That's extremely generous. But what shall we do until then? Are there any more lots you'd like to see?'

'No, m'dear,' said the older lady. 'It's only really fun when it's your own stock that's on the block. Unless you want to find out what happens to this next collection of malnourished milkers I rather think we're done.'

'At least the rain is abating, my lady,' said Maude.

'Somewhat, Denton, somewhat,' said Lady Farley-Stroud. 'You've never been to Chipping before, have you, Emily?'

'No, I never seemed to get round to it what with one thing and another. We usually go into Bristol for shopping.'

'Well, we've nothing quite so grand as they've got in Bristol, m'dear, but I'm sure we could while away an entertaining hour or more on the High Street. There's a charming dress shop I'd love you to see. Oh, and quite the most splendid bric-a-brac shop. Do you care for antiques?'

'I'm sure it will be delightful,' said Lady Hardcastle.

I could see why Lady Farley-Stroud favoured the dress shop. It seemed to cater for robustly built country ladies of a certain age but it had little to offer Lady Hardcastle. While never a slave to fashion, she nevertheless maintained an elegantly up-to-date wardrobe, something that this out-of-the-way shop seemed unable to manage.

There was a silk scarf she quite admired, but despite many 'oooh's and 'ahh's, and even one 'Oh, Emily, you'd look absolutely smashing in this' from her friend, she remained largely unmoved.

The bric-a-brac shop, however, was a completely different kettle of fish. It was the last in a small row of shops set slightly back from the rest, giving it the appearance of being hidden away in a darkened corner. The shop front was curved, and several of the small, slightly grubby panes were of dimpled glass, giving it a very old-fashioned look. But it was what was on view behind that glass that captured my attention.

I'm not a great fan of old things usually but there was a romantic quality to the mismatched collection of near-junk in the window that made me desperate to get inside and explore. Amid the usual collection of chipped china figurines, glass vases of doubtful practicality, and tarnished silverware there was an elephant's-foot umbrella stand, a brass diving helmet and a stuffed and mounted warthog head with wax oranges on its tusks. Next to that was a fish kettle, which served as a mount for a large stuffed trout.

'We're not buying it,' said Lady Hardcastle, who had noted my interest.

'Oh, but I might,' said Lady Farley-Stroud. I glanced across and saw that she was admiring the elephant's-foot umbrella stand. 'Come on, Emily, let's see if we can strike a bargain.'

She opened the door and we trooped in.

Inside was a cavern of infinite delights. I have travelled the world, seen the teeming markets in Shanghai and Calcutta, wandered the flea markets of Paris, and conducted more than my fair share of clandestine meetings in the back rooms of seedy little shops in London's East End, but there was something altogether new and magical about the collection on display inside Pomphrey's Bric-a-Brac Emporium. There's junk, and then there's a lovingly curated collection of surprising and interesting junk. And this was definitely towards the more entertaining end of the scale. There was a moose's head mounted on the wall wearing a topi and with the mouthpiece of an ornate hookah between its lips. Below it was a forest of candlesticks. There was a musical instrument section which, of course, included the usual selection of battered trumpets and euphoniums as well as a violin with faded lacquer, and a tarnished flute. But lurking among the everyday instruments were two crumhorns, a serpent and an ornate lute. One could, should one choose, start one's own Renaissance chamber group.

It wasn't something I was likely to do, though, and my gaze shifted instead to a banjo with a Mississippi riverboat painted on its resonator. I picked it up and examined it closely.

Towards the rear of the shop, a bespectacled man wearing a long velvet jacket and a matching smoking cap was talking to a gentleman wearing a rather new-looking Harris tweed suit and a matching trilby.

'. . . without losing any of its original charm,' said Velvet Jacket.

'It's very much the sort of thing I was looking for, certainly,' said Harris Tweed. 'Just not in that colour. But I see you have other customers to attend to. I'll just take this for now and be on my way.' He gestured to a model of Stephenson's Rocket which was lying on the counter. It seemed to have been fashioned from matchsticks and was quite realistic save that its boiler had been painted with the Union Flag.

'Certainly, Mr Snelson, certainly,' said the shopkeeper. He wrapped the tiny steam locomotive and took his customer's money.

Mr Snelson turned to leave. In doing so, he noticed for the first time who the new customers were.

'Why Lady Farley-Stroud,' he said. 'Good morning to you.'

'Good morning, Mr Snelson. Decorating your new home?'

He smiled. 'Yes. It was looking a bit dowdy so I thought I might enliven it with a few interesting pieces.'

'You've certainly come to the right place for that,' she said. 'Emily, dear, I don't believe you've met Mr Snelson. He moved to Littleton last month so you're no longer the newest resident of the village. Mr Snelson, allow me to introduce m'good friend Lady Hardcastle.'

'How do you do?' they said, almost in unison.

'I do hope they're treating you well,' said Lady Hardcastle.

'Who?' said Mr Snelson.

'The villagers. It can be frightfully hard to be the new bug.'

'Ah, I see,' he said. 'Yes, they've welcomed me with open arms, as it were. It's a fine place. Full of gossip, too. I hear you've been unwell. I do hope you're recovered.'

'I am, thank you, yes. Much better.'

'Splendid,' he said. 'Well, I must take my leave, I'm afraid. Good luck with your shopping.'

'Thank you,' said Lady Hardcastle. 'We shall meet again, I'm sure.'

He tipped his hat and left.

The shopkeeper approached. He was short, round and apple-cheeked, with a mischievous twinkle in the smiling eyes that peeped out through the tiny, round, blue-tinted spectacles.

'Good morning, ladies,' he said. 'Hubert Pomphrey at your service. How wonderful to see you again, Lady Farley-Stroud. And with a friend. I don't believe I've met . . .'

'Lady Hardcastle,' said Lady Farley-Stroud, turning to my mistress, 'allow me to introduce the proprietor of this splendid shop, Mr Hubert Pomphrey.'

Lady Hardcastle nodded and Mr Pomphrey bowed.

'And this is my maid, Armstrong,' said Lady Hardcastle.

'Welcome, my lady,' said Pomphrey. 'And welcome to you, too, Miss Armstrong. I see you're admiring the banjo. You have a good eye. This fine instrument was once played by Mr Zachariah Duchamp, one of the most accomplished exponents of the banjo ever to sail on the riverboats that ply the mighty Mississippi. Do you play?'

'A little,' I said.

'Then, please,' he said, with a grand sweep of his chubby arm. 'Be my guest.'

'Thank you, Mr Pomphrey,' I said. 'But not just now.' I replaced the banjo in the display.

'As you wish, miss,' he said with a smile. 'Has anything else caught anyone's eye?'

'Actually, Mr Pomphrey,' said Lady Farley-Stroud. 'I was admiring the elephant's-foot umbrella stand in the window. Reminds me of m'days in the Raj with Sir Hector, what?'

'And what a good eye you have, my lady,' he said. 'Sadly, though, I ought to say in the name of honesty that it's a mere reproduction. Cast in plaster.' He paused thoughtfully. 'But then again, perhaps not so sad. Perhaps a three-legged elephant would be a sadder sight. Would you like to take a closer look?'

'Yes, please,' she said, and he reached over the panel that backed the window display to grab the umbrella stand. It seemed heavy, and with the ornately handled umbrella still in it, also rather cumbersome. He struggled back to us and placed it on the counter for her to inspect.

'As you can see, my lady, it's in most excellent condition. Very often these plaster replicas are chipped and cracked, but this one . . . well . . .'

'It does look remarkably convincing,' said Lady Farley-Stroud. 'I'm just a little disappointed it's not the real thing.'

'Oh, Gertie, no,' said Lady Hardcastle. 'It's exactly like the real thing, a perfect imitation. This way you get an intriguing *objet* and the poor elephant gets to walk free. I agree with Mr Pomphrey – there are few sadder sights than a three-legged elephant.'

'Do they really just chop one leg off?' asked Maude innocently. Lady Hardcastle and I exchanged a glance but said nothing.

'I know from personal experience that there is a roaring trade in elephantine prosthetics on the Subcontinent, miss,' said Mr Pomphrey earnestly. 'My brother has a very successful company out there: "Pomphrey's Perfect Pachyderm Peg Legs" . . . of Pondicherry.'

'I say,' said Maude. 'Really?'

'He's teasing you, Denton,' said Lady Farley-Stroud. 'Take no notice.'

Maude looked crestfallen.

'My apologies, miss,' he said. 'Just my little joke.'

'She'll live,' said Lady Farley-Stroud. 'Now, how much do you want for it?'

Some fierce haggling ensued. Lady Farley-Stroud was not one to be trifled with over matters of money. Within minutes she had reduced the asking price by three-quarters and had persuaded Mr Pomphrey to throw in the umbrella. I had no doubt that he was still making a handsome profit, but he made a good show of gracious defeat while she clearly judged herself to have secured quite the bargain.

By the time we emerged once more onto the street with the umbrella stand wrapped neatly in brown paper and tucked under Maude's arm, the rain had ceased and the wind had eased to a more tolerable level.

'That was splendid fun, Gertie dear,' said Lady Hardcastle. 'I don't know about you, but I'm famished. What say we take you up on your generous offer of lunch? Where do you recommend?'

'Denton and I usually head for The Hayrick round the corner,' said Lady Farley-Stroud. 'Don't we, Denton?'

'We do, my lady,' said Maude, somewhat less enthusiastically than was her custom. We set off once more up the High Street.

'Hah!' roared Lady Farley-Stroud delightedly. 'Misery guts. It's hearty grub, Emily. Good, honest, English nosh in a good, honest, English pub. It's where all the farmers end up after market. Love the place. Are you a cider drinker, m'dear?'

'I've been known to tipple,' said Lady Hardcastle. 'Though I prefer a brandy.'

'At lunchtime? Well I never.'

'Oh, but darling, you should. It's never too early for the eau de vie.'

'I still insist you try the cider, m'dear. When in Rome, eh?'

'Very well, darling,' said Lady Hardcastle. 'I shall try the cider.'

'And the pie. They do a cracking beef and mushroom pie,' said the portly older woman, all but salivating as we rounded a corner into a side street and approached the pub.

Lady Farley-Stroud pushed open the door and we were almost overwhelmed by the cacophonous roar of the busy inn.

Pipe smoke. Noise. Smells of stale beer, cider, food. Laughter. Prodigious swearing. Extraordinary beards. We had entered the world of the farmers.

Maude, Lady Hardcastle and I trailed in the wake of Lady Farley-Stroud as she ploughed her way through the rambunctious market-day crowd to get to the bar. It wasn't yet noon, but the majority of the assembled rustics were already well on their way to exuberant intoxication.

The landlord had his back to us and was fussing with something on the shelf behind the bar.

'Morning, Ronnie,' bellowed Lady Farley-Stroud.

The landlord jumped. Even above the noise of the pub, her voice was enough to terrify the most redoubtable of men.

17

'Ah, good morning, m'lady,' he said, turning round. 'You gave me quite a start there.'

'Thought so,' she said. 'Dream world, eh?'

'Just keeping the place tidy, m'lady. It's bedlam in here. Always is come market day. What can I get you?'

'You have your famous beef and mushroom pies?'

'Baked 'em fresh myself this very morning, m'lady. Two, is it?'

'Four today, Ronnie. Brought some guests,' she said and indicated Lady Hardcastle and me.

'Good morning, ladies,' said the landlord with a slight bow. 'Ronald Towels at your service. Welcome to The Hayrick.'

'Thank you, Mr Towels,' said Lady Hardcastle. 'A lovely, lively place you have here.'

'Ronnie, madam, please. I'm glad you like it. Not quite what you're used to, I don't expect, but there's always a welcome here for friends of Lady Farley-Stroud.'

'I'm reasonably sure you'd be quite surprised by what we're used to, Ronnie,' she said with her warmest smile. 'And I understand that your pies and cider are the finest in the county.'

'Well, I don't know about that, Mrs . . . ?'

'This is Lady Hardcastle,' said Lady Farley-Stroud.

'Is it? Is it, indeed? Well, I'll be blowed. The one who helped you out with that business up at The Grange last year?'

'The very same,' said Lady Farley-Stroud, proudly. 'Found my jewel and helped catch a murderer.'

'That's right, I remember. Killed poor Frank Pickering, didn't they? Terrible loss, he was. One of the best fast bowlers in the district. Littleton Cotterell will miss him this season.'

'Quite,' said Lady Farley-Stroud. 'So mind you treat her well, m'lad.'

'No special treatment here, m'lady,' said Ronnie. 'You knows that. It's the finest cider, the finest pies, and everyone gets the very best there is. And a warm welcome to go with it. It's a pleasure to serve you all.' He paused and looked quizzically at me. 'And are you the famous Florence Armstrong?' he said.

'I don't know about famous,' I said. 'But I have my moments.'

'I heard as how you broke a killer's wrist with a single kick.'

'Oh,' I said. 'I did that. I bake nice cakes too.'

He laughed. 'I bet you does, an' all. Well, ladies, barge some o' they ne'er-do-wells out of the way and make yourselves comfortable. I'll send the girl out with pies and cider in two shakes. Hey!' he shouted suddenly. 'Spencer! Budge up there and make room for the ladies.'

The man looked up sullenly from his pie. I recognized him as Spencer Caradine, the skinny, bearded farmer who had bought the Farley-Strouds' cattle. He was clearly about to offer his views on the idea of budging up for anyone at all when he noticed Lady Farley-Stroud. Instead, he nodded and grudgingly shuffled along the bench to make way for us, pulling his plate and his pint with him.

'Thank you, Mr Caradine,' said Lady Farley-Stroud as she made herself comfortable. 'And I do hope the cattle will be to your liking.'

'Them's good milkers, m'lady,' he wheezed. 'Reckon I got m'self a good deal there.'

'Good show,' said Lady Farley-Stroud. 'Enjoy your pie.' She turned back to the rest of us. 'Well, Emily, what do you think? Isn't market day a hoot?'

'It's a rich slice of country life, that's for certain,' said Lady Hardcastle, looking around the crowded bar. 'Is it always this well attended?'

'I should say it's about average,' said our hostess.

'And do you know many people here? They seem to know you.'

'I suppose I'm quite easy to remember, what? Lady of the manor and all that. But I know a few. Know a few. Over there, for instance,' – she indicated a tall man with an ill-fitting hat –

'that's Dick Ackley who was bidding against Mr Caradine here for our prize cattle. And over there,' – she pointed to a surprisingly handsome middle-aged man in a well-patched jacket – 'that's Noah Lock, one of Mr Caradine's neighbours. And . . . let me see . . . ah, yes, there he is. Over there at the end of the bar next to the kitchen, short chap. That's another of his neighbours, Lancelot Tribley.'

'Quite the community,' said Lady Hardcastle.

'Got to know one's neighbours out here, m'dear. Rely on each other, d'you see?' Lady Farley-Stroud raised her voice, 'Don't we, Mr Caradine?'

He looked up from his pie. 'Beg pardon, m'lady?'

'I say we look out for each other. It's the country way. Stick together.'

'Ar,' he wheezed gravely. 'That we do, m'lady. That we do.'

'Who's that tall chap covered in flour?' asked Lady Hardcastle. 'He looks more like a baker than a farmer.'

Lady Farley-Stroud peered at the giant of a man by the dartboard.

'Not sure, dear,' she said. 'Looks familiar. Not certain where I know him from, though. The rugby club, perhaps? Hector would know.'

Conversation was briefly halted by the arrival of 'the girl' with a huge tray bearing our pies and ciders. 'The girl' was all of forty years old and was missing more than one tooth, but her gapped smile was warm and her strength impressive as she heaved the tray with its heaped plates and pint jugs onto the table.

'There you goes, m'dears,' she said. 'Four pies and four pints. Can I get you anything else? There's some mustard around here somewhere.'

'And some salt, please, m'dear,' said Lady Farley-Stroud, picking up her knife and fork. 'Come on, girls, tuck in,' she said, and hungrily followed her own advice.

The pies, despite my reservations, didn't disappoint at all. The beef was tender, the gravy rich, and I was sure that the mushrooms were chanterelles. Add to that a generous helping of mashed potato and it was a lunch fit for a farming king. The cider wasn't bad, either, but the cider served by Old Joe at the Dog and Duck at Littleton Cotterell just had the edge there.

As we ate, the two ladies swapped stories about their respective times in India. Lady Hardcastle's were certainly the more thrilling, being edited highlights of some of our less secret spying missions, but there was a mischievous glee in the older woman's stories that served as an entertaining counterpoint. I'd always suspected that in her youth she'd been a bit of a girl. It turns out she had. And sometimes rather a racy one at that.

I was catching only some of the tales, though, now that Maude, enlivened by the food and cider, was regaling me with tales of her own. Life below stairs at The Grange was a great deal more interesting than I remembered from the day I spent there. We were chuckling together as we plotted the downfall of the bullying cook, Mrs Brown, when the end of one of Lady Farley-Stroud's stories brought us both up short.

'. . . and so she just dived straight out of the window. Still stark naked, of course.'

I nearly spat out my pie.

2

Now that Lady Hardcastle was emerging from her winter-long funk and the days were beginning to get longer, life seemed altogether brighter again. Birds were building nests, unidentifiable plants were poking blade-like leaves up through the soil, and spring was most definitely in the air. We walked every morning.

'They're daffodils, dear,' said Lady Hardcastle as I pointed out some of the unknown greenery. 'They're your country's national flower. Surely you can tell a daffodil.'

'Could be a tulip,' I said, slightly sulkily. 'Or a hyacinth. Bluebells. Crocus.'

'Well, it isn't. It's a daffodil.'

We walked on.

'I got a letter from George yesterday,' she said.

'Did you, my lady?' I said. 'Is he well?'

Colonel George Dawlish was an old friend whom we had met the previous autumn when the circus he was managing had visited the village. There were 'murders and mayhem', as the press had put it, but he had left in good spirits with the circus in fine shape, despite the carnage.

'Very well indeed, it seems,' she said. 'I told you he was thinking about buying the circus?'

'You did, my lady.'

'He tells me that the sale has been completed and that he's now the proud owner of Bradley & Stoke's Circus.'

'Oh, how wonderful,' I said. 'He's keeping the name?'

'He's not sure. He says that the name was part of the sale and he thinks "Dawlish's" is too difficult to say, so he might well hang on to it.'

'Does this mean we get free tickets?' I asked. I love to be around circuses.

'I should bally well hope so,' she said. 'I'll have stern words for the boy if we don't.'

'Perhaps you could ask him for his schedule?'

'Good idea,' she said. 'I shall see what I can do. If he's visiting anywhere nice, perhaps we could arrange to spend a few days nearby.'

'Thank you, my lady,' I said.

'Speaking of visits, I wonder if Gertie would like to come over for lunch.'

'Would you like me to take a note up to The Grange, my lady?' I said.

'No, let's think about it,' she said. And then, after a pause, she continued, 'Actually, yes, I really rather think I would. She's a dear old girl and over these past few months she's been comfortingly . . . what's the female version of "avuncular"? Avunculus and . . . amita? Amitular? No, that can't be right. I always was a duffer at Latin. But anyway, she's been perfectly lovely and I should like to repay her kindness.'

'Very well, my lady, you draft the perfect note and I shall carry it bravely up the hill.'

'You're a little trouper. But not today, I think – it's Thursday.'

'Can we not write perfect notes on a Thursday, my lady?' I said.

'I shall have you know that I can craft the perfect note for any occasion upon any day of the week, but Thursday is market day so she'll not be at home. Tomorrow, definitely.'

'Very well, my lady, I shall brush my best hat in preparation.'

'You would wear your best hat to deliver a note, but not to take the air with your mistress?' she said haughtily.

'Certainly not,' I said. 'Why would I waste my best hat on an old trout like you? Lady Farley-Stroud, on the other hand, is a proper lady.'

'In very many ways,' she said thoughtfully, 'I really rather think she is.'

We reached home just as the postman was walking back down the path and we exchanged cheery 'good mornings'. Inside, I picked up the letters from the mat and made way for Lady Hardcastle to come in and remove her hat and coat.

'It's quite the week for keeping in touch,' I said, handing over the letters. 'I believe one of those is from Skins.'

'The redoubtable Skins Maloney,' she said, taking the letters with a smile of thanks. 'Either bragging of the band's continuing success or on the earhole for cash, I shouldn't wonder.'

It seemed our adventures of the previous summer had made quite an impression, not only on us, but on the others involved. Skins was the drummer in the band who had become embroiled in the affair at The Grange. We had been following his progress after striking up a friendship one drunken, musical evening back at the house after everything had been wrapped up.

'Ah,' said Lady Hardcastle, who was reading the letter. 'It's all good news. He and Dunn have a new band. He says he told us they were the best rhythm section in London. They have dates all over England. Some in Paris . . . dah-de-dah . . . would we like to come and see them in London next month . . . oh, "and give my love to

24

Flo". Well, that's all very nice. What do you think? A couple of days in London in April? We could call it a late birthday celebration for you – I haven't forgotten it's coming up. A night in a seedy club with the boys? Perhaps one of those silly shows you like?'

'Silly shows, my lady? I'm sure I don't know what you mean.'

'What was that thing you and Harry dragged me to just after Christmas? "Whoops! Oh Crikey! I've Fallen in Love with the Flower Girl Again"? I love my brother dearly, but he's got the most appalling taste in . . . well, in most things, actually.'

'You, my lady, are a frightful old snob,' I said, and went to get Miss Jones to make us a pot of tea.

The doorbell rang as we sipped our tea in the drawing room. I answered it to see an ashen Lady Farley-Stroud on the doorstep. Ordinarily a lively lady with a mischievous glint in her eye, the glint was gone, replaced by a look of distress.

'Oh, Armstrong,' she said. 'Thank goodness you're here. Is Lady Hardcastle at home?'

'She is, my lady. Please come in. You look like you could do with a sweet tea. Whatever's the matter?'

She stepped in, looking curiously about at our somewhat Spartan decor. I took her hat and coat and conducted her through to the drawing room.

'Who's that at the—?' said Lady Hardcastle as I opened the door. 'Oh, Gertie, what a delight. Do come in, I was just—'

Lady Farley-Stroud fainted. I managed to get my shoulder under her arm to stop her from falling to the ground, but I was having trouble manhandling her towards a chair. Lady Hardcastle leapt up when she saw her guest falling, and winced visibly as the wound in her stomach gave a twinge.

We got the older lady into an armchair and she began to return to her senses.

'I was just about to offer sweet tea, my lady,' I said. 'For the shock.'

'Sweet tea be beggared,' said Lady Hardcastle firmly. 'This lady needs brandy.'

'Very good, my lady,' I said, and I went to fetch both.

I returned with a tray of tea, cognac and biscuits to find Lady Farley-Stroud returned to consciousness, but looking little better. Lady Hardcastle was fussing around her friend.

'Here you are, dear,' she said. 'Flo's brought some tea and brandy. Let's get some of that down you and you can tell me all about it.'

Lady Farley-Stroud sipped at the proffered glass and began to look a little embarrassed.

'So sorry, m'dear,' she said. 'Don't know what came over me. Haven't swooned since I was a girl. Feel very foolish.'

'Nonsense, darling,' said Lady Hardcastle. 'You look like you've had a terrible shock. Whatever's the matter?'

'Oh, Emily, it was terrible. Went to the market on my own. Left Denton behind – she had things to be getting on with back at The Grange. Having lunch in The Hayrick, chatting to Mr Caradine about the cattle he bought from us last week. Poor old chap was looking very ill but he said it was just a spring cold. He looked jaundiced to me, though, I've seen that before. So I took pity on the old chap and was just about to offer him a drink when he keeled over, face down in his pie.'

'Gracious!' said Lady Hardcastle and I together.

'They tried to revive him, but he was dead as a door knocker.'

'Gracious!' we said again.

'We called the doctor, and he said it looked like . . . like he'd been poisoned!' said Lady Farley-Stroud before she fainted again, tipping the remains of the brandy over her dress.

We brought Lady Farley-Stroud round with some old smelling salts that I found at the back of Lady Hardcastle's dressing table. We let her sit quietly while I went to talk to Bert who was sitting outside in the motor car. I asked him to drive up to The Grange to fetch Maude, and to stop off in the village on the way back and collect Dr Fitzsimmons.

Back inside, I freshened the tea while we waited for Bert to return. Lady Farley-Stroud was slowly restored to her usual self (I was firmly convinced it was the tea and not the cognac that did the trick) and was soon admonishing us for making such an unseemly fuss. We were wary of distressing her again so we had to keep our curiosity in check, but it was a hellish task. How did they know it was poison? What sort of poison was it? When was it administered? Who could have done such a thing? Why would they do it?

By the time the doctor had examined her and given her into the care of her maid, I for one was definitely beginning to struggle to find things to say that weren't connected to the sudden death of Spencer Caradine. But we wished her well, promised to visit the next day, and sent them all on their way.

'Things are definitely back to normal now,' said Lady Hardcastle as we settled back in the drawing room to finish off the tea.

'Murder and mischief, my lady?' I said, brushing biscuit crumbs from my pinafore.

'Mayhem and . . . and . . .'

'Malarkey, my lady?'

'Doesn't have quite the same ring to it, does it,' she said.

'Monkey business?' I said.

'You're not helping, Flo,' she said. 'I think we shall have to settle for "misdemeanours".'

'Mucking about?'

'Remember who protected you from the evil cows with her trusty walking stick, my girl,' she said threateningly. 'I might leave it at home the next time we face a terrifying bovine menace. But a mystery might be just what I need.'

'Mystery, my lady.'

'Yes, a mystery. Oh, I see what you mean. Yes. Mystery. Mayhem and mystery.'

We raised our tea cups. 'To mayhem and mystery,' I said.

The doorbell rang again.

'Oh, who can this be?' said Lady Hardcastle. 'I was just about to indulge in some wild and ill-informed speculation upon the murder of Spencer Caradine when some inconsiderate soul comes ringing at the doorbell. Send them away with a flea in their ear for their impudence. Both ears, I say.'

The doorbell rang yet again.

'Go!' she said. 'Be maid-like. Answer the blessed door.'

I went and answered the blessed door.

'Ah, Miss Armstrong,' said the bowler-hatted man on the doorstep. 'Is your mistress at home?'

'Inspector Sunderland,' I said. 'What a pleasant surprise. Please, do come in.'

'Thank you, miss,' said the inspector. We had become friends during the investigation of the murder at The Grange. While I had a strong suspicion that his call was not a social one, it was still a pleasure to see him.

I led him to the drawing room and showed him in.

'Inspector Sunderland is here, my lady,' I said, somewhat superfluously.

'I can see that,' said Lady Hardcastle. 'Inspector. How delightful to see you. Do please come in and make yourself at home. Flo, I think we might need another pot. Tea, Inspector?'

'That would be most welcome, my lady,' he said. 'I hear you're up and about again.'

'I am, yes. And quite relieved to be so. One can't stay moping about forever,' she said.

'No, indeed, my lady. But you were shot. And then there was that business in the autumn. I think that might entitle you to a little moping.'

'You're very kind, Inspector, darling,' she said. She noticed I was still at the door. 'Tea, dear. Quick sticks. The sooner you're back, the sooner the inspector can tell us why he's here.'

I hurried to the kitchen. I could hear them chatting in the other room, but I couldn't quite make out what they were saying as I clattered about with the tea things. There were still a few biscuits left over from the batch Miss Jones had cooked that morning so I put those onto a plate and hurried back into the drawing room with the tray.

'. . . with a grapefruit in his overcoat pocket,' said Lady Hardcastle as I entered.

Inspector Sunderland chuckled. 'You are a caution, my lady,' he said. 'Like a breath of fresh air you are. I must say it's good to see you back to your old self.'

Inspector Sunderland was from Bristol CID. He had allowed us to join his investigation into a murder at The Grange when we had first arrived in the village.

He was a straightforward man who loved his work and he treated us with a level of respect it was hard to find in the rest of the world. Of course, people respected Lady Hardcastle's title, but usually only that. Inspector Oliver Sunderland valued her opinion, too. And mine for that matter.

'Florence, dear,' said Lady Hardcastle, 'do sit down. You're making the place look untidy.'

I sat in the other armchair.

'Now then, Inspector, tell all,' she said. 'Would you think me altogether too grim if I were to confess that I do rather hope it's to do with the murder of Spencer Caradine?'

'Well I never,' said the inspector with another chuckle. 'Am I to add clairvoyance to the list of your known talents?'

'Oh pish and fiddlesticks,' she said. 'Gertie Farley-Stroud was here a little while ago, all at sixes and sevens and swooning like a mopsy in a penny dreadful. She told us everything. Well, everything she could manage between swigging my best brandy and passing out, at any rate. One would have thought she'd seen more than her fair share of sudden deaths over the years, but it seems to have affected her rather badly.'

'Ah, yes, I gathered she'd been there. So you have the gist of it, then?'

'Farmer collapses in his pie, local sawbones suspects poison,' she said. 'That's all we have.'

'That's the essence of it,' said the inspector. 'Local doctor . . . doctor . . .' – he consulted his ever-present notebook – 'oh, it doesn't matter for now. Local chap, anyway. Old fellow, bit of a dodderer. He reckons it must be poison, but it's not like any poison I've ever seen. There's something not right there, I'm sure of it. I've sent the pie and the cider off to be analysed anyway, though whether they'll find anything, I don't know.'

'It's absolutely charming of you to come all this way just to tell us,' said Lady Hardcastle. 'I'm sorry Lady Farley-Stroud stole your thunder, but the thought is appreciated.'

'Oh,' he said. 'I didn't come over just to tell you, my lady. No, I'm sorry, I should have explained myself. You see, I'm rather tied up at the moment – we're on the trail of a gang of bank thieves in the city – and I . . . well, I was going to ask you for your help with the pie-eyed farmer.'

'Oh, Inspector, you absolute poppet,' she said. 'We were just saying how we could do with a mystery, weren't we, Flo?'

'You were saying it, my lady,' I said. 'I was merely mocking your stumbling attempts to remember the word "mystery".'

'You see what I have to endure, Inspector?' she said. 'Derided by a tiny Welsh mop-squeezer. Well, really. I ask you. Is that right for a woman of my station and distinction?'

'It seems most inappropriate, my lady,' he said. 'I could have a couple of the lads run her down the station, if you like. A night in the cells might teach her some manners.' He winked at me.

'You could try, dear,' said Lady Hardcastle. 'But they'd only get hurt. And who would bring up my breakfast tray?'

'As you wish, my lady,' he said. 'But will you both help? I need someone I can trust to make the right inquiries while we're busy trying to stop these lads from tunnelling under Corn Street, or whatever it is they have in mind this time. Someone with natural detective skills and a nose for crime solving.'

'You know I'm going to agree anyway, Inspector; you can drop the soft soap.'

'It's no mere flattery, my lady. You might be undisciplined, untutored and prone to wild flights of whimsical speculation, but blow me if you don't end up at the solution anyway. The pair of you proved yourselves more than once round these parts. And after last autumn's shenanigans I've a pretty shrewd idea that you're no mere effete socialite and her timid lady's maid, either. One hears things down at HQ. Probably things one isn't supposed to hear. But I've pieced a few things together and I'd be honoured to have ladies such as you on my side.'

'Then fear not, Inspector, darling, we shall do our bit. Where do we start? Who was this Caradine? Did he have a wife? Where can we find her? Who were his friends? What are the local bobbies up to?'

The inspector chuckled throatily once more. 'I knew you were the ladies for the job. Thank you. I don't have all the details yet, but I've got a couple of lads making some preliminary inquiries over in Chipping Bevington. I'll make sure you have a full report first thing in the morning. The local bobbies are . . . let's just say that I'd rather they weren't too closely involved. Well-meaning chaps, but not among Nature's great thinkers. Be polite, but don't rely on them for anything. Your own local man, Sergeant Dobson, will be able to contact me at Bristol CID if you need me. I'll pop by in a couple of days to see how you're getting on.'

'Right you are, Inspector,' she said. 'Of course you know what we're going to have to fetch out now, don't you?'

'Your infamous crime board, my lady?' he said with a smile.

'The very same,' she said. 'Flo, why does everyone have that look on their face every time they mention the crime board?'

'Because it's the most preposterously silly idea they've ever heard, my lady?' I said.

'Heathens!' she said. 'Heathens and philistines! You don't have the trained minds of the scientist, that's all. Clarity of thought, that's what's required. Organization. Connections. Reasons. The board helps me think. We shall fetch it from the attic this very evening, Inspector, and begin our analysis.'

'She means I'll fetch it,' I said.

'I'm poorly,' she said weakly, clutching her side. 'I was shot in the stomach, you know. I try not to talk about it, but it prevents me from fetching blackboards and easels from the attic.'

'And she means that we'll begin our analysis tomorrow when we have your officers' report and know what there is to analyse.'

The inspector put down his teacup and stood.

'It seems it's all in hand then,' he said. 'I shall take my leave. Good afternoon, my lady, and thank you again.'

I stood too, and went to see him out. When we were in the hall, I spoke quietly. 'Thank you, Inspector,' I said. 'I don't know if you really do need our help, but this is the most animated she's been in quite a while. You're something of a breath of fresh air yourself.'

He shook my hand and I opened the front door for him.

'You really were my first thought when I realized I needed help,' he said. 'But I'm glad I could be of some small service in return. I shall be in touch presently.'

He walked down the path to the waiting police car in the lane.

3

'I've been thinking,' said Lady Hardcastle as we enjoyed breakfast together in the morning room. 'What we really need is a telephone.'

'We do?' I said, picking up another crumpet.

'We do,' she said. 'Think how much more quickly the inspector could have contacted us yesterday if we had a telephone. And think how easy it would be to ask him questions and give our reports.'

'True, my lady,' I said. 'But it was lovely to see him in person again.'

'Oh, telephones won't stop people paying calls on each other,' she said dismissively. 'But think of the convenience, the immediacy, the . . .'

'The bills, my lady? And the intrusion?'

'Oh, Flo, you are a fuddy-duddy. No, I have made up my mind. We shall have a telephone. I shall write to . . . to . . . Actually, to whom does one write?'

'They have a telephone at The Grange, my lady. Sir Hector will know.'

'Sir Hector is the sweetest old buffer ever to wear a hat,' she said. 'But we both know he won't know anything of the sort. Gertie's the girl to go to for information about the household. I shall ask her. Perhaps we could pop up there this morning to see how she is.'

'I think we should, my lady,' I said. 'Should we take her a gift?'

'How very thoughtful. What have we got?'

I thought for a while. 'I made a cake this morning,' I suggested.

'We'd offend Mrs Brown,' she said. 'Now there's a cook I wouldn't want to get on the wrong side of.'

'Some brandy?'

'She is partial to a little brandy.'

'A little?' I said.

'Do we have any to spare?'

'An unopened bottle, my lady? Actually, I don't think so. The vintner's order is due at the end of the week.' I sat for a moment in contemplation. 'Oh, I know. A caricature. She loves your drawings. We must have an old frame somewhere that we can use.'

'What a splendid idea,' she said enthusiastically. 'At the cattle market, I think. Give her an uplifting image of the place so she's not always dwelling on poor Mr Caradine. I'll decamp to the dining room and get sketching. You find the frame.'

'Right you are, my lady,' I said as I gathered up the breakfast things.

She worked fast, and by eleven o'clock we had a framed pen-and-ink sketch of Lady Farley-Stroud surrounded by cows. She signed the picture and titled it 'Cattle Market'.

'There,' said Lady Hardcastle. 'That should put a smile back on the old girl's face. I'm rather pleased with that.'

'And rightly so, my lady,' I said. 'You have a rare gift.'

'Then let's get our hats and coats and take a stroll up to The Grange where we can give the gift created by my gift to—'

Thankfully, the doorbell rang before she could get too far with that particular out-of-control thought.

It was Constable Hancock from the village police station.

'Mornin', Miss Armstrong,' he said, touching the peak of his police helmet with a fingertip. 'Is Lady Hardcastle at home?'

'She is, Constable, she is. Do come in. She's in the dining room.'

'Oh, I hope I haven't interrupted her lunch,' he said.

'Not at all, she was sketching. Come through.'

I led him to the dining room.

'Constable Hancock is here, my lady,' I said as I ushered him in.

'My dear Constable,' she said as she put her pens and pencils into the lacquered box on the table. 'To what do we owe the pleasure? Would you care for some tea?'

'Never been known to refuse the offer of tea, my lady,' he said with a smile. 'That would be most welcome.'

'Do the honours, would you, Flo,' she said, and I took myself off to the kitchen.

By the time I returned with the tray, Lady Hardcastle was leafing through the contents of an official-looking manila folder.

'Admirable diligence from the city detectives, Constable, but it doesn't appear they were able to discover much,' she said as I set the tray down on the table.

'No, m'lady,' said Hancock. 'I took a look at the reports and I reckon they must have asked everyone as was there that lunchtime. Don't look like no one saw a thing.'

'Any report from the police surgeon?'

'Not yet, m'lady, but that'll go to Bristol CID with a copy to the station at Chipping. We'll not see it 'less we asks. And even then I don't reckon as they'd let us. Not much love lost 'tween us and the boys in the town. Sergeant Dobson reckons they's a bunch of idiots, and I can't say as I disagrees with him. And they thinks we're nobodies 'cause we're based over here in the village, like it makes us second-class coppers or somethin'.'

'We know the truth though, eh, Flo?' she said.

'We do, my lady. Finest police officers in the county we've got here.'

'You're both very kind,' said Hancock, taking the tea that I'd poured for him. 'Don't suppose you'd mind if I helped myself to one o' they biscuits? I'm famished.'

Lady Hardcastle invited the constable to help himself to biscuits and invited me to take a look at the report from the Bristol detectives. She picked up a small notebook and a mechanical pencil from the table and made some notes while I read the file. The notebook and pencil had been a 'get well' gift from Inspector Sunderland after the shooting. He was never without his own trusty notebook and she took it as a sign of his approval of her detective skills that he had chosen to give her a notebook of her own.

The pub had been packed, as was usual for a Thursday, and Inspector Sunderland's men had interviewed them all. Dismayingly though, not one of the several dozen witnesses had witnessed anything at all. No one was behaving oddly, there were no arguments, no one was seen with a bottle made of dark glass with a label bearing a skull and crossbones and the word 'Poison' in shaky writing. No one knew of anyone with a particular grudge against Spencer Caradine. There was, though, a carefully written note to the effect that the detectives couldn't be sure that this was definitely the case. 'It is usually noted in cases of recent death that no one cares to speak ill of the deceased nor to suggest that there might be any reason for anyone to dislike him. In cases of murder, no one wishes to say anything which might be construed as an accusation.' They made a good point. Unless folk had grudges of their own to be settled, most people would tend to keep mum.

'Well,' I said when I'd finished reading. 'That doesn't tell us much.'

'No, not really,' said Lady Hardcastle. 'There are a few names to follow up, I think, but I do wonder if it's just because I've heard them before. Gertie pointed out a few of them to us, do you remember? They were all neighbours, though, so perhaps it might be worth speaking to them. And the widow . . . what's her name?'

I looked at the file. 'Audrey,' I said.

'Audrey,' she said. 'Yes, that's it. It will be awkward, but I think we ought to start with her.'

'Should we clear it with the Chipping Bevington police?' I asked.

'I shouldn't bother if I were you, miss,' said Constable Hancock. 'They's a bunch of idiots and they'll only give you a hard time if you tries. You've got the go-ahead from Inspector Sunderland so I suggests you just does what you wants and treads lightly round they Chipping lot. That Sergeant Boyce is a right one. I'd give him a wide berth if I were you.'

'Very well, Constable, we shall,' said Lady Hardcastle. 'There's just one problem we need to overcome.'

'What's that, my lady?' I said.

'Transportation,' she said dejectedly. 'How the devil do we get to all these blessed farms?'

'Aha,' said a triumphant Constable Hancock. 'I have the answer to that one.'

'You do?' said Lady Hardcastle.

'Indeed I do, m'lady,' he said, and he produced a letter from his tunic pocket.

Lady Hardcastle read the note.

'Oh, what a splendid woman dear old Gertie is,' she said, beaming. 'Bert and the motor car are at our disposal. She's sending him over at noon and I am to treat him as though he were my own. Well, that's just perfect. We shall go and visit the Widow Caradine first, then call on Lady Farley-Stroud on the way back.'

Without Lady Farley-Stroud in the motor car, Bert was a far more adventurous driver and we made much more rapid progress than I had been expecting. The hedgerows rushed by and I was rather enjoying the sensation of speed.

As we rounded a bend and began to climb the hill to Top Farm we caught sight of a man leaning against a gate and watching the progress of the motor car.

'I say, Bert,' said Lady Hardcastle. 'Who's that?'

'That's Lancelot Tribley, m'lady. He owns Bottom Farm.'

'Just down from Top Farm?' she said.

'You got it, m'lady,' he said with a smile.

'Can you stop the car, please. I'd like a quick word with him.'

'He's not on the list, my lady,' I said. 'He wasn't at The Hayrick when Caradine died.'

'No, I know. But he's their next-door neighbour. He might have seen something.'

Bert had stopped as soon as he'd been asked and had already reversed the car back down the road to the gate. We climbed out and Lady Hardcastle introduced herself.

'There aren't many people around here who don't know who you are, my lady,' said the short, powerfully built man at the gate. He was in his forties, I estimated. His flat cap and rumpled jacket gave him the appearance of a farmer, but something about his manner suggested that he might be more comfortable in blazer and flannels.

'You might be right, actually,' said Lady Hardcastle. 'I'm not certain whether fame becomes me, but it does save time on introductions.'

'I can see it would be an advantage,' said Tribley. 'And what can I do for you?'

'You've heard about the unfortunate death of Mr Caradine?'

'I have at that. Though I'd be hard pressed to think of many who might think of it as "unfortunate".'

'No?' she said.

'No. He wasn't well liked, our Spencer.'

'Oh? And why was that?'

'No one likes to speak ill of the dead, but in the case of old Spencer Caradine, it's pretty much all that's left you: there aren't a great many nice things one can say about him. He was a miserable old codger who never had a good word for anyone. Well, actually that's not true. He had plenty of good words for most of the people he met, but not ones I can repeat in front of ladies. He could start a fight in an empty room, that one.' He seemed almost wistful at the memory.

'I see,' said Lady Hardcastle. 'The thing is, there's a suspicion that he might have been murdered. The Bristol CID have asked us to ask around and see if we can find out a little bit more about him and what might have happened to him. Did you know him well, even though you didn't get along?'

'Well enough, I suppose.'

'Did you see him often? Speak to him?'

'We passed the time of day. You know how it is.'

'When did you last see him?'

'Early in the week, I believe,' he said, after a pause. 'It would have been Monday or Tuesday.'

'What did you talk about?' she asked.

'This and that, you know. Nothing of any consequence.'

'I see,' she said. 'And you didn't see him again?'

'No, that was the last.'

'You weren't at The Hayrick the day he died, were you?'

'No. I didn't have cause to be at the market last week and I had matters to attend to elsewhere.'

'I see,' she said. 'Anything interesting?'

'Just a small business matter in Gloucester.'

'That must have made a nice change.'

'Anything to get away from this place for a bit,' he said, looking round at the field behind him.

'You're not keen on the farming life, then?'

He laughed bitterly. 'I inherited this wretched place from my brother when he passed away five years ago. I've been trying to get shot of it ever since.'

'Oh,' said Lady Hardcastle. 'What did you do before that?'

'I'm a chef by training. I've worked in some of the finest hotels in Europe. Now look at me. Instead of roasting pigs I'm chasing round after the little blighters. I ask you.'

'Surely there must be people willing to buy a profitable farm, Mr Tribley,' I said.

'Or rent it,' suggested Lady Hardcastle.

'You'd have thought so, wouldn't you? There's some interest. But there's always something in the way, some reason they back out of the deal. And, to be truthful, the rental income wouldn't be so helpful. I should like some capital.'

'That's a terrible shame, Mr Tribley,' I said. 'It must be awful to be trapped in an occupation you have no fondness for.'

'True enough. But in the end one just has to get on with it. A chap has to eat.'

We all fell silent for an awkward moment.

'Well, you've been most helpful, Mr Tribley,' said Lady Hardcastle eventually. 'Thank you. You've been most generous with your time, but we mustn't take up any more of it. We should leave you to get on.'

'No trouble at all. Nice to see a friendly face.'

We both thanked him again and returned to the car. Bert had been watching and was already out of his seat and cranking the engine to life.

'Thank you, Bert. On to Top Farm as soon as you're ready, please.'

It was less than a mile up to Top Farm, and we were pulling into the farmyard before I'd even managed to settle properly into my seat.

Lady Hardcastle waved Bert back into his driving seat as he made to get out.

'You're most kind, Bert, but I don't see any great profit in us all getting muddy. It's not as though I can't open a car door.'

'Thank you, m'lady,' he said.

'We might be a little while,' she said. 'Do make yourself comfortable.'

'Thank you, m'lady,' he said. He had brought a newspaper and seemed unconcerned about how long we might be. I got the feeling he was looking forward to a day of dozing broken up by occasional driving.

The farmhouse was solid and well maintained, a whitewashed family home to be proud of. Lady Hardcastle knocked on the sturdy front door. A few moments later it was opened by a short, plump, grey-haired woman. She was in her late fifties, I judged, and her face, though etched with sadness, was still pretty. In her youth she would have turned heads, I was certain.

'Yes?' she said suspiciously. 'Can I help you?'

'Mrs Caradine?' said Lady Hardcastle warmly. 'I'm Lady Hardcastle, from Littleton Cotterell, and this is Florence Armstrong. Inspector Sunderland of the Bristol CID has asked us to—'

'I've heard of you,' interrupted the widow, still on her guard. '"Amateur detectives", they say, whatever on earth that means. You've come to poke your noses into my Spencer's death?'

'I want to help you find out the truth, Mrs Caradine. I lost my own husband at the hands of a murderer. I understand all too well how you must feel.'

'Begging your pardon, my lady,' said Mrs Caradine with more than a hint of bitterness, 'but you don't understand nothing.'

'Then help me to understand, Mrs Caradine. Please may we come in and talk?'

Audrey Caradine eyed us both appraisingly for a while longer until finally she said, 'You'd better both come in, then.'

The inside of the farmhouse was as clean and well looked after as the outside. She led us into a warm, cosy kitchen.

'I've just made a pot of tea,' she said, fetching clean cups from the hooks on the Welsh dresser.

We sat at the large kitchen table while she fussed with the tea things.

'You must be devastated, Mrs Caradine,' said Lady Hardcastle kindly. 'I do so hate to intrude, but if we can catch your husband's killer—'

'What makes you so certain he was killed?' interrupted Mrs Caradine, sitting down with us.

'The doctor insists it was poison,' I said.

'Dr Manterfield, was it?' said Mrs Caradine derisively. 'That old quack from Chipping? What does he know? Not a patch on our Dr Fitzsimmons. Spencer was ill. He'd been ill a couple of days 'fore he even went to the market.'

'So you don't think he was murdered?' asked Lady Hardcastle.

'There's plenty as would have liked to murder the old buzzard, that's for sure,' said Mrs Caradine. 'But that sort of thing don't happen in real life, does it? Not round here.'

'You'd be surprised, Mrs Caradine,' I said.

'Like as not, I would be,' she said. 'But that don't make it so.'

'I gather your husband was not a popular man,' said Lady Hardcastle.

Mrs Caradine shook her head. 'Spencer was a curmudgeon and a bully, Lady Hardcastle. He was a humourless old goat whose only real pleasure came from trying to make everyone around him just as miserable as he was.'

We sat in embarrassed silence.

'Shocked you, a'n't I?' said Mrs Caradine. 'I can't say as I'm glad he's gone. I loved him once and I never really wished him ill, but a lot of people's lives'll be just that little bit brighter without his dark cloud hanging over them.'

'People like whom?' said Lady Hardcastle.

'"Whom",' said Mrs Caradine with the first near-smile I'd seen her give. ''Ark at she.' She chuckled drily. 'Be quicker to give you a list of people who liked him.'

Lady Hardcastle produced her notebook and pencil from her voluminous handbag. She leafed through the first few pages until she came to the notes she had made earlier. 'Can you tell me anything about your neighbours, Mrs Caradine? Would any of them have a grudge?'

'Pretty much all of them, I'd say,' said Mrs Caradine. 'But let's see, there's Lance Tribley over one side.'

'Yes, we met him on the way here. Nice enough chap. Doesn't seem to relish the life of the farmer, but he seems a decent sort. How did Mr Caradine get on with him?'

'Like I said, no one really got on with Spencer.'

'But did they have any special disagreements?' said Lady Hardcastle.

'Same as everyone else as far as I knows. They had a row down by the boundary gate this last week, I think.'

'What about?' I said.

'Couldn't say. Didn't hear, didn't care. Spencer was always arguing with someone.'

'I see,' said Lady Hardcastle, looking at me quizzically. 'And on the other side?'

'Noah Lock's our neighbour on t'other side. Lovely bloke.'

'No arguments there, then?'

'Look,' said Mrs Caradine wearily. 'I knows you means well, and despite all as I've said, I really does want to find out if it was murder, but you i'n't listening, are you? Spencer Caradine, my late husband, was a miserable old codger who rowed with everyone. 'Course he rowed with Noah.'

'What about?' said Lady Hardcastle.

'Whatever he could think of.'

'Anything recent?'

'Noah pops by a couple of times a week . . . just . . . to be neighbourly, like. I 'spect Spencer found cause to harangue him about sommat.'

'I see,' said Lady Hardcastle. 'And what about other neighbours? Does anyone else come to call?'

'No, them's our only actual neighbours as you might say.'

'What about . . .' Lady Hardcastle flicked back a page or two in her notebook. 'Ah, yes, here he is . . . Dick Ackley? Did you ever see him?' she asked.

'Old "friends", as you might say. He's from over Woodworthy but they knowed each other for ages.'

'And what did they argue about?'

'Now you're getting it,' said Mrs Caradine. 'You name it, love, they argued about it. 'Twas like it was their favourite pastime. Latest was when Spencer's bull won a prize and Dick accused him of nobbling his bull.'

'Mr Caradine beat Mr Ackley at the auction last week, too,' I said.

'Don't I know it, love. Dick came round here shouting the odds that night. "You knew I wanted them cows, you bribed the auctioneer." They was at it for ages.'

'And did he?' said Lady Hardcastle.

'Did he what?' said Mrs Caradine.

'Did he bribe the auctioneer?'

'I wouldn't put it past him, but I don't reckon so. Dick Ackley was just a bad loser.'

'I see,' said Lady Hardcastle, making a few more notes. 'Do you have any other regular visitors, any other friends?'

'None as I can think of,' said Mrs Caradine. 'Farmers tends to keep close to their neighbours case they needs help when things go bad. But that i'n't to say they's friendly. No one travels miles for social calls, not like in your world. Them's the only ones as we see and I reckon you got a picture now of how Spencer didn't exactly get along with any of 'em.'

'Thank you, Mrs Caradine,' said Lady Hardcastle. 'I understand you have children.'

'Two daughters and a son, yes,' she said, a little more warmth returning to her voice. 'The girls both married and moved away. I've written to them but I don't know as they'll come for the funeral. One's in Portsmouth, married a sailor. T'other's in service in London; lady's maid, she is, and her fella's a valet.'

'I worked in London myself,' I said, looking over at Lady Hardcastle.

'Done all right for yourself now, a'n't you?' said Mrs Caradine. 'It don't seem such a bad life. Better than this, sometimes, I reckons.'

'And your son?' said Lady Hardcastle.

'Our Morris? He's still here. He'll be out cleaning the sheds.'

'Will he take over the farm?'

'I should have liked to think so,' said the widow sadly. 'But I just don't know. He could make a good living for hisself, and lord knows I can't run the place on my own.'

'But . . . ?' prompted Lady Hardcastle.

'But he hates the place. He only ever stayed for me. Now that his father's gone, don't seem like there's nothing to keep him here. He'll be off soon enough, I reckon.'

'Did he get on with his father?' asked Lady Hardcastle. Mrs Caradine simply raised her eyebrows and shrugged as though to say, 'Really? Have you really not been listening?'

46

We sipped our tea in silence for just a few moments longer, but it was clear that there was little more to say.

'Well, Mrs Caradine,' said Lady Hardcastle, 'we oughtn't to take up any more of your time. Once again, I'm sorry we had to intrude upon your mourning, but we really do want to get to the bottom of all this.'

'I do understand, missus,' said Mrs Caradine. 'But I hopes you does, too. Like I said, there's shock and a little sadness like there always is when someone passes, but in the long run he'll not be sorely missed.'

'Well, that was a little odd,' said Lady Hardcastle as Bert drove us to The Grange.

'Not quite the grieving widow I was expecting to meet,' I agreed. 'She was upset, but I wouldn't say that her husband's death was the cause of it. She was pleased to be rid of him.'

'There was certainly an element of that, yes. We should have a proper ponder. Perhaps Gertie will have some insights. She must have known them all for years.'

The journey from Top Farm was a short one. It wasn't long before the tyres were scrunching on the gravel drive outside the impressive, but endearingly higgledy-piggledy manor house, where Tudor chimneys loomed behind symmetrical Georgian walls, which in turn sat beside a Gothic Revival wing replete with turrets and impressively arched windows.

The brakes squealed, the car stopped, and Bert stepped smartly out to open Lady Hardcastle's door. I let myself out of the other side as he helped her to clamber out and waited while she straightened herself out.

'Oh,' she said abruptly. 'The picture.' She leant back inside the car looking for the drawing we had brought for Lady Farley-Stroud. I let her rummage around for a short while before tapping on the window and pointing at the brown-paper package I had picked up when I got out.

'Is this what you're looking for, my lady?' I said innocently.

She scowled, and struggled back out of the motor car.

'I expect you think that's rather amusing,' she said as we walked towards the front door.

'Pardon me, m'lady,' said Bert.

Lady Hardcastle turned. 'Yes, Bert?'

'I was wondering if I might go down to the kitchens for a cuppa, my lady.'

'Why, Bert, of course. How silly of me to forget. Yes, please do. I shall ring for you when we're ready to leave. Until then, you have my permission to lounge and idle.' She winked, and with a smile and a touch of the peak of his cap, he set off for the servants' entrance at the back of the house.

'I say, Flo, we really must get one of those,' said Lady Hardcastle as he walked out of sight.

'A chauffeur, my lady?' I said.

'No, you goose, a motor car. Can't you just picture me behind the wheel with you by my side? Free to come and go as we please. Roaring down the highways and byways . . .'

'Crashing into ditches and trees,' I said.

'O ye of the tiniest amount of faith,' she said, aiming a flick at my ear. 'It can't be all that difficult. Bert manages it and he's scarcely possessed of the keenest of minds.'

'I agree he's something of a plodder, my lady, but he has a certain single-mindedness about him. He has the advantage of having a dogged determination to concentrate on the task at hand. He's not a flighty old biddy who always has her mind on something else.'

'Pfft,' she said. 'I know a lady's maid who might not get any supper.'

'And I know a grumpy old widow who might struggle to cook supper for herself,' I said, dodging another flick.

She laughed and rang the doorbell. 'A telephone and a motor car, that's what we need.'

Jenkins, the Farley-Strouds' butler, answered the door.

'Lady Hardcastle,' he said with a welcoming smile. 'And Miss Armstrong. Please do come in.' He opened the door fully and ushered us inside. He helped both of us with our hats and coats and put Lady Hardcastle's walking stick into the new elephant's-foot umbrella stand. 'Lady Farley-Stroud had hoped you might be calling. She asked me to take you to the drawing room.'

He led the way, though we had spent enough time in the house by now to know our own way.

'Please make yourselves comfortable,' he said, indicating the chintz-covered chairs.

'Thank you, Jenkins,' said Lady Hardcastle. 'Are you well?'

'Passing well, thank you, my lady. How very kind of you to ask. I shall tell my lady that you're here.'

He bowed and left.

The room, like the rest of the house, was slightly dated and dowdy, with a faintly melancholy air of faded elegance. But it was warm and welcoming for all that, and it was surprisingly easy to become very comfortable very quickly.

Lady Farley-Stroud arrived with Jenkins after only a few minutes and waved me back into my chair as I attempted to stand up.

'Sit down, m'girl,' she said. 'Wouldn't have one of me own servants sitting on the best furniture, but Emily treats you as part of the family and who am I to make a fuss.'

I nodded my thanks.

'Hello, Gertie, darling,' said Lady Hardcastle. 'I do hope you don't mind us dropping in.'

'Not at all, dear,' said our hostess. 'Glad to see you. Jenkins? Coffee for three, please. And some cake if Mrs Brown has any.'

'Certainly, my lady,' said Jenkins, closing the door behind him as he left.

'So sorry about yesterday, Emily,' said Lady Farley-Stroud when he had gone. 'Don't know what came over me.'

'You'd had a shock, darling,' said Lady Hardcastle. 'Perfectly natural. Think nothing of it. How are you feeling now?'

'Much better, m'dear, much better.'

'I'm pleased to hear it. You had us quite worried.' She picked up the gift that had been lying on the sofa beside her. 'We brought you a little something to cheer you up.'

She handed over the brown-paper package, which Lady Farley-Stroud opened eagerly.

'You shouldn't have, m'dear,' she said as she struggled with the string. 'But thank you. Much appreciated. Don't get many presents.' She finally freed the framed picture from its wrapper and laughed delightedly. 'Oh, I say. How wonderful. You've quite captured me. You're a very clever lady. Thank you. We'll have to put it in the hall where everyone can see it.'

She carried on examining the sketch, beaming with pleasure.

'Sorry to have made such a fuss, Emily, dear. Not like me, not like me at all.'

'Pish and fiddlesticks,' said Lady Hardcastle. 'I'd be more worried if it hadn't affected you. It must have been awful.'

'Oh, it was, m'dear, it was.'

'What happened, exactly? Had you been at The Hayrick long?'

'Got there early, about eleven, I'd say. Found a table with Mogg—'

'The chap we met last week, your estate manager?'

'That's the fella. Ambrose Mogg. Salt of the earth. He was bringing me up to date on the cattle herd. Dour chap, little dry, but witty when he wants to be.'

'You said yesterday you were sitting with Mr Caradine,' said Lady Hardcastle.

'"Sitting near" would be more like it,' said Lady Farley-Stroud. 'You remember those long tables in the public bar? Mogg and I were opposite each other at one end, Caradine was a little further down, on Mogg's side.'

'Was he with anyone?'

'Caradine was never "with" anyone, m'dear. Not a popular man.'

'So we gathered.'

'Oh?' said Lady Farley-Stroud with a raised eyebrow.

'We've just come back from talking to the Widow Caradine,' said Lady Hardcastle.

'That poor woman. Can't say I ever spent much time with her m'self,' said Lady Farley-Stroud, finally setting the picture down on a side table. 'She never came to market.'

'No, I don't suppose she did. She gave us quite an unexpected picture of her late husband, I must say.'

'Spencer Caradine was an unpleasant old goat. Doesn't do to speak ill of the dead, I know, but it can't be helped. Man could start a fight in an empty room.'

'You're not the first person to say that today, dear,' said Lady Hardcastle.

'No, heard it in the pub one day. Thought it apt. Not kind, but it did make me chuckle at the time.'

'Which is why he sat alone, one presumes.'

'Exactly so, m'dear. Difficult man to be with.'

'Did he look well?'

'Not really, dear, no. Quite peaky.'

'But you talked?' asked Lady Hardcastle.

'Briefly. One minute he was grumbling about his new cows, the next minute he was dead.'

'Just like that?'

'He shuddered a bit, then fell forwards into his pie.'

'He didn't clutch his throat at all? Did he struggle for breath?'

'Choking, you mean? No, just an almighty spasm and then gone.'

'And was there anyone near him? Had anyone spoken to him?'

'Not as far as I recall, dear, no. Solitary man. No friends that I know of. Always wondered about the wife, how she ended up with him. Well liked as far as I know. And beautiful, too. Turned more than a few heads in her day, I can tell you.'

'She's rather striking even now,' said Lady Hardcastle. 'I was wondering: did she have any admirers?'

'I should jolly well say so.'

'Noah Lock?' suggested Lady Hardcastle.

'Oh, I say, you are good, aren't you?' said Lady Farley-Stroud appreciatively. 'How on earth did you reach that conclusion?'

'Oh, just the way she stumbled over explaining why he "popped round" a couple of times a week "to be neighbourly, like".'

'It's been an open secret for years, m'dear. But she's devout. "Till death us do part", it said in her vows and she was never going to break a promise she'd made before God.'

'But if Caradine were suddenly to die, she'd be free to marry Lock. Interesting.'

'You think she killed him herself?' asked Lady Farley-Stroud excitedly.

'I'd not rule it out,' said Lady Hardcastle. 'But she wasn't at the pub, so how could she have poisoned him?'

'So it was Lock?'

'Again, possible. He was certainly at the pub that day. But so were several other people. Dick Ackley, for instance.'

'Oh my gosh, yes,' said Lady Farley-Stroud. 'They hated each other. Lots of tension over the cattle sale.'

'And the prize bull,' I said.

'The prize bull,' she said. 'Completely forgotten that. Yes. It has to be Ackley. He could have slipped something into Caradine's cider at the pub and no one would have noticed.'

Lady Hardcastle laughed. 'Steady on, Gertie, darling. We can't go accusing them all. What about Morris Caradine?'

'The wet lettuce son?'

'He's a wet lettuce?' said Lady Hardcastle.

'Of the very limpest sort,' said Lady Farley-Stroud. 'Don't mind a chap not wanting to get his hands dirty on the farm if his heart lies elsewhere, but he's so spineless about it.'

'How do you mean?'

'Never stood up to his father. Just went along, looking droopy and miserable. Dashed good painter, by all accounts. Could give you a run for your money, Emily, what? But he never said, "Papa, I am moving to the city to be an artist, and to the Devil with your blessed farm." No, he just sullenly accepted his lot.'

'Was he afraid of his father?' I said. 'Was he bullied by him?'

'Spencer Caradine tried to bully everyone, m'dear. But, yes, Morris got the worst of it.'

'They always say poison's a woman's weapon,' said Lady Hardcastle thoughtfully. 'But perhaps it's a wet lettuce's weapon, too.'

'Oh, dear lord, it could be any of them,' said Lady Farley-Stroud.

'What do you know about their other neighbour?' said Lady Hardcastle. 'Lancelot Tribley. We met him this morning on the way to Top Farm.'

'Funny chap, Tribley,' said Lady Farley-Stroud. 'Fits in everywhere but the farm. Chairman of the rugby club, you know. Ask Hector about him. But he hates that farm. Made a lot of fuss about a year ago about how he was selling up and moving on. Big plans for a business venture in Gloucester, I think. Twelve months on and he's still here. Dreamer. Head in the clouds.'

I had a sudden thought. 'No one's mentioned Toby Thompson,' I said.

'Dear old Toby,' said Lady Hardcastle. 'Of course. Well done, Flo. Did I ever tell you he was the first person we met on our first morning walk after we moved in, Gertie? Lovely chap. Why isn't his name on my list? He must be a regular at the market.'

'Oh, he is, m'dear, but not so much recently. His sister's ill. He's been spending every spare moment with her up in North Nibley. Not that he has many spare moments, you understand. But when he has nothing to sell, market day's an indulgence the poor chap can't afford.'

'Oh, how sad,' said Lady Hardcastle. 'But why didn't Mrs Caradine mention him? He's one of her neighbours, surely?'

'No, m'dear. I'd have to get the map out to show you, but his farm's the other side of Noah Lock's. Not strictly her neighbour.'

'Aha,' said Lady Hardcastle. 'That would account for it.'

'And what are your thoughts, m'dear?' said Lady Farley-Stroud. 'Who did it?'

'Oh, Gertie, you are funny. We've only spoken to two people, the police haven't found any evidence that they've told us about, and the police surgeon hasn't even confirmed he was poisoned yet. Mrs Caradine said he'd been ill.'

Lady Farley-Stroud looked dismayed. 'Getting overexcited, eh?'

'Just a tad, darling,' said Lady Hardcastle kindly.

There was a knock on the door and Jenkins came in with the coffee tray.

'I say, Jenkins, what took you so long?' said Lady Farley-Stroud. 'Been to Brazil for the coffee?' She chuckled.

'I believe this particular blend comes from the West Indies, my lady.' Jenkins was a straightforward fellow, almost entirely un-encumbered by a sense of humour.

'Does it, by jove?' she said. 'I say, ever been to the West Indies, Emily?'

'No, dear. But my aunt used to go out there quite a bit.'

'Jamaica?' said Lady Farley-Stroud.

'No . . . Antigua,' said Lady Hardcastle. 'My uncle worked in the sugar business.'

'Cook sends her apologies, my lady,' said Jenkins. 'But the egg delivery was late and she's only just now finishing off the cake she had intended to make. She asks if you might like some of this shortbread instead.'

'I should bally well say so, Jenkins,' said Lady Hardcastle enthusiastically. 'We've had Mrs Brown's shortbread before. Thank her very much.'

'Yes, Jenkins, do,' said Lady Farley-Stroud.

'Will that be all, my lady?' he said.

'Yes, thank you,' said Lady Farley-Stroud. 'Oh, have you seen Sir Hector?'

'He's in his study, I believe, my lady. Would you like me to convey a message?'

'No, don't wake him up. Will you stay for dinner, Emily?'

'Thank you, dear, but no. We ought to be getting back. I still have one or two things to do back at the house. Another evening, perhaps?'

'That would be splendid,' said Lady Farley-Stroud. 'We shall be just two for dinner as usual, then, Jenkins. Would you like the motor car, Emily?'

'If you wouldn't mind, darling, that would be lovely.'

'Tell Bert, would you, please, Jenkins,' said Lady Farley-Stroud.

'Thank you, my lady,' he said with a bow. He left quietly.

Back at the house I prepared a light meal which we ate together while Lady Hardcastle speculated wildly on the subject of poisons and poisoning.

'You see,' she said, gesticulating with her fork, 'there are poisons that act almost instantly, and some that take hours. It would be so much easier if we knew what it was that killed Caradine. Then we could work backwards and establish when the poison was administered. And then, of course, we'd have a better idea who our suspects might be.'

'What are the most likely poisons, then?' I asked.

'Well, there's our old friend arsenic,' she said, tapping the medical book that was the source of her newfound expertise. 'A large enough dose can take as little as half an hour and it's not frightfully hard to acquire. We don't know how Caradine was feeling just before he died so we can't know if the symptoms match, but it's possible that someone could have slipped him some while he was in the pub.'

'Isn't there something in the report about him looking a bit peaky all morning, though, even before Lady Farley-Stroud saw him?' I said.

'There is, but Mrs Caradine said he'd been ill, so that might not mean anything. Unless of course she'd been giving it to him for a while. You can slowly poison someone with a small, steady dose.'

'So we can't rule out arsenic,' I said.

'No. And then there's cyanide, of course. That can be very quick indeed. Someone wandering past the table could have dropped some in his cider . . . and then . . .'

'Lady Farley-Stroud did say that he just keeled over.'

'She did, she did.'

'What about strychnine?' I said.

'Slower acting, but it does lead to convulsions. Gertie said he spasmed before he collapsed.'

'And they're all fairly easy to get hold of,' I said.

'That's the problem. I do wish the police surgeon would get on with it.'

'Perhaps we could contact Inspector Sunderland in the morning,' I suggested.

'I think we might have to,' she said. 'Or put it in the hands of someone who actually knows about these things. I've got a pal at the hospital, chap I knew up at Cambridge. I'm sure he'd have it sorted out in two shakes.' She munched contemplatively on her dinner for a few moments. 'I say,' she said. 'This trout is delicious.'

'Thank you, my lady. It's the cyanide that makes the difference. Some people use flaked almonds, but I find that a touch of prussic acid adds a piquancy that can't be matched.'

'You'd never get away with it, dear. Sunderland would be onto you like a shot.'

'We're in it together, my lady. He's tired of being shown up by your brilliance.'

She laughed. 'If only I were brilliant. I feel like an absolute duffer at the moment. I don't have the faintest idea how we're going to solve this one.'

'We've only just begun, my lady. Wait until we've spoken to a few more of the farmers, then you'll feel better.'

'I suppose so,' she said. 'When did Bert say he'd be here tomorrow?'

'I suggested ten o'clock, my lady. I thought it would give us time to do a few things about the house and for the farmers to be back at home after their early start.'

'Good thinking. What do you think, Ackley or Lock first?'

'Ackley was a bad loser over the auction, but would that be enough to want to kill a man? Lock had more to gain if he could free the Fair Audrey from her loveless marriage and take her for his own.'

'He'd be doing them both a favour,' agreed Lady Hardcastle. 'Shall we toss a coin?'

'Only if you have one, my lady, for I am but a poor servant girl with no money of her own.'

She laughed again, the smile transforming her face, making her seem sunnier and more alive than I'd seen her for a long while. 'You're lively today, Flo,' she said. 'What's got into you?'

'Honestly? I have no idea. Perhaps it's the relief of finding that you're properly on the mend.'

'I'm sorry I worried you, dear. One gets wrapped up in oneself and forgets that it's hard on everyone else, too. I ought to write to Harry and let him know how things are going.'

'You ought, my lady.'

'But how shall we choose whom to visit?' she said. 'We need something governed entirely by chance.' She looked around. 'Oh, I know: the book. You riffle through the pages and I'll shove my finger in at random. A page number ending one or three will be Lock first, five or seven will be Ackley.'

'And if it's a nine, my lady?'

'Then Bert takes us into Bristol where we have a slap-up lunch, an afternoon of shopping and try to catch a show at the Empire. And hang the murder investigation.'

'Really? You're on.'

I lifted the front cover of the book out of the way and then riffled through the pages. Lady Hardcastle's finger darted between them as they fell and I opened the book fully to see what fate had chosen for us.

'Page two five seven,' I said disappointedly. 'Looks like we'll be speaking to Dick Ackley tomorrow morning.'

'It seems that way. We'll have to have our day out another time.'

'Pfft,' I said. 'Stupid murderers and their stupid murders.'

'Quite so, dear, quite so. Now let's get cleared up and we can update the crime board. And then I think a little music is in order. Perhaps we can compose some bawdy music hall songs to make up for our missed trip to the Empire.'

'She was only a fishmonger's daughter . . .' I sang as I gathered up the plates.

4

I was up with the lark on Saturday morning, and resolved at once to make enquiries as to the sleeping habits of larks. Do they really rise early? 'Up with the lady's maid' might be just as evocative of early rising but perhaps open to unfortunate misinterpretation.

By the time Lady Hardcastle rang for her morning coffee, I'd completed quite a few chores that I had been putting off and was feeling rather pleased with myself as I took it up to her.

She was sitting up in bed, reading, when I entered.

'Good morning, Flo, dear,' she said.

'And good morning to you,' I said. 'At last. Coffee?'

'"At last", eh? Are you calling your mistress a slugabed?'

'If the nightcap fits.'

'Harrumph,' she said. 'It's Saturday. Surely a lady can rest on a Saturday.'

'That would be true, my lady, were it not the case that the lady in question takes her ease on the other six days of the week as well.'

'You, my girl, are a puritan. And a . . . a . . .'

'A perfectly charming and wonderful woman, my lady?'

'If you like,' she said with another harrumph.

'It's actually only eight o'clock, my lady,' I said. 'Breakfast will be ready in fifteen minutes and Bert won't be here until ten. I've laid out some clothes and polished your boots.'

'You seem to have everything well in hand. Thank you.'

'You're welcome, my lady. I shall yell uncouthly when breakfast is served.'

'We need a gong.'

'Nonsense, my lady. A good strong pair of Welsh lungs is all we need. See you presently.'

I excused myself and went back downstairs.

Breakfast and dressing passed without major incident. There was a moment of slight drama over a loose button on the dress, but Flo's Magic Sewing Box came to the rescue there.

'I swear he must arrive early and wait round the bend in the road,' said Lady Hardcastle as the doorbell rang. 'How can a man be so perfectly punctual all the time?'

I opened the door. 'Good morning, Bert,' I said. 'How do you manage it?'

'Morning, miss,' said a slightly puzzled Bert. 'Manage what?'

'To be so perfectly on time,' I said. 'You always ring the bell just as the clock chimes.'

He chuckled. 'Well, I has our Dad's pocket watch – keeps excellent time, that does – so that gets me here near enough . . . and then you has the loudest hall clock in Christendom. If I gets out of the car as soon as I hears it start to chime, I can ring the door just as it starts to strike the hour.'

'Oh,' I said, stepping aside so that Lady Hardcastle could get out of the door. 'How mundane.'

'Sorry to disappoint you, miss,' he said with a grin.

We arrived at Dick Ackley's farm in Woodworthy just as Mr Ackley was walking back up the lane from one of his more distant fields.

Lady Hardcastle asked Bert to stop and let us out so that we could walk with him. Mr Ackley, too, stopped in the lane. He regarded us with suspicion as we both clambered out of the motor car.

'Good morning, Mr Ackley,' said Lady Hardcastle, approaching him. 'I'm Lady Hardcastle and this is Miss Armstrong.'

'And good mornin' to you, m'lady. I knows who you are,' he said, knuckling his forehead. 'I seen you with Lady Farley-Stroud down The Hayrick t'other week. Heard about you 'fore that, o' course. What can I do for you?'

'We're trying to find out a little more about the death of Mr Caradine,' she said.

'That old buzzard? Shouldn't speak ill and all that, but good riddance to him.' He resumed his trudge back to the farmhouse and we fell in beside him.

'You're not the first person to say that to us, Mr Ackley,' she said. 'And we only started asking about him yesterday.'

'Don't reckon you'll get many different opinions round here,' he said. 'On the day the Good Lord was handing out charm and happy-go-lucky personalities, Spencer Caradine was round the back trying to start a fight with St Peter over sommat or other, I reckons.'

'When did you last see him?' she said.

'Thursday, down The Hayrick. Saw him sitting there, hunched over his pie, glaring at everyone. Then a little later he was face down in it.'

'And when did you last speak to him?' I asked.

'I went over to his place last week after he cheated me at the auction. Gave the old codger a piece of my mind.'

'What did you say?' I said.

'Told him I'd not stand for none of his nonsense no more and if he bilked me again I'd give him what for.'

'And what was his reaction?'

'Told me to . . . beggin' your pardon, ladies, but I can't say what he told me to do in present company.'

'We get the gist,' said Lady Hardcastle with a smile. 'But why did you think he'd cheated you?'

'Well,' he said thoughtfully, 'now I comes to tell it to someone else, I i'n't certain no more that he did. It was just every time I thought I was about to get a little bit ahead, there was Caradine, putting the kibosh on it. Like he was doing it on purpose. He didn't need them cows from off the Farley-Stroud estate. He just wanted 'em so I couldn't have 'em. Good milkers they was. I could-a done with they.'

'Where did this altercation take place?' she said.

'Out in his yard.'

'He didn't invite you in? Offer you a cup of tea and talk it over?'

Ackley laughed. 'Spencer Caradine? Genial host? He wouldn't give you the steam off . . . begging your pardon, ladies.'

'Was Mrs Caradine there?' I asked.

'Audrey?' he said, slightly wistfully. 'She didn't come out, but I seen her through the window, like.'

'And she didn't invite you in?'

'She never done nothing without Spencer's say-so.'

'So you had your row in the yard,' I said. 'And then what?'

'I just left him to it,' he said. 'I'd said my piece, so I just left him to stew on it. It weren't going to do no good, like, but I felt all the better for having said it.'

'And you didn't see him again until the next market day?' said Lady Hardcastle.

'No, m'lady, didn't have no cause to. He weren't the sort of bloke you'd seek out for company if you knows what I mean.'

We had arrived at the farmhouse gate where Ackley stopped, plainly unwilling to invite us further.

'Do you keep any poisons, Mr Ackley?' I said abruptly.

He stared at me, first in surprise, and then with mounting anger.

'I beg your pardon?' he said coldly.

'Poison, Mr Ackley. Do you keep any?'

'I hope you're not accusing me, miss . . .'

'Armstrong,' I said. 'No, Mr Ackley. I'm trying to find out where the poisons are around these parts. We're new round here.'

'Every farmer has poison, Miss Armstrong. Rats. They eats the feed, damages the barns. Pests. We kills 'em,' he said, looking me defiantly in the eye.

'And what do you use?' I said, returning his stare.

'Arsenic.'

'Thank you,' I said.

'Yes, Mr Ackley, thank you,' said Lady Hardcastle.

We stood in silence for a few moments.

'I got to be getting on,' said Ackley. 'Good day.'

And with that, he opened the gate, walked through and then closed it behind him without giving us a second look.

'Well, that told us,' said Lady Hardcastle as we walked back towards the motor car and the ever-patient Bert. 'Nice job rattling him at the end there. Caught him off guard.'

'Didn't help us much, though,' I said disappointedly.

'Oh, I don't know. You goaded him into giving you a defiant and definite answer.'

'I suppose so,' I said as we clambered into the car.

'Where to now, m'lady?' said Bert as we settled into our seats.

'Let's go and see Noah Lock,' said Lady Hardcastle. 'Audrey Caradine's forbidden love.'

We hurtled along the lanes towards Noah Lock's farm. Well, perhaps 'hurtled' is overstating it a bit. Bert had little regard for the twenty miles per hour speed limit, but the little car was hardly a racing model. Still, we made good time and we arrived at the farmhouse gate just as Lock was coming out of his front door.

He was a tall man, built like a sportsman – a rugby player, perhaps – and he looked as though he might be in his early fifties. He smiled a greeting when he noticed us standing at his gate.

'Come on in, ladies,' he said with a smile. 'Mind the mud, the path needs a sweep.'

I opened the sturdy wooden gate and stepped aside to allow Lady Hardcastle to enter.

'Good afternoon, Mr Lock,' she said as we approached him. 'I'm Lady Hardcastle and this is Miss Armstrong.'

'I know,' he said, still smiling. 'I've been expecting you. Would you like some tea?'

'If we're not interrupting your work,' she said, 'that would be splendid.'

He led us into the farmhouse and through into the kitchen. It wasn't as neat and prim as Audrey Caradine's kitchen, but it was tidy and clean. He waved us to chairs at the large oak table and we sat.

'You were expecting us, you say?' said Lady Hardcastle.

He laughed, his smile illuminating his face once more. 'Word travels fast, my lady, even out here. They say you're investigating the death of Spencer Caradine. Old Sergeant Boyce down in Chipping is none too pleased about it, I can tell you.'

Lady Hardcastle frowned. 'No, I didn't expect he would be. Still, it can't be helped – we're doing a favour for a friend.'

'He doesn't speak too kindly of Inspector Sunderland, either,' said Lock.

'Poor man. He must feel quite humiliated by the whole thing,' she said thoughtfully. 'Perhaps we should try to make peace.'

'It's an admirable sentiment, but you'd be wasting your time. He likes to feel hard done by. Thrives on it, you might say. Best to leave him to stew – he'll be happier in the long run.'

Lock put a kettle on to boil and prepared the tea things.

'You don't sound like a local man, Mr Lock,' said Lady Hardcastle as Lock placed cups and saucers on the table.

'No, my lady,' he said. 'My people are from Hertfordshire.'

'And how did you end up here, if you don't mind my asking?'

'Resigned my commission, took my pension and went looking for a farm somewhere nice and quiet.'

'Oh,' she said. 'Where did you serve?'

'Here, there, and everywhere,' he said. It was apparent that he didn't really want to talk about his military service and he said nothing further as he filled the teapot and set it down on the table. He pulled out a chair and sat down.

'Have you seen Audrey Caradine since her husband's death?' asked Lady Hardcastle.

He looked at her appraisingly.

'I shan't insult your intelligence, Lady Hardcastle,' he said, 'by trying to pretend that I have no idea what you're talking about. Of course I've seen Mrs Caradine, and I'm sure you know exactly why.'

'More than once?' she said.

'More than once a day, most days,' he said, regarding her levelly. 'Look, half the county knows how we feel about each other. I have no desire to see her name sullied by grubby rumours and insinuations, but I also see no profit in denying that I'm in love with Audrey Caradine and that I fully intend to marry her as soon as is seemly.'

'It's very convenient that Mr Caradine has finally died,' said Lady Hardcastle.

'There's a sense in which it very much is, yes. And I know that that makes me a suspect in his murder—'

'We're not yet certain that it is murder,' she interrupted.

'That's true,' he said. 'But the Bristol CID wouldn't have loosed their favourite hounds on the case if they didn't at least think there was a possibility that it might be.'

'You flatter us,' she said.

'Nonetheless, I had nothing to do with his death. You've met Audrey. Do you think she would consent to spend the rest of her life with a murderer? Killing him might have brought us together all the sooner, but once she found out it would have pushed us further apart than ever.'

'You make a good case,' she said.

Lock poured the tea.

'Which poison do you use for your rats?' I asked as he offered me the sugar.

'For my what . . . ? Oh, I see.' He smiled. 'I use strychnine. There's a bottle in the shed.'

'Thank you, Mr Lock,' I said with a polite smile.

'My pleasure, I'm sure,' he said. 'Does that make me more suspicious, or less?'

'To be perfectly frank, Mr Lock,' said Lady Hardcastle, 'we have absolutely no idea. The police surgeon is dragging his heels and no one yet knows what killed Mr Caradine. For all we know it could be natural causes. We could have been sent on a wild goose chase by Inspector Sunderland, upsetting our neighbours and wasting everyone's time into the bargain.'

'But you don't really think so,' he said, taking a sip of his tea.

'Honestly?' she said. 'No, I don't. The witness statements all seem to point to unnatural causes. What did you see on Thursday?'

'I'm afraid I didn't see anything. I was on the other side of the room.'

'Had you seen Mr Caradine earlier in the day?'

'No, I was busy selling a few sheep. I didn't even know Caradine was in Chipping until all the kerfuffle in The Hayrick.'

'And so when did you last see him?' she asked.

'To speak to?' he said.

'Or at all. I get the impression that few people spoke to him. At least not without some sort of quarrel ensuing.'

He laughed. 'You have that right,' he said. 'I last spoke to him on Monday afternoon when I called round to ask him if he needed any feed. I'd over-ordered and I was happy to let a neighbour have some.'

'How did he seem?'

'Ill-tempered and ungrateful as ever.'

'Did he take the feed?'

'Like a shot. He was a grumpy old codger, but he wasn't stupid.'

'And did you see him after that at all?' I asked.

'I saw him across the field on Wednesday as I was . . . ah . . .'

'Making your way home from your assignation?' suggested Lady Hardcastle.

'You have a charming way of making our perfectly innocent meetings sound sordid and grubby, Lady Hardcastle.'

'How would you describe it, then?' she asked.

'A cup of tea and a chat,' he said. 'She was trapped in a loveless marriage with a charmless bully. He had chased all her other friends away and no one else had the nerve to stand up to him. I was all she had for company other than her son, and Morris tried to spend as much time away from the house as he could.'

'But you didn't speak to Caradine on Wednesday,' said Lady Hardcastle. 'Was he far away? How did he look?'

'Like a miserable old goat.'

'In himself, Mr Lock. Did he look ill?'

'Come to think of it, he did look a bit less robust than usual. Did you meet him when he was alive? He was a thin, insubstantial-looking man, but quite vigorous. Now you ask, I suppose he looked a little . . . diminished on Wednesday.'

'Pale?'

'I've no idea, I'm afraid, he must have been a couple of hundred yards away across a field, but there was something about his walk. Why?'

'I'm not sure,' said Lady Hardcastle. 'Mrs Caradine said he'd been ill, that was all. I was just wondering whether it might have been an illness sufficient to kill him. I just thought you might have got an impression, something that might give us more of an idea of the state of his health.'

'Well, I'm no doctor, I'm afraid. And I didn't get a terribly good look. Just an impression, you know.'

'I do,' she said. 'And then on Thursday you sold your sheep and retired to The Hayrick for lunch?'

'In a nutshell.'

'Do you have many friends there?'

'Where? The pub? A fair few, I suppose.'

'It's a rather welcoming community, isn't it?'

'It is. They're not at all troubled by the arrival of incomers,' he said.

'As we can attest,' she said.

'It doesn't hurt to be a farmer, either. Once the frosts come and the lambs are freezing, we're all in it together. When the storms come and blow down the pig sheds, we all rally round. No one cares about the Royal Engineers or the family name then, I'm just another farmer, a neighbour in need, or a pair of strong arms to pick up the pieces.'

'You make it sound rather romantic,' she said.

He smiled. 'I suppose I do.'

'And were many of your friends at The Hayrick?'

'Most of them, I should say. It's always lively on market day.'

'Yes, I remember,' she said.

'Ah, yes, I was wondering where I'd seen you. Heard of you, of course, but I couldn't place where I'd seen you. You were there with Lady Farley-Stroud.'

'We were.'

'Is it always the same crowd, Mr Lock?' I said.

'More or less,' he said. 'Not everyone is there every week, but it's not like we take roll-call.'

'You've been very patient,' said Lady Hardcastle, putting her cup emphatically back into its saucer. 'But we mustn't take up any more of your time.'

'My pleasure, I'm sure,' he said, with a nod and a wry smile.

Lady Hardcastle stood and Mr Lock and I rose, too.

'Thank you for speaking to us, Mr Lock. May we call again if anything else comes up?'

'Of course, my lady,' he said. 'My door is always open.'

He saw us to the door and waited there, watching, as we tiptoed along the path to the waiting car at the gate. Bert had already cranked the engine to life and was settling into the driver's seat as we approached.

'Where to now, m'lady?' asked Bert as we clambered into the back of the motor car.

'Heavens, Bert,' said Lady Hardcastle. 'Do you know, I haven't the faintest idea. There are still a couple of people we need to talk to, but I hadn't really made any plans beyond these two visits. What do you think, Armstrong?'

'I've no idea, my lady,' I said. 'Home for lunch and a ponder?'

'Would you think it impertinent of me to make a suggestion, m'lady?' said Bert, regarding us warily in his rear-view mirror as he set off.

'Not at all, Bert, suggest away,' said Lady Hardcastle.

'Lady Farley-Stroud did say this morning that she would welcome another visit. She seemed to be hinting heavily that I should try to persuade you to come for lunch. Would that be acceptable?'

'Bert,' said Lady Hardcastle delightedly, 'that would be nothing short of absolutely perfect. To The Grange for lunch and don't spare the horses.'

With a crunch of gears and a fierce revving of the engine, we were off.

Jenkins answered the door almost as soon as Lady Hardcastle had rung the doorbell, and led us straight through to the dining room with barely a word of greeting. Lady Farley-Stroud was at the sideboard, filling her plate.

'Lady Hardcastle, my lady,' said Jenkins, ushering us inside.

'Emily! Come on in, m'dear. So glad you could come. Grab a plate. Help yourself. Plenty of nosh.'

Lady Hardcastle kissed her in greeting and picked up two plates, handing one to me. She didn't ask if Lady Farley-Stroud minded if I ate with them but I tried to be as unobtrusive as possible.

'Will Hector be joining us?' she said as she helped herself to a slice of pie.

'No, m'dear,' she said. 'Gone over to the rugby club in Chipping. Big match today. Not back till supper time. I usually go with him but there's a parish council meeting later this afternoon so I'm having to miss the match. Do help yourself, Armstrong. Don't stand on ceremony.'

I put a few bits and bobs on my plate and sat down next to Lady Hardcastle.

'So, my dears,' said Lady Farley-Stroud. 'Tell Auntie Gertie all. What have you discovered?'

Lady Hardcastle recounted the details of our two meetings while Lady Farley-Stroud listened attentively.

'Gracious,' said Lady Farley-Stroud when she'd finished. 'So that means Lock killed him for love. How romantic.'

Lady Hardcastle laughed. 'How did you get there?' she said.

'It's plain as the bulbous nose on Hector's face, m'dear. He and Audrey Caradine are in it together, putting strychnine in the old boy's food so they can be together.'

'Arsenic would be better for that,' said Lady Hardcastle. 'Lots of low doses over time, slowly poisoning him, making it look like he was just ill.'

'Oh,' said Lady Farley-Stroud, crestfallen. 'But Ackley had the arsenic. So it was him?'

'But what if,' said Lady Hardcastle with a mischievous smile, 'the Caradines used arsenic as their rat poison and there was plenty at their own farm? Or Lock was lying? Or Audrey slipped some strychnine in his porridge before he went to market? What if it was young Morris Caradine? We've not spoken to him yet. And there was such chaos at The Hayrick that day that it could have been anyone there – people we've not even thought of talking to.'

'Oh, Emily, you're just teasing me now.'

'A little tiny bit, dear, yes. But do you see? It's not nearly as simple a matter as one might hope. We do still need to speak to Morris. And we're still waiting to hear from the police surgeon about the nature of the poison – if indeed there was any poison at all.'

'How on earth do you keep it all clear in your head? I swear you must be the cleverest person I ever met.'

'It's just patience, darling,' said Lady Hardcastle. 'If you wait long enough the solution usually presents itself.'

'And what about you, Armstrong? D'you think she's the cleverest?' said Lady Farley-Stroud, turning towards me.

'Of course, my lady,' I said. 'I've always thought so.'

'Quite right, too,' she said. 'Proud to be able to call you m'friend, Emily, dear. We should see more of you, you know. You really must come to dinner again soon. You promised last week that you would.'

'Oh, that's right, I did,' said Lady Hardcastle. 'But perhaps you and Hector should come to the house. It's my turn, surely. I came here during our first week at the house, do you remember?'

'I do, I do. We had a few people over. Lovely evening, as I recall. Didn't you play for us?'

'I might have done. Put me anywhere near a piano and I'm bound to play it eventually. But if that was the last time we dined together then it really is my turn. I've been very remiss.'

'Nonsense, you've been recovering from wounds received in action, what?'

Lady Hardcastle laughed. 'I suppose I have at that. But it's still my turn.'

'Very well, m'dear, if you insist. Shan't argue with a free supper. Name the day and we'll be there. Be good to get out.'

'We'll organize it soon, darling.'

They chattered inconsequentially for the rest of the meal. At length Lady Hardcastle asked if she could ring for Bert, and there followed a brief and awkward discussion of payment for his services, or at the very least for the costs of running the motor car. Lady Hardcastle insisted it was only right and proper and Lady Farley-Stroud wouldn't hear of it.

But it was a ritual exchange, intended to save face. The Farley-Strouds weren't nearly as wealthy as the villagers believed and of course she would be only too grateful for any financial help, but it would be humiliating to say so. So they danced around the subject for a while before Lady Hardcastle wrote a generous cheque. Lady Farley-Stroud insisted it was far too much before putting it in her purse while Lady Hardcastle discreetly looked the other way.

By the time they'd finished, Jenkins was at the dining room door announcing that Bert was ready whenever we needed him.

'Thank you for lunch, Gertie, darling,' said Lady Hardcastle as she kissed her goodbye.

'Entirely my pleasure, m'dear. Thank you for keeping an old girl company. Where are you off to now?'

'As a matter of fact, we have no plans at all. I was thinking of getting out into the studio and messing about with some "animation" ideas I had.'

'"Animation", eh?' said Lady Farley-Stroud. 'Sounds frightfully exciting. Will we ever get to see any of your moving pictures, m'dear?'

'One day, perhaps. One day.'

'You should show them at the village hall. We'd get people from miles around to come and see them.'

'Well, I don't really—'

Sir Hector blustered into the hall.

'Did I hear someone say Bert has the motor out?' he said. 'Oh, what ho, Emily, m'dear. Coming or going?'

'Just on our way home, Hector,' said Lady Hardcastle.

'I thought you left hours ago,' said Lady Farley-Stroud to her husband. 'You could have eaten with us.'

'Sudden change of plans,' said Sir Hector. 'Biffo couldn't host – memsahib's mother came to stay or some such. We agreed to meet at the club instead.'

'Well, I've agreed that Bert should drive Emily and Armstrong back home,' she said. 'You'll have to wait.'

'Nonsense,' said Lady Hardcastle. 'We can all squeeze in together. It's your motor car after all. Is the rugby club far?'

'Not far, m'dear, not far,' said Sir Hector. 'But not our club today. Match is at Chipping. Big match, big match. Can't miss it. D'you like rugger?'

'Roddy used to play in our youth and I always enjoy watching when I can,' she said. 'Armstrong's quite an enthusiast, though.'

'Are you, m'dear? Marvellous. Why don't you both come along? Gertie's having to miss out, poor thing.'

'Actually,' said Lady Hardcastle, 'it sounds like it might be fun. What do you think, Armstrong?'

'I'd love to,' I said.

'Settled,' said Sir Hector. 'Last one in the motor buys the beer.'

We arrived at the club in plenty of time. And a good thing, too, as it turned out. It was, as Sir Hector had said, an important match. Against all expectations, plucky little Littleton Cotterell had beaten Clifton in the semi-final of the Wessex Challenge Cup and today was the day of the final. The other semi-final had also resulted in a surprise upset so that our village team was playing against North Nibley. The final was being hosted, rather conveniently, by Chipping Bevington RFC.

Sir Hector had once been the chairman of Littleton Cotterell RFC and had recently been appointed Grand Eternal Poobah. It was a purely ceremonial title, which mostly seemed to entitle him to wear a splendidly outrageous blazer in the club colours of blue and gold. More usefully, it granted him certain hospitality privileges at local rugby clubs, which meant that we were greeted most warmly.

'Well then,' said Sir Hector. 'How about a beer? D'you drink beer? Or cider, perhaps. The memsahib loves her cider.'

'Cider would be lovely, Hector, thank you,' said Lady Hardcastle.

He returned moments later with a tray.

'You like rugger, then, Miss Armstrong?' he said as he handed out the brimming glasses.

'It's our national game, sir,' I said. 'My brothers all played, and they even let me and my twin join in their practice sometimes.'

'Did they, by jingo!' he exclaimed with a chuckle. 'Where did y'play?'

'On the wing,' I said. 'Small and fast, see? Some of the lads wanted us to cut our hair and pretend to be boys so we could play in matches, but it never happened.'

Sir Hector was highly amused by the idea. He called one of his pals over and told him about it. Within a few minutes we were at the centre of a good-naturedly boisterous group of ageing rugby players. They introduced themselves as the Old Codgers and adopted us as their honoured guests for the rest of the afternoon.

There was a balcony on the first floor of the white-painted clubhouse which afforded a splendid view of the pitch. Chairs had been set out for club officials and their guests. Sir Hector, naturally, bagged three of the best. We settled in to watch the match in the company of some extremely entertaining old men.

The match itself was a corker. It was a hard-fought contest between two village teams who would ordinarily have had no business playing in such a prestigious final. We all became quite caught up in the excitement of it all.

At one point the referee blew his whistle and awarded a penalty against Littleton. Lady Hardcastle leapt to her feet and began yelling her protests in the most indelicate language, suggesting that the beleaguered official was favouring Nibley. I tugged on her sleeve, urging her to sit down.

'It was a fair call, my lady,' I said. 'The curly-headed chap was in front of the ball when it was kicked so he wasn't allowed to run forwards and take it like that.'

There were murmurs of agreement from the Old Codgers.

'Yes, well,' she said huffily. 'I still don't like him. He has shifty eyes.'

This elicited guffaws from our new friends who, as they became increasingly drunk during the course of the rest of the match, took to calling the referee 'Shifty'.

'Sir Hector?' I said. 'That chap running up and down the touchline. Is that Mr Tribley from Bottom Farm?'

'Yes, m'dear,' he said. 'The very same. Club chairman and team coach. One of the best we've had. Glad he came to the village. Splendid chap.'

'And is that Dick Ackley at outside centre?'

'Yes, m'dear. Seems to attract the farmers, this game. Strong lads.'

The match ended with Littleton Cotterell having scored twelve points to North Nibley's nine, and the celebrations began. Our elderly hosts were well on the way to inebriation by the end of the match, but Littleton's victory saw them tucking in to the ale with renewed vigour. Class barriers were broken down by the sporting event and they supped with men from the villages and neighbouring farms as equals as the celebrations got properly underway. When the players returned to the bar, things became even more rowdy. Mr Tribley led them in to roars of congratulation. Soon he and Mr Ackley were laughing together. They were joined by Mr Lock, who I hadn't seen until then, and the three of them seemed to be leading the merriment.

There were women there, too, but mostly wives and sweethearts of the players and supporters, and all of us left as soon as the ribald singing began. Rugby songs tend towards the smutty, and although both Lady Hardcastle and I found them terrifically amusing, we thought we might save the gentlemen some embarrassment by leaving them to their fun, not to mention salvaging something of our own reputations. It wouldn't do to be seen to be enjoying Rabelaisian revelries when the other women had decorously fled.

We said our goodbyes to Sir Hector, promising to send Bert back for him later.

'Cheerio, m'dears,' he slurred. 'I say, you must come to the club dinner next Friday. The memsahib can't make that one, either. You can be my guests.'

'Both of us, sir?' I said, slightly dubious that I should be welcome at a rugby club dinner.

'You especially, m'dear,' he said. 'The Old Codgers were very taken with you – thought you knew a lot more about the game than a lot of the chaps. They insisted you be invited.'

'Then we shall be delighted,' said Lady Hardcastle, kissing his cheek. 'Thank you so much for the hospitality, Hector, darling, we've had simply the most wonderful afternoon. Do give my love to Gertie, won't you. Cheerio.'

'Shall do, m'dear, shall do. Toodle-pip,' he said with a cheery wave, and he tottered off to join his chums.

5

On Wednesday morning, Lady Hardcastle arrived at the breakfast table already in her overalls.

'The muse is upon me, Flo, dear.'

'Is she, my lady? Which one?'

'Do you know, I'm not at all certain. Tall girl, Greek clothes. I was hoping it might be Thalia. Comedy, you see. I should like so much for my little film to make people laugh.'

'Does she have a shepherd's crook? Thalia carries a crook, doesn't she?'

'Possibly. Or it might be a mop. Is there a muse for mop-squeezers?'

'We're taken care of by St Zita, my lady.'

'Are you, by jingo? The breadth of your knowledge never fails to delight me.'

'A childhood misspent haunting the nation's libraries.'

'Hardly misspent, dear, if you can talk of saints and muses with equal facility.'

'I was supposed to be mastering the arcane arts and secret skills of the circus.'

'From what I've seen over the years, you can count many of them as well and truly mastered. Do you remember that time in Budapest when you pinned that chap to the wall by his coat sleeve? With a fruit knife. From five yards away.'

'He was about to shoot you, my lady.'

'Thanks to you, he ended up shooting a rather elegant chandelier instead.'

'Which fell on that Prussian colonel,' I said.

'Oh, it did, didn't it? You see? Circus arts mastered. Knife throwing, trick shooting and slapstick comedy. All we lacked was a lady on horseback.'

'And elephants, my lady. You can't have a circus without elephants. This muse, though. I presume you and she will be installing yourselves in the orangery for the foreseeable?'

'That's certainly my intention, yes. What do you have planned?'

'Edna and Miss Jones have been set to work. Your dresses are mended—'

'That reminds me, dear. There's a slight rip in the organdie blouse. Would you be a poppet?'

'Another one? How do you manage to cause so much damage, my lady?'

'I swear it's not me. They just appear.'

'Very well, my lady,' I sighed. 'I shall deal with it before I go out. I thought I might take a stroll across the green at lunchtime and see Daisy. She works at her father's butcher's shop in the mornings so it's difficult to talk there. But we can snatch snippets of conversation while she's working in the pub at lunchtimes.'

'You've become quite pally lately, you two.'

'She was very sweet while you were indisposed, my lady,' I said. 'She could gabble for England, but she has a good heart. And she's quite the best source of local gossip.'

'Splendid,' she said, getting up. 'You enjoy your lunch. Could you get Miss Jones to bring me some sandwiches at around noon, please. I'm off to make art.'

Daisy was busy. Rushed off her feet, in fact. Over the winter, the Dog and Duck had been quiet at lunchtimes. I'd grown accustomed to being able to sit at the bar and gossip with my new pal in between occasional calls of 'another couple of pints over 'ere, my love'. But the lighter mornings meant the local farmers were finishing their labours earlier so that by the time I arrived the place was heaving.

I caught Daisy's eye and gave her 'the signal'. A few moments later she arrived at my table in the corner with a small cider and a cheese sandwich that could chock a dray cart – my usual order.

'Yacky da, love,' she said cheerfully as she placed the food and drink down.

I laughed. 'Close enough. *Iechyd da* to you, too, *fach*.' I raised my glass. 'I suppose you're too busy to join me?'

'Sorry, love. Frantic in 'ere today. Up and down like a dog at a fair, I am. Lovely to see you mind. I'll chat later if I gets a chance.'

She was gone.

I sat back and looked around. It wasn't quite market-day-at-The-Hayrick, but for a tiny village pub, it was certainly busy. I'd been lucky to find somewhere to sit. Joe kept a tiny table in the corner for solitary drinkers. Today, it seemed, was not a day for quiet contemplation, and so it had been unoccupied. All around me there were rambunctious farmers and labourers supping cider, smoking pipes and roaring with laughter at jokes I couldn't quite hear.

At the next table were a few faces I recognized. There was Dick Ackley, the cow buyer 'from over Woodworthy'. Sitting next to him was the Caradines' neighbour and Littleton Cotterell RFC club chairman, Lancelot Tribley. We'd met him on our visit to Top Farm, and I was struck once more by how ill-suited he was to his rumpled tweed jacket. Opposite the two of them, also looking as though he came from another world entirely, was Noah Lock. Mrs Caradine's handsome neighbour wore the clothes of a farmer but had the bearing of a military gentleman.

'Nearly a week since old Spencer kicked the bucket,' said Ackley. 'Here's to him.' He raised his pint.

'May the miserable old cuss rest in peace,' said Tribley. 'Though I doubt anyone else on the other side will have any peace once he turns up.'

'To Spencer,' said Lock. 'And long life and happiness to Audrey.'

They all drank.

'You'll be getting married at last, then, you two,' said Tribley. 'Good luck to you both.'

'Thank you,' said Lock. 'As soon as it's seemly. How about you, Lance? It's long past time you found a companion to grow old with.'

'I'll be asking a girl soon enough,' said Tribley. 'Lovely woman.'

'Anyone we know?' asked Ackley.

'Can't say yet. I'll be making an announcement as soon as I get one or two things sorted out.'

'Here's to you two as well, then,' said Lock. 'And good luck with your "things".'

They drank yet another toast.

'I hears young Morris got an offer for Top Farm already,' said Ackley. 'He'll not be hanging around.'

'Two offers,' said Lock. 'Spencer got one a while ago – I gather that one still stands. Then just the other day some new chap from the village came up to see him and made him another. The lad's spoilt for choice.'

'Good for him,' said Ackley. 'To Morris.'

They raised their glasses once more. Their talk turned to the recent cup win. Lock congratulated Tribley and Ackley on Littleton's performance.

I finished my sandwich. I was draining the last of my cider when Bert pushed his way over to my table.

'Afternoon, miss,' he said. 'Lady Hardcastle's compliments, but have you finished your lunch and would you mind coming up to Top Farm with her?'

'Yes, and yes, Bert. In that order. Give me a moment to give my apologies to Daisy and I shall join her. Is the motor car outside?'

'Engine running, miss.'

'Nice lunch?' asked Lady Hardcastle as Bert drove us through the lanes.

'Could have been better, my lady,' I said. 'Daisy was too busy to chat so I just sat on my own in the corner.'

'Perfect earwigging spot,' she said.

'Well, it would have been, but all I could hear was Lock, Ackley and Tribley.'

'Our three farmers. Did they have anything to say for themselves?'

'Not really,' I said. 'They're pleased that Lock and Audrey are finally free to be together. Oh, and Tribley has a lass, too, apparently, but he wouldn't say who.'

'And they say it's only women who sit around and discuss their romances.'

Bert took us to Top Farm by a new route along roads that we'd never travelled before. We passed through a small hamlet that I didn't even know was there – a couple of houses, a chapel and a pub by a small stream. Clearly Lady Hardcastle hadn't known it was there, either.

'You see this is why we need a motor car of our own. We've lived here nearly a year and this is the first I've ever even heard of this place. There's only so much exploring one can do on foot.'

'Quite so, my lady,' I said.

'I say, Bert,' she said, raising her voice so that he could hear her in the front.

'Yes, m'lady?' he said, looking up to regard us in the rear-view mirror.

'What sort of motor car would you recommend for a country lady to go gadding about in?'

'It depends on what you wants it for, m'lady.'

'For gadding about in,' she said.

He laughed. 'I means, do you want to impress people, or do you want something that's easy for a chauffeur to look after and will get you about the place with the minimum of fuss?'

'Wouldn't any motor car impress people, Bert?'

'I dare say it would, m'lady, but there's "Blimey, look, there's a lady in a motor car", and then there's "Blimey, look, there's a motor car. Oh, and it's got a lady in it." Do you see what I means?'

'Sort of. So if I just wanted to pootle around the countryside with my maid by my side, visiting, exploring, flitting hither and yon, with no need to impress the impressionable, what should I get?'

He looked a little surprised. 'You intends to drive it yourself, m'lady?'

'But of course, Bert, dear. Why ever not?'

He seemed dubious. 'If you say so, m'lady. In that case, I hear tell that the Rover 6 is a capable little motor car and it's small enough for even a lady to drive.'

'Even a lady, eh?' said Lady Hardcastle. 'Does it come in red?'

His doubts about the ability of women to understand the complex engineering of the motor car were no doubt confirmed. 'I dare say they can paint it any colour you wish, m'lady. You'd still need a man to look after it, mind, whatever colour they paints it.'

'You hear that, Armstrong? We need a red Rover 6 and some instruction on motor maintenance. Make a note.'

'You have the notebook, my lady,' I said.

'I do? Oh, I do. Remind me to make a note.'

'I shall do my utmost.'

'Splendid, thank you,' she said. 'Oh, I say, I think I know where we are now.'

'Yes, m'lady,' said Bert. 'That's Top Farm up yonder.'

'So it is. Make a note of this route, Armstrong, we shall come out here in the new motor car.'

'You still have the notebook, my lady.'

'And we shall get you a blessed notebook as well.'

'Thank you, my lady,' I said. 'You're a kind and generous woman. I've always said so.'

'Pish and fiddlesticks,' she said. 'You've never said anything of the sort. Have you ever heard such tommyrot, Bert?'

'No, m'lady,' he said.

With a squeal from the brakes, the car drew up in the farmyard and we stepped out into the mud.

Lady Hardcastle leaned down to speak to Bert through the window.

'We might not be too long if Morris Caradine isn't in, but it's worth a try. Don't nod off.'

'I shall remain alert and ready, m'lady,' he said, touching the peak of his cap.

'Good man,' she said, and led the way up to the farmhouse door.

She rapped smartly on the black-painted door and we didn't have to wait long before it was opened by a timid-looking man in his mid-twenties. He was tall, and skinny, and very much resembled his late father. This was clearly Morris Caradine.

'Yes?' he said suspiciously.

'Good afternoon,' said Lady Hardcastle. 'I'm Lady Har—'

'I kn-n-now who you are,' he stammered. 'What do you w-w-want?'

'May we come in, please, Mr Caradine?'

'C-c-can I s-s-stop you?'

'Of course you can, but I'd rather you didn't. We just want a few words and then we'll leave you in peace.'

'You'd b-b-better c-come in, then,' he said, and he stepped aside so that we could enter.

'Is your mother at home?' asked Lady Hardcastle as we made our way towards the kitchen.

'N-no, she's gone over to see N-Noah Lock.'

I had thought when he opened the door that it was just nervousness, but his stammer was quite serious.

'Has she, indeed? Good for her,' said Lady Hardcastle with a smile.

He looked blankly at her. I didn't mention that she'd have no luck finding him unless she went down to the Dog and Duck.

'I wouldn't say no to a cup of tea if there's one going,' she said, continuing to smile warmly. 'How about you, Armstrong?'

'I never say no to a cup of tea, my lady,' I said.

He meekly set about preparing tea for us all.

'Do you mind if we sit down?' said Lady Hardcastle. 'I've had a busy morning and I find I still tire easily.'

He waved to the kitchen chairs and we sat in silence while he continued with his tea making. He seemed thoroughly absorbed in his task and it was plain that he would be too distracted to answer any questions. At length, he banged the teapot on the table, where he had already placed three cups, a jug of milk and a bowl of sugar. He sat down and stared at us.

'Will you pour, please, Armstrong?' said Lady Hardcastle.

I stood and took care of the pouring while she addressed Morris.

'You have our utmost sympathies on the passing of your father,' she began.

He snorted.

'I understand that you were not especially close,' she continued. 'But I know from a lifetime's experience of such things that you will feel the loss nevertheless.'

He continued to stare blankly.

'My friend Lady Farley-Stroud tells me that you're a talented artist,' she said.

'I paint a bit. N-nothing you'd like, I don't s'pose.'

'Oh, I don't know. I have quite catholic tastes when it comes to the visual arts. I might surprise you.'

He stared.

'Now that your father has gone, I suppose you'll be taking over the running of the farm.'

His stare changed to a quizzical frown, and then his face split into a broad grin.

'That's where you'd be wrong,' he said. 'As s-soon as we s-sell this place I'm off to London. I've got a p-place at art college.'

'Good for you,' said Lady Hardcastle. 'And your mother?'

'Our Ma's going to marry N-Noah.'

'Wonderful,' she said. 'But how are you going to sell the farm? I understood from Mr Tribley that he couldn't find a buyer for his place.'

'Got two offers already,' he said proudly. 'N-nothing to worry about. Be glad to get out of the place.'

'From all I've heard, I'm sure you will,' she said. 'But I'm intrigued. How have you managed to be so lucky when Mr Tribley can't find a buyer? Is Top Farm so different?'

'Can't s-say,' he said. 'Sworn to s-secrecy. But it'll be fine, you'll see.'

'Well, I'm delighted for you. I'm sorry to have to bring the subject back to your father but do you remember anything odd happening in the days before his death?'

'N-nothin' I can think of,' he said. 'But then I stayed away from the house as m-much as I could when he was at home.'

'So you wouldn't have seen any visitors?'

'No one visited our Dad. He was a b-b-ba—'

'Yes, dear, I gather he was.'

We all three sipped our tea, almost in unison.

'What do you do about rats on the farm, Mr Caradine?' I said.

'About what?' he said, so surprised by the change of direction that it seemed to shock the stammer out of him.

'Rats,' I said. 'Which poison do you use to kill them?'

'Oh, I see. No p-poison. Our Dad used to use traps. Sometimes he'd sh-shoot them with an airgun.'

'Thank you,' I said with a nod.

'I say,' said Lady Hardcastle. 'You make a smashing cup of tea.'

'Oh,' he said, nonplussed by yet another change of tack. 'Thank you.'

'It's surprisingly rare in a young man. In any man, come to think of it. My brother makes a simply revolting cup of tea, doesn't he, Armstrong?'

'I promised myself I'd never mention it, my lady – after all, he's your brother and you must stand by him no matter what – but Harry's tea is quite the most disgusting liquid known to man.'

'You'd never know if he'd put poison in it,' she said. 'His tea could hide the taste of anything.'

Morris Caradine simply stared again.

'Well,' said Lady Hardcastle, putting her teacup in its saucer with a clink. 'We ought to leave you to get on. We just wanted to see if there was anything you could tell us that might help us to work out who killed your father, and you've been most helpful.'

'I h-have? I d-don't feel like I've s-said anything. I don't know n-nothing.'

'And yet you've been most helpful, dear,' she said, patting his hand. 'Give our regards to your mother, and I hope everything works out for you just the way you hope. You'll love London. We were very happy there for many years. And when things are more settled I'd love to see some of your paintings if you'd care to show them to me.'

'Oh. Oh, all r-right, then,' he said. He tentatively held out his hand.

We both shook it and took our leave.

The next day, we decided to take a break from the bewildering complexities of Mr Caradine's death. We had received a wire from Inspector Sunderland, but only to say that the police surgeon was utterly baffled. The cause of death was unclear, though there was evidence of kidney failure and liver damage. He was provisionally suggesting poison, though he wouldn't be drawn to say anything more definitive, being completely unable to say what manner of poison it might be. There was nothing further for us to do.

Instead we were consumed by the bewildering complexities of Lady Hardcastle's two new pet projects. These were: the installation of a telephone and the purchase of a motor car.

The first was going to take quite some time, but we now had confirmation that matters had finally been set in motion. The approval of various bodies was being sought. The installation of a marching line of telegraph poles to extend the line from the heart of the village along the lane to the house needed to be planned.

We anticipated some grumbling from people who complained that we were marring the beauty of the countryside. I couldn't help but agree to a certain extent, but the promise of being able to call The Grange, or to talk to Lady Hardcastle's brother, Harry, in London soon overcame my own objections. The village grumblers would find something else to grumble about long before work was due to commence. It would be weeks, possibly months, before we had our telephone, but at least things were moving.

The second project, the purchase of a motor car, proved to be equally problematic in its own way. We prevailed upon Bert to drive us into Bristol where we had an appointment with a motor dealer.

'Good morning, madam,' said the sharp-suited man as we entered the small showroom.

'Good morning,' she said. 'I'm Lady Hardcastle. I wired you that I was coming.'

'Ah, yes, my lady. Of course. Would you care for some tea while we wait for your husband?'

'Tea would be splendid, thank you. I'd like to talk to you about the Rover 6.'

'I really must insist that I speak to your husband about this, my lady. This really is a matter for him.'

'Very well. Might I trouble you for the use of your telephone? I shall need to engage the services of a medium so that we might organize a séance.'

'I . . . er . . . I do beg your pardon, my lady. I . . . er . . . of course. The Rover 6, you say?'

'Yes, please.'

'Have you already engaged a chauffeur, my lady? Or will you be waiting until the motor car has been delivered?'

'I shall be driving and maintaining it myself,' she said in her most infuriatingly amiable tone.

'Yourself, my lady?'

'Or my maid, perhaps. I rather think we might want to take it in turns.'

I smiled in response to his questioning look.

'In all conscience, my lady, I really can't recommend the purchase of something as complex as a motor car. Not to—'

'Not to whom, Mr Haggett?'

'Not to . . . ah . . . to . . .'

'Not to a pianist? Might I damage my fingers?'

'No, my lady. To . . . ah . . .'

'To a Londoner? I can understand that. We can be a bit over-confident sometimes. It comes from growing up in the capital of the Empire, I think.'

'No, my lady. Please. I really must—'

'I'm torn, Mr Haggett. Part of me wants to carry on teasing you and making you squirm. Another part wants to scream and shout and berate you in a most unladylike fashion for not taking me seriously. But honestly, the most powerful part of me just wants to buy a motor car. What do you say we start again? I'm interested in the Rover 6. That's one, there, isn't it? The pillar-box red one? What can you tell me about it?'

He sighed, but relented.

An hour later, papers were signed, a cheque was handed over. Delivery was arranged for the next day on the strict understanding that she should return the car as soon as she found that it was unsuitable and that he would happily agree favourable terms.

6

We dressed formally for the rugby club dinner, which was to be held at a hotel in Chipping Bevington. Littleton Cotterell lacked the facilities to provide a grand dinner, although Daisy told me that Joe had offered them exclusive use of the snug of the Dog and Duck. Sir Hector, naturally, was being driven to the do by Bert and had generously offered to pick us up on the way.

'Heard about your motor car from Gertie. Delivered today, she said. But best to get Bert to drive us,' he said. 'I know a lot of chaps do it, but I don't hold with driving when you've had a few. Knew a fella in India, had a skinful at the club, completely pie-eyed, tried to ride his bicycle back to his bungalow, fell off and got mauled by a tiger.'

Lady Hardcastle laughed.

'I really don't think there are many tigers in Gloucestershire, Hector, and I can't imagine how one might fall off a motor car.'

'No, m'dear,' he had insisted. 'The principle still holds. Can't control a machine when you've had a few drinks and it would be a shame to miss out on the wine. The Grey Goose has the most excellent cellar. Landlord's a bit of an oenophile. Used to be a wine steward in London.'

And so we had accepted his kind offer and were ready and waiting when, at seven o'clock on the dot, Bert rang the doorbell.

The journey had been swift and comfortable. Sir Hector was in voluble mood (I suspect he'd already had a pre-prandial gin or two). Bert, though professionally discreet as always, rolled his eyes at his employer's more outrageous stories.

We were soon outside the Grey Goose. Young men from the rugby club, dressed in white tie, but with waistcoats in the same shades of blue and gold as Sir Hector's, held the doors of the motor car open for us.

There was champagne in the bar where we were introduced to several of the team members. Dick Ackley we already knew, of course.

'Why, Mr Ackley,' said Lady Hardcastle. 'How splendid to see you. Congratulations on your win.'

'Thank you, m'lady,' he said. 'We certainly never expected to be champions.'

'So I'm told. Quite the David and Goliath story, they tell me.'

He laughed. 'I reckons it is at that. Us and Nibley both. No one would have put so much as a farthing on either of us getting to the cup at the beginning of the season. Just goes to show, don't it?'

'It does indeed. Everyone loves it when the outsider wins.'

We moved away from the current team and were immediately accosted by several of the Old Codgers. They seemed genuinely delighted to see us.

They set about regaling us with tales, some of manly derring-do, some of childlike silliness. The club's glories – of which there seemed to be quite a few – were relived in fantastical detail. These were interspersed with stories of japes and pranks, many of which seemed to involve petty theft. Tales were told of stolen boots, stolen trophies, stolen trousers, even a stolen goat that had been serving as the mascot of a visiting Welsh team. My attention drifted slightly and I found myself listening to Noah Lock, Lancelot Tribley and some of the team members we'd met earlier.

'Not like in your day, eh, Noah?' said a skyscraper of a man.

'No, Lofty,' said Lock, 'in my day we considered ourselves fortunate to suffer only a fifty-to-nothing drubbing on a Saturday afternoon. I believe I hold the honour of captaining the least successful team in Littleton Cotterell's history. But never mind that, you haven't introduced me to your charming companion.'

'Ah, yes, right,' said the tall man. 'This is Winnie Marsh. Winnie, this is Noah Lock. He owns Chapel Farm, over t'other side of Top Farm.'

I thought the freckle-faced girl might have blushed to be the centre of attention but she smiled confidently.

'How do you do, Winnie?' said Lock. He looked thoughtful for a moment. 'Are you Dennis Marsh's daughter, by any chance?'

'That's right,' she said. 'You know my father?'

'Of course. He helped me out with some feed last winter after my hay barn caught fire.'

'That was you? I remember that,' she said. 'Terrible thing to happen. Did you ever find out what caused it?'

'A lamp,' he said. 'I would have sworn I'd put it out, but apparently not.'

'I wouldn't put it past old Spencer Caradine to have done it,' said Dick Ackley.

'We'll never know now that the poor old chap's dead, though, will we?' said Lock.

'I know you shouldn't speak ill of the dead and all that,' said Winnie, 'but he was a nasty piece of work, and everyone knew it. To tell the truth, I don't know why we have to pretend every dead person was a saint. It's not like our lies are going to help them in the afterlife. They'll be judged on what they did, not on what we say after they've gone.'

It looked as though her talk was making Lofty a little un-comfortable. He clearly thought that speaking ill of the dead – even when it was the truth – was a terribly bad idea. Lancelot Tribley, on the other hand, seemed more than a little impressed by her.

'Quite right too, Winnie,' he said. 'Can't be having with all this tiptoeing around a chap's reputation. If he was a bad un, we should be free to say so.'

The Old Codgers' conversation suddenly intruded.

'. . . with a cobbler's last,' said one of them. 'I say, who's that chap over there, m'dear? Don't think I recognize him. Is he one of ours?'

'That's Mr Thingummy,' said Lady Hardcastle. 'Do you remember, Flo? We met him in Mr Whatsit's junk yard.'

'Mr Snelson,' I said. 'A fellow customer at Pomphrey's Bric-a-Brac Emporium.'

The Old Codger laughed. 'Fellow sufferer, eh? Never could remember chaps' names m'self. What's he doin' here, though?'

'New chap in the village,' said Sir Hector. 'Met him the other day while I was walking the dogs. Thought he might like to come along. Poor chap said he never gets out. Come on over, lads, let me introduce you all.'

He led them away but we could still hear fragments of their conversation.

'. . . and Lady Hardcastle over there said she saw you in Pomphrey's,' said a Codger. 'Get yourself anything nice?'

'As a matter of fact,' said Snelson, 'I did. I found a rather charming little model of Stephenson's Rocket.'

'That's right!' exclaimed Sir Hector. 'The memsahib mentioned it. I knew there was something rum about you, what!' He laughed and slapped Mr Snelson on the shoulder.

'Rum, Hector?' said the Codger. 'What's rum about a model steam engine? I love steam engines m'self.'

'This one, though,' said Sir Hector, still chuckling, 'was made of matchsticks with a giant Union Jack painted on the boiler.'

'Well, you know how it is,' said Mr Snelson ruefully. 'Sometimes a fella just can't help himself. It reminded me of a toy I'd had when I were a nipper.'

The Codgers laughed and congratulated Mr Snelson on his excellent purchase.

When the gong sounded for dinner, Sir Hector returned. He offered Lady Hardcastle and me an arm each to escort us into the dining room. As the special guests of the Grand Eternal Poobah we were seated at the top table where the linen was crisp and white, the cutlery silver and the glassware crystal. Quite a luxurious setting for a rugby club dinner.

The food was certainly above average but, as promised, it was the wine that really set the Grey Goose apart. Glass after glass of the most perfectly matched wines accompanied each course, and by the time we arrived at the port (for which the ladies were allowed to remain), both Lady Hardcastle and I were really rather squiffy.

The company, too, had been most convivial. The club chairman, Lancelot Tribley, was a good deal more humorous than he had been when we'd met him at his farm. Here he seemed much less out of place. He had a quick wit and a stock of anecdotes which became racier and racier as the evening wore on and the level of wine remaining in the bottles went down.

His speech of congratulation to the First XV for their unexpected victory had been short and heartfelt, and with enough good-natured humour to save it from ungracious boastfulness.

Shortly before midnight, Mr Tribley stood and called for order. 'Gentlemen,' he said in a loud, clear voice. 'I fear our time here is coming to an end. The good folk of the Grey Goose wish us well, but wish us gone. They have homes to go to, and have requested in the friendliest and most respectful terms, that we sling our collective hooks and leave them to tidy up.'

There were mixed calls of 'Shame!' and 'Good for them!'

He waited for the commotion to die down. 'And so I should like to propose a vote of thanks to the chef, the staff and to the landlord for laying on this sumptuous feast.'

Cries of 'Hear, hear!'

'I further propose,' continued Mr Tribley, 'that we repair to the clubhouse to end the night in the traditional manner.'

Cheering ensued.

'There's a charabanc to take the gentlemen back to the club. Taxicabs and carriages have been arranged to take those ladies home who do not have their own transport.'

There was more cheering and a good deal of kerfuffle as goodbyes were said to wives and sweethearts and the gentlemen of the club readied themselves for the serious business of . . . whatever it was that rugby club members got up to when the ladies weren't around.

We found Bert asleep in the motor car a short way down the High Street. Having woken him and given him time to collect his wits and start the engine, we asked him in as sober tones as we could manage if he would be an absolute poppet and take us home.

We slept in on Saturday morning.

As we tumbled into the hall and struggled with our coats and hats after dinner the night before, we had agreed that I should leave Edna and Miss Jones to their own devices in the morning. And so it was eleven o'clock by the time I stumbled blearily into the kitchen in my dressing gown and asked Miss Jones if she wouldn't mind making some breakfast. Nice and quietly.

'Good morning, Miss Armstrong,' said Edna loudly.

I smiled weakly.

'Nice dinner?' she said, still at a level more suited to calling in the dogs than conducting a friendly conversation in the kitchen.

'Very pleasant, thank you.'

'Nice to get out,' she said.

'It is. Did you do anything nice?'

'Me and our Dan went to the Dog and Duck like usual. Lovely evenin'. Eunice and Fred Spratt were there, an' all. We had such a lark. Old Fred's a card. Had us in stitches all night, he did.'

'Sounds as though it was great fun,' I said.

'Oh, it was. Eunice was sayin' as how her Daisy said you was tryin' to find out about Spencer Caradine croakin' in his pie. I said that was right. I said you and the mistress was investigatin' like billy-o. You'll have to explain the blackboard thing, though. I tried tellin' her about it but to tell the truth I hasn't got an idea what you two makes of it.'

'I'll run you through it one day,' I said. 'You might be able to help us.'

She laughed. 'Oh, I doubt that. You looks a bit peaky, mind. There's some aspirin in the cupboard. You want me to get you some?'

'Thank you, Edna, that would be most welcome. What else did Eunice say about Mr Caradine? She's never said anything to me.'

'There you goes, love,' she said, handing me the aspirins and a glass of water. 'Well, she didn't know you was involved, did she? She said first she heard about it was from her Daisy.'

'Daisy and I talk about it all the time in the shop,' I said.

'Well, you knows Eunice. Going deaf, she is, but she won't admit it. She don't hear half the things you says to her direct, never mind when you two are over t'other side of the shop. Her earwigging days are behind her now. But she reckons it was Morris as done for his dad. Terrible bullied he was. Bound to snap in the end. It's always the quiet ones, i'n't it?'

'It often is.'

'I said as how you thought it might be Noah Lock but she weren't having none of that. Got a soft spot for Noah, has Eunice. We all have, really. He's such a handsome man. Never been a handsome murderer, has there? You can tell a murderer. All that evil clouds their faces. Ugly, the lot of 'em.'

I didn't have the energy to argue.

''Course,' she continued, 'I always thought it was Lance Tribley. Been at each other's throats for ages, them two. Always arguin' and whatnot.'

I couldn't stop myself. 'And what whatnot?' I said.

'Oh, just little bits of petty nonsense, you know. Leavin' each other's gates open so the animals wander off. You know the sort of thing.'

'Ah,' I said. 'But nothing nasty?'

'That's nasty enough if your livelihood depends on 'em, i'n't it?'

'You're right, of course.'

The doorbell rang.

It was becoming something of a routine, this 'interrupting Flo while she's doing something else' thing. I joked to myself as I trudged through to the hall that it was probably Sergeant Dobson with news of a baffling crime which had happened overnight and which he was powerless to solve. I opened the door.

'Mornin', miss,' said Sergeant Dobson. He noticed my state of dress. 'Sorry to bother you so . . . early . . . but is your mistress at home? There's been a bit of a to-do up at the rugby club.'

I smiled ruefully. 'Come on in, Sergeant,' I said. 'Make yourself comfortable in the morning room and I'll see if I can rouse her. Miss Jones is making tea. I'll get her to bring you some.'

I left him to find his own way and went upstairs. Lady Hardcastle was just beginning to stir as I drew the curtains and let the morning sun bring life to the room.

'What ho, Flo, dear,' she croaked. 'Was that the door?'

'I'm afraid so, my lady,' I said, picking up her dressing gown and holding it for her. 'Sergeant Dobson with news of a "to-do" at the rugby club.'

'That's scarcely news,' she said as she shrugged into the silken robe. 'We saw them all setting off there last night after dinner. There was bound to be a to-do of some sort.'

'That's what I thought, my lady, but I doubt he's come over to tell us that some rugby players got a little drunk and sang filthy songs. I suspect that something else has happened.'

'As long as this "something else" comes with tea and aspirin, I'm game for anything.'

'That's certainly the talk in the taverns, my lady,' I said, and we went downstairs together.

The sergeant stood as we entered the morning room.

'Good morning, Sergeant, dear,' said Lady Hardcastle. 'Please sit down. I say, is that tea fresh?'

'Yes, m'lady,' he said. 'Your Miss Jones just brought it through.'

'Pour me one, would you, Flo. Would you care for another, Sergeant?'

'I'd not say no, m'lady. Never do, to tell the truth. I probably drinks too much of the stuff.'

'I know what you mean,' she said with a smile. 'So what's this "to-do" at the rugby club?'

'There's been a burglary.'

'Has there, indeed? But the First Fifteen and half the rest of the club were up there last night. How on earth did anyone manage to burgle the place?'

'That's the baffling part, m'lady. That's why I come over here. I called Bristol for a detective, and Gloucester too, but they said they can't spare anyone for something as trifling as a few rugby trophies. They said I should do my best on my own, like. I thought, seein' as how Inspector Sunderland already had you lookin' into the Caradine death, you might like to, you know . . .'

'You're never on your own in Littleton Cotterell, Sergeant,' she said bracingly. 'We shall help, shan't we, Flo?'

'Of course, my lady,' I said. 'Anything and everything we can do.'

'I knew I could rely on you two,' said the sergeant with evident relief. 'Thank you.'

'So tell all. What actually happened?' asked Lady Hardcastle.

'Well,' he said, 'I gathers you was at the Grey Goose with 'em last night.'

'We were,' I said.

'Right. And you left about midnight when the lads all went back up to the club.'

'Exactly so,' said Lady Hardcastle. 'I presumed the beer would flow and hijinks would ensue.'

'And so they did, m'lady. I woke Lance Tribley this morning after the theft had been reported, and he said a rollicking good time was had by all. Well, he did once he'd stopped . . . beggin' your pardon, ladies, but he was a little the worse for wear.'

'I can very well imagine,' said Lady Hardcastle, sipping her tea.

'According to Lance, they was all there till about five this mornin' when he locked up and staggered home.'

'So the burglar struck after it had started to get light? And when there were potentially dozens of burly men around to see him. Intriguing. Perhaps he was watching the place to see when everyone left. Or perhaps he was a lucky opportunist. How did he get in? What did he take?'

'There's a storeroom on the side of the clubhouse. They keeps groundskeeping tools up one end so there's a door to the outside, and crates of beer and whatnot down t'other so there's an inside door an' all. It don't look like either door was locked.'

'If Tribley were three sheets to the wind when he left, it's not beyond the bounds of possibility that he might have neglected his custodial responsibilities,' said Lady Hardcastle, thoughtfully. 'Were there any other possible means of entry?'

'Maybe, m'lady, but to tell the truth we stopped looking.'

'Oh?' she said. 'Why's that?'

'Footprints. Seems friend burglar stepped in a puddle of oil from the lawnmower and left a trail clear as day.'

'How very inept of him,' she said.

'Or suspiciously convenient for us,' I said.

'Well, quite,' she said.

'As for what he took,' resumed the sergeant, consulting his notebook, 'that's interestin', too. He left the beer, the spirits, and the cash behind the bar, and helped himself to the Wessex Challenge Cup, a runner-up shield won by the Second Fifteen in last year's Severn Vale Tournament, a jersey worn by Ripper Henderson in the Great Brawl of ninety-eight, and the penny the club originally paid for the land they built the club on in 1895. Everything that was in the trophy cabinet in the committee room, it seems.'

'Well I never,' she said. 'Sentimental value only, then?'

'Well, the Wessex Cup is silver – that'd fetch a few bob. But you're right, m'lady, the rest is only special to the club.'

'Well, now that makes it all rather fascinating, eh, Flo? Oily footprints and missing trophies. Right up our street.' She paused for a moment. 'Righto, Sergeant,' she said, 'here's the plan. Don't let anyone interfere with the scene of the crime until Flo and I have had a chance to look round. We'll get dressed and make our way over there as soon as we can.'

'Right you are, m'lady. I've left young Hancock at the club. He knows what to do. I appreciates your help.' He got up to leave.

'It's entirely our pleasure, Sergeant. We had nothing planned today, did we, Flo?'

'No, my lady,' I said. In fact, I had been planning a lazy Saturday of reading and tea drinking, but it was true that we had no formal plans. Ah, well.

'Then I shall see myself out and leave you to your . . . preparations,' said the sergeant. 'Thank you again.'

The rugby club was a mile or so on the other side of the village, just off the road to Bristol. After the excesses of the previous night, we decided that the walk would do us good. We made good time despite our weariness and the weight of Lady Hardcastle's canvas art bag, and we soon spotted the tall goalposts of the rugby pitch.

The lane up to the clubhouse was rutted, but mercifully free of mud, and as we rounded the last bend we finally saw the clubhouse itself. It was a large, white-painted, wooden building, much like the one we had been at the previous week, and, indeed, very much like most of the sporting pavilions I had ever seen. Steps led up to a small verandah where players might sit, and above it a balcony for spectators. A small clock tower showed the time as almost one o'clock.

We mounted the wooden steps and entered the building. The main space formed a communal room with a bar along one wall. It was sparsely decorated but felt homely with its mismatched tables and chairs and a handful of well-worn armchairs over by the large heating stove. It was in some disarray, with overflowing ashtrays, half-empty beer glasses and assorted other detritus lying about on the tables and the floor. The whole place could have done with sweeping and airing, but it still felt very welcoming. A sign indicated that dressing rooms were to the right, while another pointed to the committee room to the left and the 'Grand Eternal Poobah's Dining Room' upstairs.

'What ho!' called Lady Hardcastle. 'Are you there, Constable Hancock?'

The constable hurried in from the door on the left.

'Good afternoon, m'lady,' he said, knuckling his forehead. 'Sergeant Dobson found you in, then?'

'And almost ready for visitors,' she said. 'As soon as he'd told his tale, we hurried over here as fast as our shapely legs would carry us.'

The constable blushed slightly.

'Take no notice, Constable,' I said. 'She just likes to see how much she can discomfort people with her inappropriate remarks. Mind you,' I whispered conspiratorially, 'she's right – we do have very shapely legs.'

He flushed a brighter shade of crimson and Lady Hardcastle laughed. 'Why don't we forget about legs,' she said, 'and concentrate instead on feet? The sergeant says you have some footprints to show us.'

'I do indeed, m'lady,' said the tall young constable. 'Follow me.'

He led us out through the door through which he had just entered the bar, past the bottom of the staircase and along a corridor with windows on the left-hand side looking out onto the verandah and the pitch. There were higher windows on the right which presumably provided further illumination for the committee room. As we neared the door to the room, I noticed the footprints on the polished floorboards.

I stopped to look more closely. 'It seems he came in through that door at the end of the corridor . . .' I said, indicating the closed door several feet in front of us, '. . . and walked this way . . . He stood on tiptoes here, look, probably to look in through the window to check that the room was empty . . . then doubled back to the committee room door.'

'I can't argue with that,' said Lady Hardcastle. 'Huge feet, too.'

'Size twelve, I reckons,' said the constable. He indicated his own boots. 'I wears tens but they's much bigger than mine.'

'And how tall are you, Constable?' she asked.

'Six foot exactly, m'lady.'

'So our thief would almost certainly be taller than that. It does rather narrow the pool of suspects, eh, Flo?'

'There can't be many men in the area above six feet tall, my lady, no.'

'And most of 'em plays for the rugby team,' said Hancock.

'Do they?' said Lady Hardcastle. 'Do they indeed? Well, well, well.'

'What's through there?' I asked, indicating the door at the end of the corridor.

'That's the storeroom, miss,' he said.

'We'll look at that in a moment,' said Lady Hardcastle. 'I'd like to take a look at the trophy cabinet first if I may.'

Stepping carefully around the oily bootprints, we entered the committee room. In contrast to the spartan functionality of the main bar, the committee's accommodations were a great deal more comfortable. The room was rectangular, with the windows looking out onto the corridor along one long, oak-panelled wall. There were boards along the other bearing the names of past chairmen and honouring various club members past and present for their achievements on the field. The leather-topped table and luxuriously upholstered chairs were polished and apparently undisturbed by the intruder, but he had left oily bootprints on the floor. There was a fireplace on the short wall at the other end of the room that clearly shared a chimney with the stove in the bar and that seemed to have been his destination. There was a heavily laden, deep-shelved bookcase set in one of the alcoves, with the trophy cabinet in the other.

'So, he comes in here . . .' I said, '. . . walks along this wall around the edge of the carpet . . . and stops . . . here.' I was standing in front of the right-hand alcove and the empty trophy cabinet built into it.

The cabinet was extremely well fitted, clearly the work of a craftsman. It stood from floor to ceiling and filled the alcove precisely without the tiniest fraction of an inch to spare. It was made of a dark wood, polished to a high sheen, with gleaming, glass-panelled doors.

I went to open it. 'Is it all right to touch things, Constable?' I said. 'Do I have to be wary of fingerprints?'

'There i'n't none as I can see, miss,' he said. 'Very careful, he was.'

I opened the doors and looked inside. The shallow shelves were clean and polished, just like the exterior, though a shade darker, giving a pleasing feeling of texture to the design. There was a length of beading along the front of each shelf forming a lip that seemed like a splendidly clever way to prevent things from rolling out. Other than that, the cupboard was bare. I closed the doors.

Lady Hardcastle, meanwhile, had been looking around the room and came over to rummage in the bag hanging over my shoulder for her sketch pad and pencils. While I followed Constable Hancock to the storeroom, she stayed behind to sketch the scene of the crime.

The store was dark and musty. There was a lantern hanging from a hook but the constable ignored it and walked across to the large double doors at the other end. He threw them open and the dingy room was illuminated by the bright afternoon sun.

Occupying pride of place near the doors was a massive Ransomes lawnmower. I'd seen such a machine before at the country estate of one of Lady Hardcastle's friends, but never in the hands of a tiny country rugby club. It must have stood nearly as tall as me and weighed over a ton. There was a wide-based oilcan lying on its side beside it, and its spilled contents were clearly the source of the footprints we had been following.

'So,' I said. 'The rest of the trail is of two sets of muddled prints, with the boots facing in opposite directions . . . but between here and the outer door there's just one set, heading out. It seems that our thief came in through the door, stepped in the oil, went to the corridor, took a peek through the window, entered the committee room, pinched the trophies and then retraced his steps back out through the store.'

'That's how I sees it, miss,' Hancock said.

'I suppose you had a rootle round outside?' I said.

'I rootled like a good un, miss,' he said with a chuckle. 'Didn't find nothin', mind. The grass wiped his boots clean and the trail disappears. He was headin' back to the road, though, I reckons.'

'It certainly looks like it, doesn't it?' I agreed. 'Ah, well, nothing much else to see here. Let's go and see how Lady Hardcastle is getting on.'

'I'm fine, thank you, dear,' she said from the doorway. 'What have I missed?'

I explained my thoughts on the trail as she looked around the storeroom for herself, sketching as she went. 'It was certainly very obliging of him to leave such obvious spoor,' she said as she crouched to examine the spilled oilcan.

'I wouldn't read too much into it, m'lady,' said Hancock. 'No one ever lost money bettin' on the stupidity of the average criminal. Like as not he really was too gormless to realize what a trail he was leavin'.'

'I dare say,' she said pensively. 'Who found that they'd been burgled?'

'Caretaker, m'lady. Luther Redick.'

'Trustworthy chap?'

'Trustworthy as they come, m'lady,' he said. 'He i'n't so bright, but he's the salt of the earth. He come in this mornin' to clear up. He took one look at the bar, but decided to come out to check the committee room first, start himself off gentle, like. And that's where he finds the bootprints. He follows them into the room, he finds the cabinet empty and then he was straight back out on his bike to fetch me and the sergeant. He was in a bit of a state so we sent him home.'

'Very thoughtful of you,' said Lady Hardcastle with a smile. 'Well, I confess I'm no expert on the scenes of crimes so I'm not entirely sure I know what else to look for. I think we ought to leave that to you, Constable.'

'Thank you, m'lady,' he said. 'But to tell the truth I don't reckon there's much more to be seen. I was plannin' to lock up and head back to the station.'

'Right you are,' she said. 'We'll walk with you.'

Then we heard the sound of the main doors opening. 'Is anyone there?' called a man's voice. I recognized it as belonging to Lancelot Tribley.

'In the storeroom,' called the constable in reply.

We left the storeroom and met Mr Tribley in the corridor. He wanted to see the empty cabinet for himself. We left him to it, telling him that we'd wait for him in the main room where Lady Hardcastle and I made ourselves comfortable in the armchairs near the stove. Constable Hancock milled restlessly about, clearly unable to make up his mind whether to stay or go, and eventually ambled outside into the sunshine.

At length Mr Tribley finished his examination of the scene of the crime and joined us in the main room. He flopped into a chair. Lady Hardcastle raised an eyebrow but it took a few moments for Mr Tribley to notice.

'I'm so sorry, Lady H,' he said lazily. 'Don't mind if I sit down? It's been a bit of a morning.'

'Help yourself,' she said with a faint hint of frostiness. 'It's your clubhouse.'

He made no reply but just sighed theatrically and rested his head on the back of the armchair with his eyes closed. After gathering his wits for a few moments, he opened his eyes once more and looked towards Lady Hardcastle.

'If you don't mind my asking,' he said in a tone that carried no genuine concern whether she minded or not, 'what on earth are you doing here?'

'We're investigating your burglary,' said Lady Hardcastle politely.

'You're doing what?' he said with some astonishment.

'Investigating your burglary,' she said again affably.

'And why on earth . . . ?'

'Sergeant Dobson asked us to. He thought we might be able to help him get to the bottom of this little mystery.'

He laughed. 'Well I never. First old Caradine, now this. You'll forgive me if I suggest that there's not really much of a mystery here, though. Some passing scallywag tried the back door, found it open, and came in to help himself to the contents of the trophy cabinet.'

'That much is true,' she said. 'But it ignores a couple of interesting things. Not only did he go directly to the committee room as though he knew that's where the trophies were, but he passed straight by two cases of scotch, one of gin, several cases of wine, two barrels of beer and one of cider – all eminently marketable items. Instead, he went straight for some memorabilia with value only to the club and a very recognizable trophy which will be almost impossible to sell.'

Tribley sat a little straighter and his look of condescension faded away. 'Well I never,' he said again. 'You really are rather good, aren't you? My apologies if I seemed rude, my lady. It's been a disappointing morning.' His tone had changed from mockery to weariness.

'Please, think nothing of it,' she said with a smile. 'Have you had a chance to have a good look round? Is anything else missing?'

He smiled ruefully. 'Not as far as I can tell. This is more like the sort of pranks chaps used to get up to in the nineties. We had a fellow here, "Jester" Dunleavy. Always pinching the silverware. Just pranks then, mind you.'

I remembered the stories the Old Codgers had been telling us the night before at dinner. Petty larceny seemed to be part of the club's traditions.

'So no money was stolen?' asked Lady Hardcastle.

'No,' he said. 'We'd never keep club money on the premises, even if we had any.'

'Not even behind the bar?'

'What? Oh, I suppose so.'

'Was that stolen?'

'It doesn't appear so, no,' he said frostily.

'You said the club has no money, and yet you have that frightfully expensive lawnmower.'

'Gift from an old member. Made his fortune in the colonies in oil, or tin, or rubber, or something. Said he wanted to give something back to the club that had brought him so much joy as a young man. Completely useless if you ask me, but some of the fellows like it. It keeps the pitch looking smart, I suppose.'

'I see,' she said. 'So tell me what happened last night.'

'There's a reason we leave the ladies behind,' he said. 'A chap's got to have one or two secrets from the missus.'

'In general terms, then, without betraying any confidences. I'm not sure we're quite ready for the gorier details.'

'Very well,' he sighed. 'We arrived here by charabanc at around a quarter to one, I'd guess. Strong liquor was taken, yarns were spun, songs were sung, pranks were played and the gentlemen of the club began to drift off to their homes and their slumbering loved ones at about three. By a quarter to four only Bats Ackley, Big Jim, Lofty and I remained, so we did our best to tidy up' – he ruefully indicated the chaos of the room – 'and then let ourselves out of the front door, carefully locking it behind us.'

'Without checking the storeroom door?' I asked.

'We barely managed what we did, my dear,' he said. 'I fear that remembering to check the back doors was quite beyond us.'

'And you walked home?' said Lady Hardcastle.

'Yes, the four of us staggered out onto the road and wended our weary way back to the village.'

'You stayed together?'

'We parted at the end of the lane. I made my own way back to Bottom Farm,' he said. 'Bats went off towards Woodworthy. I imagine Lofty and Big Jim would have walked most of the rest of the way together.'

'Did you see anyone else?'

'Not as far as I recall.'

'No one at all? No one you didn't recognize? No mystery miscreants?' she said.

'We could barely recognize each other by then,' he said. 'But no, no lurking lawbreakers or vagrant villains.'

'Any nefarious ne'er-do-wells?' I said.

'No, nor any felonious footpads,' he replied with a smile.

Lady Hardcastle had taken out her notebook and pencil. 'These other three chaps,' she said. 'What were their names again? They sounded like a gang of rogues and ruffians themselves.'

He chuckled. 'Couldn't be further from the truth. There was Dick "Bats" Ackley. He's our outside centre but in real life he's a dairy farmer from Woodworthy. Then there was "Big Jim" Meaker. He plays in the front row at weekends but his beef herd keeps him busy the rest of the time. And last but by no means the least substantial, there was Donovan "Lofty" Trevellian. He's a baker and a lock forward.'

'I see,' she said, scribbling down the details. 'Mr Ackley we know already. Do you have addresses for the other two? I should like to speak to them.'

'Of course. But if you can wait until Monday evening they'll all be here for training.'

'Training?' I said. 'I thought the season was over.'

'Not for a good few weeks yet,' he said. 'It's one of the oddities of the rugby calendar that the big cup competitions are settled long before the end of season. We still have the league to play for.'

'If you have no objections, then,' said Lady Hardcastle, 'we shall come over and have a quick word with them, just to see if any of them remembers anything useful.'

'You'll both be more than welcome,' he said. 'We start at around six o'clock and we'll likely be here until at least nine.'

Lady Hardcastle put her notebook back in her bag and stood. I rose, too, and this time Mr Tribley was more mindful of his manners and leapt to his feet.

'We shall see you on Monday evening, then,' she said.

'I look forward to it,' he replied, with a little bow. 'Is it all right if Redick comes over and cleans the place up now?'

'Check with the constable,' she said, 'but tell him I have no objections.'

'Thank you, Lady Hardcastle,' he said. 'Good day to you.'

'And good day to you, Mr Tribley.'

We went back out into the sunshine and looked for Constable Hancock. He was nowhere to be seen so we set off for home, stopping at the police station on the way to make a brief report to Sergeant Dobson.

Sunday. Ah, Sunday. What would life be without Sundays? That melancholy day that seems to stretch out forever and yet still seems to be over too soon. There was no particular difference for me between any one day of the week and any other, but there was always something about Sunday that seemed to be different for the rest of the world. Somehow that difference managed to seep in through the cracks around the windows and doors, no matter how hard we worked to keep it out.

We endured another Sunday, sustained by the pleasure of spending several hours in the dining room after lunch creating another crime board. The Caradine case seemed to have stalled indefinitely so we turned the blackboard around and started afresh on the clean side in an attempt to resolve the mystery of the purloined trophy.

'It seems to me,' said Lady Hardcastle, gazing at the blackboard, 'that our thief must have had an extra-special reason to steal only the cup and the other tat. The first thing anyone says when they see what happened is, "Why didn't he take the booze and the cash?" He walked past some very saleable loot and went straight for the junk and the cup. He never made any attempt to go through to the bar to steal the cash. Anyone would assume there was cash behind the bar.'

'It does seem very odd, my lady,' I said. 'And he definitely knew where he was going, too. He even knew he could take a look in through the window to make sure the coast was clear.'

'It's an inside job, isn't it?' she said.

'I can't see any reasonable alternative. It's someone who knew the club and had some special reason for pinching the memorabilia and the cup. No passing opportunist would have done that.'

'Nor would they have been so foolish as to step in the oil and leave such obvious tracks,' she said. 'Even the most dullardly thief would take care over something like that.'

'A drunken rugby player on the other hand . . .'

'Well, quite,' she said, standing up. 'We must definitely go along to their training tomorrow evening and see what Tribley's three friends have to say for themselves.'

'Right you are, my lady,' I said. 'Tea?'

'What a splendid idea,' she said. 'And perhaps some toast and marmalade.'

'Coming right up.'

7

Monday passed in a blur of laundry, grocery shopping and nagging Lady Hardcastle to tidy the papers in her study. We had taken tea in the garden and by the time I had tidied up and made sure Miss Jones had left us something interesting in the pantry for supper, I was exhausted. I wasn't at all looking forward to the trip to the rugby club.

'Oh, come on,' chivvied Lady Hardcastle. 'Don't be such a misery guts. It'll be fun, I promise. There's a mystery there, just waiting to be solved.'

'And sweaty men in rugger togs,' I said with a grimace.

'That too. It'll be a lark. Best foot forward, missy. The sooner we get there, the sooner we're back.'

And so we strolled in the warm evening air back to the rugby club.

Training had already begun by the time we arrived, and we sat on the verandah of the clubhouse for a while watching as Mr Tribley put the team through its paces.

'Who's that girl on the other side of the pitch?' said Lady Hardcastle. 'Do we know her from somewhere?'

'Looks like Winnie Marsh to me, my lady,' I said. 'She was with that terribly tall chap at the dinner.'

'Ah, yes,' she said. 'Well done. Lofty, wasn't it?'

'That's the fellow.'

'It must be love if she's even prepared to watch him training,' she said.

'There's no accounting for it.'

While the players caught their breath after a particularly strenuous exercise, Mr Tribley approached us.

'Good evening, ladies,' he said amiably. 'Glad you could come.'

'Thank you for inviting us,' said Lady Hardcastle. 'Are the men here that we wish to speak to?'

'They are, my lady,' he said. 'Your best chance of speaking to them alone would be if I were to send them over one at a time. If you wait until we're finished they'll all be in the bar and you'll never get a chance to speak to them.'

'That would be most helpful, Mr Tribley,' she said. 'Thank you.' She took out her notebook and pencil. 'Do you think we might start with . . . with . . . ah, here we are . . . with Mr Ackley? Let's start with a familiar face.'

'Of course. I'll send Bats over,' he said.

'"Bats"?' she said.

'"Battering Ram". Not a wily player, Ackley. Takes the ball and just charges the opposing three-quarter line head-on. Barges as many as he can out of the way and then goes down like a sack of spuds when they finally stop him. Takes two or three of them, mind. Makes a lot of ground. Good lad, old Bats. Wish he'd offload to the wing once in a while, but you can't have everything.'

He walked off and spoke to Mr Ackley. He directed the team to their next drill, but his attention seemed continually to be drawn by the freckle-faced girl on the other side of the pitch.

'Good evening, Mr Ackley,' said Lady Hardcastle.

'Good evening, m'lady,' said Ackley. 'What can I do for you?'

'Do sit down. I understand you were among the last to leave the club on the night of the dinner.'

He sat in the remaining chair. 'That I was.'

'Did you see anyone or anything unusual?'

He thought for a moment. 'No, not really. There weren't really anyone about at all.'

'I see,' she said, making a note. 'Have you been with the rugby club long?'

'Quite a while, yes, m'lady. It was my old dad as got me into it when I was a lad. "They needs strong uns like you," he says. So I come along. Been here ever since.'

'It means a lot to you?'

'It does, my lady. It's like a great big family, if you get my meaning.'

'I do,' she said. 'How is the farm?'

'Not so bad, I s'pose,' he said. 'We could all do with a few more bob in our pockets, couldn't we? No matter what we does, there's always bills to pay. But somethin' will turn up.'

'I dare say it will,' she said. 'Well, thank you for your time, Mr Ackley. We shan't keep you from your training any longer. Would you be kind enough to send Mr . . . Mr Meaker over?'

He stood. 'My pleasure. That's Big Jim over there.' He pointed to a stocky man by the touchline. 'Looks like the tubby old gundiguts could do with a break.'

He trotted off to confer with his teammate.

'It was him,' I said. 'He stole the trophy to melt it down and sell the silver to cover his bills. He loves the club and he wanted the other stuff as souvenirs.'

Lady Hardcastle laughed her warm, infectious laugh. 'And he ignored the booze and cash because he didn't want to rob the club. The cup belongs to whoever it is that organized the competition – and he doesn't care about them – and the insurance would cover the cost of replacement anyway,' she said.

'Exactly,' I said. 'Case closed.'

'Hold your horses there, Flo,' she said with another chuckle. 'Let's see what "Big Jim" has to say for himself before we lock Ackley in the chokey.'

Big Jim was already lumbering towards us. I had assumed that 'Big' Jim would be tall, but this chap was shorter than Lady Hardcastle by a couple of inches. No, in his case, 'big' referred to his girth – he was almost as broad as he was tall. His head seemed to be connected directly to his body without the complication or inconvenience of a neck.

He clumped up the wooden steps. 'You wanted to see me?' he said.

'If you wouldn't mind,' said Lady Hardcastle. 'Do please sit down.'

He did as he was bidden. I winced as the chair creaked a little under his weight.

'We're just trying to get to the bottom of the theft the other night,' she said. 'And since you were one of the last to leave, we wondered if you might have seen anything.'

'I'm not sayin' I's proud of it, mind – our Ma drummed it into us as kids that strong drink was the path to wickedness – but I was drunk as a wheelbarrow. I could barely see me feet to find me way home, never mind noticin' no strangers nor nothin'.'

'Nothing at all? No strange sounds? Unusual movements in the hedgerows?'

He thought for a moment, staring earnestly at his boots. 'Well . . .' he began hesitantly. 'I suppose there might have been some rustlin' in the trees along by the track there.' He nodded towards the track that led out onto the road. 'But it might just have been Old Mr Fox on his way back from raidin' some poor blighter's hen house. Or a hedgehog, maybe.'

'Possibly,' she said, making a careful note. 'Of the four of you, yours is the house furthest from the club?'

"S right,' he said. 'T'others had all gone their separate ways by the time I got back to the farm.'

'You own the farm?'

He laughed. 'No, m'lady, I'm one of Sir Hector's tenants. Took over from our Dad when he passed on.'

'Aha,' she said, making another note. 'Did you wake your wife when you got in?'

Another laugh. 'No, m'lady, I i'n't married.' He looked down at his immense body. 'Who'd have an old lump like this?'

She smiled. 'You shouldn't put yourself down, Mr Meaker.'

He smiled in return, but didn't seem properly convinced.

'We're just trying to get a picture of what happened that evening,' she said, 'so we shan't hold you up any longer, but I take it you won't mind if we need to speak to you again?'

'Not at all, m'lady,' he said, getting up. 'Glad to be of service. I needed a break anyway.' He nodded towards the team who were doing something frightfully energetic on the pitch. 'You want me to send anyone else?'

'That would be most kind,' she said, consulting her notes again. 'Mr Trevellian, please.'

'Right you are,' he said and he clumped back down the steps. 'Oi!' he yelled. 'Lofty! Get over here, ya gurt lanky bean-pole. Lady here wants a word.'

Lady Hardcastle sighed. 'I could have done that,' she said.

'No, my lady, your voice isn't anywhere near that loud.'

'Yours is. If I want uncouth yelling, you're always my first choice.'

'I'm flattered, my lady.'

If you put 'Big Jim' on a floured kitchen workbench and rolled him out, the result would be Donovan 'Lofty' Trevellian. He must have been at least six-foot-four, and although he appeared strong and athletic, there was nothing of the bulk of Jim Meaker. He trotted towards us with some grace, but as he sat at Lady Hardcastle's invitation, there was a certain ungainliness as he folded himself into the chair.

She introduced our purpose as before and once again asked him what he had seen that morning as he went home. Much like the others, it was evident that he had been too tipsy to notice anything very much.

'I take it from your accent that you're not from Gloucestershire,' said Lady Hardcastle when we had explored the very little he knew about the events of early Saturday morning.

'No, ma'am,' he said. 'Cornish through and through. Our family's been fishin' out of Mousehole since the 1600s.'

'You didn't join them?'

'No, ma'am. I never could get on with the boats – I gets seasick, see? And then when I grew to be this tall, I was more of a hindrance than a help, so I chucked it in, like.'

'And what do you do now?' she asked.

'Baker's apprentice,' he said proudly.

'Forgive me,' she said with a smile, 'but aren't you a little old to be an apprentice?'

'You could say that, I s'pose,' he said with a grin. 'I wasn't much use as a kid, fell into some bad ways, had more'n my share of trouble. But one day our local bobby – lovely old bloke he was – one day he caught me pinching lead off the church roof and he sat me down and gave me a talkin' to like I'd never had before. Turned me round, he did. Saved me from goin' bad altogether, I reckon. And he said he knew a bloke up in Gloucestershire as would take me on and teach me a trade. If I stayed, he said, I'd end up doin' hard labour in Truro gaol. Or worse. So I packed up and come up here. Best thing I ever did, I reckon. I've got a girl up here and everything.'

'Well, good for you,' said Lady Hardcastle. 'I believe we've just seen the lucky girl across the pitch.'

'Winnie, she is, Winnie Marsh. Her dad farms a few acres over t'other side of the village.'

'Well, I'm delighted for you, Mr Trevellian,' she said. 'We wish you all the happiness you so obviously deserve.'

'Thank you, m'lady,' he said, beaming.

We said our goodbyes and he trotted back to the field.

'I'm none the wiser,' she said as we gathered our things and made ready to return home.

'Nor I, my lady,' I said. 'Big Jim might have taken the cup to raise the money to impress the ladies. Lanky there is a reformed scallywag, but he might well have reverted to his old ways in a moment of drunken madness.'

'Suspects with motives and opportunities abound. They all had the means, too, since the door was left open for them. Heigh ho. We'll work it out eventually.' She looked over at the pitch. 'I don't want to interrupt them again so let's just wave to Mr Tribley and be on our way.'

I agreed, and with a cheery salute to the men on the pitch, we set off for home.

As we walked along the lane back towards the village, we heard angry yelling coming from around a bend. Someone, it seemed, was not at all happy with his companion's behaviour. Lady Hardcastle and I exchanged glances and hastened our pace a little – someone might need our help.

We rounded the bend to see an exasperated Sir Hector Farley-Stroud, purple of face and with his hands on his hips, berating three madly cavorting springer spaniels who had evidently just returned from an unauthorized excursion into the nearby field.

'What ho, Hector,' called Lady Hardcastle, laughing heartily. 'Having trouble with the girls?'

'What? Oh, good evening, Emily, m'dear. Trouble? You don't know the half of it. You wouldn't care to give a home to three delinquent dogs, would you? They'll be the death of me.'

'Oh, pish and fiddlesticks,' she said. 'You'd be lost without these three. Wouldn't he?' She ruffled the ears of the three friendly and inquisitive gun dogs. 'Yes, he would.'

'You're right, m'dear,' he said cheerfully. 'But it would be so wonderful if at least one person in my life did as I asked. Ever.'

'They're adorable. Aren't you? Yes, you are, you're adorable.'

The dogs wagged and sniffed. Abruptly, they pricked up their ears and dashed off together to investigate something else.

'It's delightful to see you, m'dear,' said Sir Hector. 'Where are you off to this fine evening?'

'We're just on our way home as a matter of fact. We've been to your rugby club.'

'Have you, by jove? Well, well. Bad business that. You investigating for us?'

'We are, dear, yes,' she said.

'Good, good. I dare say the insurance settlement would come in handy, but it's a bad show to lose a trophy like that.'

'It was insured?'

'Of course, of course,' he said. 'Whole club's insured. Stony broke, but worth a fortune if anything gets pinched.'

'That's very interesting,' said Lady Hardcastle.

'Is it?' he said. 'Vital clue, eh?'

She laughed. 'I wouldn't say that, but it's always helpful to know as much as possible.'

'Of course, of course. Shame it had to happen just as we were winning trophies, though. Haven't ever won anything before.'

'Is it an old club?' I asked.

'Not very, m'dear, no. Got the club diaries back at The Grange if you're interested.'

'Well, we—' began Lady Hardcastle, but I interrupted.

'That would be lovely, Sir Hector,' I said. 'If you wouldn't mind?'

'Not at all, m'dear, not at all. I'll send Bert over with them soon as I can. But I'm afraid I must dash – can't leave the gels to their own devices for too long or who knows what they might get up to.'

'Right you are, Hector,' said Lady Hardcastle with a smile. 'Give our love to Gertie, won't you.'

'Certainly, m'dear, certainly. Toodle-pip.'

With that, he trotted nimbly down the lane and out of sight in pursuit of his wilful dogs.

'The club diaries?' said Lady Hardcastle, watching him go. 'Really?'

'You saw how chuffed he was that someone was interested in his silly old rugby club. We don't have to read them.'

She smiled. 'You're very sweet. As for the case . . . how very disappointing. It could well be just a squalid insurance fiddle. I'm sure things will seem a little clearer once we've had some supper. And wine.'

'Supper and wine it is, then, my lady,' I said, and we set off once more for home.

I cobbled together a light supper of bread and cold meats, with a little cheese I found lurking in the larder and some experimental chutney Miss Jones had made the previous weekend. Lady Hardcastle opened a bottle of wine and we sat in the dining room discussing the theft.

'An unknown tall man enters the storeroom, steps in oil, steals a cup and some tat, and goes back out the way he came,' said Lady Hardcastle as she nibbled a piece of Double Gloucester and put the finishing touches to the last of her sketches of the men we'd spoken to earlier in the evening. 'He does it on the one night of the year when the club is occupied by all of the First Fifteen and assorted club dignitaries, but nobody sees him.'

'The timing does seem odd,' I said. 'Burglars don't usually wait till dawn.'

'No, indeed. It could be a carefully planned theft that got delayed when the thief turned up and found the place full of drunken sportsmen, but why not just come back another night?'

'So it's an opportunist who just happened upon the place as he wandered past, or it's an inside job as we thought earlier,' I said.

'Hmmm, yes. Inside job. But why?'

'All the night owls seem to have had motive or opportunity,' I said.

'They do rather, don't they? If only we knew where the thief went after he left. Those oily footprints just peter out; it would be nice to know which direction he set off in.'

'It would be even better if one of the late birds had seen him.'

'Hmmm,' she said again. 'It's so very odd that they didn't. It would have been perfectly light by the time they staggered out and there's not much cover. A chap could hide behind that line of trees along the side of the club I suppose, but he'd have to be very careful. Getting there and back would leave him exposed to even the most casual of glances from the drunkest of oafs.'

'What about—' but my ruminations were interrupted by the ringing of the doorbell.

Lady Hardcastle glanced at the clock on the mantel – it was almost ten o'clock. 'Who on earth could possibly be calling at this time of night?' she said, affronted.

I laughed. 'I shall find out,' I said and got up.

I opened the door to find Bert, the Farley-Strouds' chauffeur, standing there with a stack of books in his hands.

'Oh, Bert, it's you,' I said. 'We wondered who on earth could be calling at this hour. Is everything all right?'

'Quite all right, thank you,' he said with a rueful smile. 'Sorry to be calling so late but Sir Hector insisted that you needed these urgently.' He proffered the books.

I gave him a puzzled frown as I took them. I opened the topmost book and glanced at the first few pages. 'Ohhh,' I said as I realized what I was reading. 'The rugby club diaries. I'd forgotten all about them. Oh, Bert, I'm so sorry you had to drive all the way down here with these. It's very sweet of Sir Hector but they really could have waited until the morning. Can I offer you some tea?'

'Very kind, miss,' he said cheerfully. 'But I'd rather be getting back if you don't mind. Got to be up early to take Sir Hector to Gloucester.'

'Right you are,' I said. 'Well, thank you again, and drive carefully on the way home.'

'I shall, miss,' he said, and with a smile and a tip of his cap he turned on his heel and returned to his motor car.

I took the books back through to the dining room.

'Bert?' said Lady Hardcastle, looking up from her notebook.

'You heard?' I set the diaries down on the table. 'He brought the rugby club diaries.'

'So I gather,' she said. 'Here's a plan then: we decamp to the drawing room, I'll have a tinkle at the old Joanna – I do find I think better when I'm playing the piano – and you can scour the diaries for . . . for . . . lawks, I have no idea what you might scour them for. Background information, I suppose. How does that sound?'

'It sounds rather pleasant, actually, my lady,' I said, and I began clearing away the supper things. 'Coffee?' I called from the kitchen a few moments later.

'At this time of night?' she called back. 'I'm pouring brandy, you silly thing.'

We settled in the drawing room and as I listened to Lady Hardcastle's beautiful interpretation of a selection of Chopin nocturnes, I leafed through the diaries. For the most part they seemed to contain accounts of matches (which Littleton Cotterell almost invariably lost) and notes of the more interesting decisions from otherwise rather dry committee meetings. This rather prosaic fare was interspersed with tales of some of the more entertaining goings-on at the club, usually involving jolly japes and drunken adventures.

'I say, listen to this,' I said.

Lady Hardcastle stopped playing, mid-Chopin. 'Found something, dear?' she said.

'I think so. Did Mr Tribley say something about a chap called Dunleavy?'

'Something like that. Prankster or some such, I believe he said.'

'A prankster indeed,' I said. 'He was Jonathan "Jester" Dunleavy, it says here. Club chairman and benefactor.'

'They do love their nicknames. Never especially oblique, though, are they? Billy "Frightfully Big Chap" McGillicuddy. Dan "Wonky Nose" Fitzwarren. I take it Dunleavy liked a joke.'

'It seems he did, my lady,' I said. 'He was something of a star in his day. "A scrum half of considerable skill", according to one match report here. It seems that when he retired from the field he continued to be involved in the running of the club. Apparently he contributed to the cost of much of the club's furnishings from his own pocket.'

'Not quite as funny as I was hoping, to be honest,' she said, distractedly riffling through the pile of music beside the piano.

'I'm getting to that. Most of the reminiscences in here are about the pranks he played. Or instigated. Apparently his favourite was to pinch trophies from opponents when Littleton visited them for away matches. He brought them back and displayed them in Littleton's own trophy cabinet as "spoils of war".'

'Charming,' she said. 'I wonder where one draws the line between jolly japes and mere petty thievery.'

'It says they were always returned eventually. In the meantime, though, he was never caught, nor could the victims ever work out what happened to the missing loot.'

'I can see why the current theft struck a chord with Tribley, then. Perhaps it's someone from North Nibley. I'd wager the whole district came to know of Dunleavy and his japes. It could be revenge.'

'Revenge is a dish best served cold, my lady, but that would be cold and starting to grow mould.'

'It's better than anything we've come up with so far,' she said. 'Now then, what do you fancy next? How about this?' She showed me one of the ragtime pieces she had bought the previous summer after meeting the boys from Roland Richman's Ragtime Revue.

'Oh, that looks fun,' I said. 'How about you, though, my lady? Has the music loosened your cogitations?'

She laughed. 'I'm not certain one should enquire as to the state of a lady's cogitations, dear. It seems impertinently personal. But give me a moment with this delightful-looking two-step and we shall see if anything develops.' She began to play.

'Like castor oil for the soul, my lady,' I said.

She stopped abruptly and turned around. 'I've been such a dunderhead,' she said. 'That's it. Come, we must retire at once. We've an early start in the morning.'

I frowned confusedly.

'Quick sticks,' she said, scooping up the music and closing the lid of the piano. 'We need to be at the rugby club by six in the morning at the latest. To bed!'

And she bustled off, leaving me to pick up the brandy glasses and lock up for the night.

We were awake at five o'clock on Tuesday morning. I was an habitual early riser so I found it no hardship at all to be washed, dressed and ready for the walk before six. Lady Hardcastle, by contrast, clearly found it a struggle. Nevertheless, her enthusiasm for her scheme – whatever it was – carried her through. At the appointed hour we arrived at the deserted club. The early morning sunlight glinted on the dew-damp grass and mystery birds sang in the hedgerows.

'Here we are, then, my lady,' I said as we walked up to the pavilion. 'Just after dawn at the rugby club, the dew still wet on the grass.'

'Exactly,' she said, waving her finger in the air. 'Exactly so.'

Intrigued, I followed her round to the side of the pavilion, obeying her exhortation to remain as close to the wall as possible. As she reached the corner, she motioned me to join her and we both peered round together.

'What am I looking at, my lady?' I said, feeling more than a little foolish to be sneaking up on what appeared to be nothing more than a locked door.

'The grass, Flo. Look at the grass.'

I did as she said and looked down at the grass in front of the big double doors that led into the storeroom. The oily bootprints were still visible, just as they had been on Saturday morning, and they still faded away where the grass had brushed the oil from the soles of the boots. But now, in the low sunlight making the dew shine as though the grass had been dusted with jewels, I could see that the footprints continued. Although the oil wasn't dark enough to see, there was still enough of it to repel the dew. It was possible to trace the tracks beyond the door and, finally, to see where the burglar had gone. Moving my head this way and that to best catch the light on the grass, I followed the line of the prints as it moved away from the pavilion towards the hedgerow and then, to my astonishment, looped round and returned to the door.

'He didn't go anywhere,' I said. 'He turned round and went back inside.'

'So it would appear,' she said with a grin of triumph.

'Whatever made you think of this?' I asked as we continued to examine the prints.

'It was when you mentioned taking castor oil last evening,' she said. 'I thought about how the water runs off when one tries to rinse the spoon. Then I wondered about making the grass wet to see the tracks and realized that just after dawn it would be lightly damp without our having to contrive anything ingenious at all.'

'You're a genius,' I said.

'Hardly,' she laughed. 'But sometimes a little inspired. Come on, let's get back for some breakfast, then we can call on Sergeant Dobson to see if they still have a key to the storeroom. I think we need a proper look round in there.'

Having fetched Sergeant Dobson, we went through to the storeroom and threw open the double doors to let the daylight in so that we might begin our search.

'What are we looking for, my lady?' I said as we split up.

'Well, the trophy would be nice,' she said.

'Really?' I said. 'In here?'

'Perhaps. But anything, really. We'll know when we find it. Something that's not supposed to be here.'

'Right you are,' I said and I began my search.

We clattered about, moving groundsmen's tools, old rugby balls, spare parts for the lawnmower, broken furniture waiting to be repaired, all the while looking for 'something that's not supposed to be here'.

After about ten minutes of otherwise fruitless search, Sergeant Dobson let out a cry of triumph. 'Hullo!' he said. 'And what do we have here?'

I looked over to see him holding a pair of large, well-worn, black work boots. He sniffed the soles.

'Oil,' he said. 'I reckon these is our thief's boots.'

'I say, Sergeant, well done,' said Lady Hardcastle.

He folded down the tongue of the boot. 'And look here,' he said. 'He's been kind enough to write his name in them.'

Lady Hardcastle looked where the sergeant indicated. 'Lofty Trevellian,' she said.

The sergeant was very pleased with himself. 'I'll get down the bakery and arrest him at once.'

He made to set off.

'Just a moment, Sergeant,' said Lady Hardcastle. 'I'm not sure that's the correct course of action.'

'I'm grateful to you for all your help, m'lady,' he said. 'But I can take it from here.'

'But Sergeant—' she said. He was already gone.

'It's not Lofty, is it, my lady?' I said.

'No, that would be most odd. Why would he leave his boots behind? How did he get home with no boots?'

'The sergeant will say he left them because they were covered in the oil he used to lay a false trail. After taking them off, he changed into some other boots. But he won't know anything about these other boots and he won't ask why he left the oily ones where they could be found.'

'Well, quite. It's all very convenient, isn't it? One might argue that he would have had some difficulty taking them with him when they left the celebrations, of course. But that wouldn't explain why they were still here a few days later. Surely he would have retrieved them – he's had ample opportunity. I'm not at all convinced. I think someone wants to incriminate poor Lofty.'

8

Lady Hardcastle's muse, whichever she turned out to be, seemed to have Wednesday mornings free. She called upon her again on the 24th so that once again Lady Hardcastle arrived in the morning room for breakfast in her overalls.

'Good morning, my dearest old friend,' she said as she sat down. 'And Happy Birthday.' She produced a card from one of the oversized pockets of her overalls.

'Oh, thank you, my lady,' I said. 'I'd quite forgotten.'

'No, you hadn't,' she said, producing a small package from another pocket. 'And neither had I.'

As usual she had eschewed a commercially printed birthday card in favour of something she had painted herself. It was of two black-and-white cows outside our house. Underneath was the caption, 'Happy Birthday, Flo. Can we come in? We're Friesian out here'.

'You're a very silly lady,' I said. 'Thank you very much.'

'Open it up,' she said.

Inside, along with the usual birthday wish, was a folded note. The note told me that an appointment had been made with a dressmaker in Bristol where I was to be fitted with a gown of my choosing.

'Oh,' I said. 'You're very silly and very lovely. Thank you.'

'Open the box, open the box.'

I opened the box, which contained a beautiful ornate silver brooch.

'For your new gown,' she said.

'Goodness me,' I said. 'This is wonderful. But you really shouldn't have.'

'I really should,' she said. 'You've been an absolute poppet all winter and I wanted you to know how much you mean to me. Now before we get too sentimental, pull on that section at the edge of the brooch.'

I did as I was told, and out popped a pair of picklocks.

'Just in case,' she said. 'A girl should never be without a picklock. You taught me that.'

I had one or two things to do in the village, so as soon as Lady Hardcastle had retired to the orangery and breakfast was cleared away, I put on my hat and coat and sallied forth.

I was surprised to find Daisy outside the Dog and Duck rather than inside her father's shop.

'*Bora da*, Daisy, *fach*,' I said as I drew alongside her.

'Hello, love,' she said. 'Many happy returns.'

'Thank you very much.'

'What do you reckon to this?'

She was appraising the effect of a large poster she had just put in the window.

I looked at the neatly painted poster. 'An Evening with Madame Eugénie, England's Foremost Medium and Psychic.'

'What a marvellous idea,' I said. 'When is it?'

'When is . . . ? Oh, blow it. I forgot to put the day on.' She seemed to find this terribly amusing. 'I'd forget me own head if it weren't nailed on. Sunday. Next Sunday night. Do you think you and Lady H might come along?'

'I can certainly ask,' I said. 'I'd love to come along myself, that's for certain. You know I've always been interested in spiritualism. My grandmother had the sight, you know.'

'I remember you sayin',' she said. 'You also said you knew some charlatans, mind. From the circus. She i'n't one o' they. She's clairvoyant, too. She'll do you a private reading for a shillin'.'

'A shilling! I might not be doing that. But I'll ask Lady Hardcastle if she wants to come to the séance.'

'Right you are,' she said cheerfully. 'It'd be lovely to have our local dignitaries here.'

I laughed at this. 'Sir Hector and Lady Farley-Stroud not good enough for you these days?' I said.

'Oh, they's charming and all,' she said. 'But they a'n't got that air of glamour like you has.'

I laughed again. 'I shall endeavour to persuade Lady Hardcastle to bring her air of glamour, then. But even if she is otherwise engaged, I shall be there myself.'

Daisy's mother rounded the corner.

'Hello, Ma,' said Daisy. 'What do you reckon?'

Mrs Spratt regarded the poster for a moment. 'You've not put a date on it, you buffle.'

Daisy laughed. 'Flo said that, didn't you, Flo?'

''Least one of you's got the brains you was born with,' said Mrs Spratt. 'You all right, Flo, dear?'

'Fine, thank you, Mrs Spratt. How about you?'

'Mustn't grumble, dear, mustn't grumble. What's all this I hear about a burglary up the rugby club?'

I told her everything we'd discovered so far, though that, honestly, wasn't much.

'Tch, I don't know,' she said. 'What with that and Spencer Caradine being murdered, I don't know what this village is comin' to.'

''T'i'n't nothin' new, Ma,' said Daisy. 'We had all that business last year, an' all. All they murders.'

'You're just provin' my point, Dais,' said Mrs Spratt.

'And anyway,' said Daisy, 'Flo says they don't even know Spencer was murdered.'

''Course he was. Stands to reason. Someone as mean-spirited as that was bound to come to a sticky end. Not murdered indeed. Poisoned, he was. You mark my words.'

'The police surgeon is having the Devil's own job confirming that, though, Mrs Spratt,' I said. 'Lady Hardcastle keeps pressing Inspector Sunderland for more information but the police surgeon is baffled. She's so frustrated that she's thinking of asking one of her old friends to look into it.'

'He wants to come to me,' said Mrs Spratt, setting off once more towards her husband's shop. 'I'll set him straight. Poisoned, he was, and serves the old snudge right. It was that Morris. He's a weird one. You can tell your inspector I says so.'

I returned home and tried to settle to some chores, but by lunchtime I grew too bored to continue. I went out into the garden and let myself into the orangery. Lady Hardcastle was hard at work.

'What ho, Flo dear,' she said, looking up from the table. 'How's Daisy?'

'Very well indeed,' I said. 'She was putting up a poster for a séance at the pub.'

'Was she, was she?' she said distractedly as she fiddled with a model on the table beneath her enormous moving picture camera. 'What do you think?'

The model was of a woodland scene. She was putting the finishing touches to a lifelike figure of a mouse. Lifelike, that is, apart from the fact that it was standing on its hind legs and wearing a waistcoat.

'It looks adorable, my lady. I love his little cane.'

'He's Town Mouse. He's visiting his friend in the country.'

'He's quite the dandy,' I said.

'He's a fiddly little beggar is what he is,' she said. 'I think it'll be worth it, though.'

'One photograph at a time, did you say?'

'One blessed frame at a time,' she confirmed. 'I think I have about forty-three seconds' worth now. Let's hope nothing happens to the camera, eh.' She touched the tripod affectionately.

'This "animation" is quite the thing, is it?' I asked.

'No,' she said. 'In fact I'm not sure it'll catch on at all. Monsieur Méliès has made some marvellous films but he's a genius and I'm just an old dabbler. Still, it keeps the natives gossiping. I'd rather they were talking about "that strange lady and her moving pictures" than "that dangerous lady and her spying shenanigans".'

'Nothing wrong with a bit of dabbling, my lady,' I said as she shooed me out of the way and clicked the button on the camera. 'The Empire was built by dabblers. And by spying shenanigans, come to that. You're a—'

I was cut short by a distant clap of thunder.

'Bother!' she said as the skies began to darken. 'There goes my light. Help me pack up, would you, dear. I may as well retire to the study if there's going to be a storm.'

By evening the hatches were battened against the storm. I had sent Edna and Miss Jones home even earlier than usual so that they might try to beat the worst of the rain. I suggested that if it were wretched the next day, they should save themselves the unpleasantness of coming over.

'Will we be paid just the same?' asked Edna.

'You'll be paid, and you'll be dry,' I said.

She gave a single, sharp nod and stomped off into the gathering gloom.

This left Lady Hardcastle and me alone in the house. This wasn't in the least bit unusual, but there's something about a storm that makes one feel trapped. We would almost certainly have chosen to remain indoors, but the torrential rain had taken the choice away.

We settled down in the drawing room together with our books after my delicious birthday supper. Miss Jones had prepared everything for me so that I didn't have to do anything. She had also made a cake, which Edna had helped to ice.

I was reading a local history that Dr Fitzsimmons had lent me when a passage caught my imagination. I looked up from the book and saw that Lady Hardcastle had also stopped reading and was staring into the fire.

'Do you believe in ghosts, my lady?' I asked.

'Do I what?' she asked distractedly.

'Ghosts,' I said. 'Do you believe in them?'

'Believe, dear?' she said, looking over at me. 'No, I don't "believe". My mind is open to the possibility that there's something going on that we don't understand, but I do try awfully hard not to believe in things. I'm an empirical girl. You know me. Show me some evidence and I'll be excited as a puppy, but a few credulous folk hearing bumps in the night isn't enough for me.'

'Oh,' I said, feeling strangely disappointed.

'Why do you ask?'

'Just something I was reading,' I said.

'I thought you were reading that local history the doctor gave you.'

'I am. Chipping Bevington has a ghost.'

'Does it, by goodness?' she said, sitting up. 'Why doesn't Littleton Cotterell have one?'

'That's not recorded, my lady,' I said. 'There's just a story about the Chipping Bevington ghost.'

'Well go on then, you're dying to tell me.'

'There's a long, dreary section about the town and its history, about the market and the pubs. Did you know there were seven pubs, my lady?'

'It doesn't surprise me,' she said with a smile, warming to my own enthusiasm.

'And then there's this quite recent bit about the ghost of Sir Samuel Lagthorpe,' I said as I picked up the book and began to read.

The Chipping Bevington Ghost

Sir Samuel Lagthorpe was an energetic man who spent many years abroad managing various colonial enterprises. By the time he returned to England at the beginning of 1873 he had amassed a fortune large enough that he need never work again. He moved to the West Country where he bought a modest, but comfortable, house just outside Chipping Bevington in the village of Littleton Cotterell. He settled into country life, enjoying his new role as the exotic village squire 'from overseas'.

Always interested in the comings and goings of his new neighbours, he accompanied his friend John Stallard, a local farmer, to the cattle market in Chipping Bevington to experience for himself the commercial realities of the men among whom he now lived. It was there that he met a beguiling and beautiful young woman named Charlotte Dunnett. Her father owned land near the town. He encouraged her to attend the cattle market to learn more about his tenants so that she might one day take over the management of his estate. So popular was she that few ever questioned her ambitions and she was a welcome and regular sight at the cattle market.

Sir Samuel soon managed to get himself introduced to the young woman. By and by their shy meetings at the cattle market grew to courtship. Before summer's end they were engaged to be married.

His forthcoming marriage sealed Sir Samuel's resolve to make his home in England after years of wandering the Empire. Accordingly, he made arrangements to spend several days in London settling all his affairs. He knew that life with a woman as sparkling and wilful as Charlotte would never be predictable but he was determined that, whatever other adventures they might have, their financial future would be as secure as he could make it.

He travelled to London by train on Monday the 27th of October, intending to return two weeks later when everything was settled. He took rooms at his club and spent an industrious yet enjoyable few days going through papers with his solicitor by day and dining with old friends and companions by night.

He returned to his club on the Thursday evening, the 30th, to find a telegram waiting for him that had been delivered earlier that day. It told him that Charlotte had gone for her morning ride as usual. She was an adventurous, some might say reckless, rider and Sir Samuel had often begged her to take more care. She always laughed and told him not to be so silly. Today, his worst fears were realized. She had fallen from her horse and now lay gravely ill at her father's house. Sir Samuel, said the telegram, was to come at once.

He left hurried instructions for his belongings to be packed and sent on, settled his bill and took a hansom to Paddington. He managed to catch the last train to Bristol but by the time he arrived there was no connecting train north to Chipping Bevington and so he roused a local cabman and hired a brougham to take him the twenty miles to Charlotte.

The journey was long. Sir Samuel fidgeted and fretted as the carriage made its way along the Gloucester Road. At length he arrived at the Dunnetts' house but even as he hurried inside he knew he was too late.

He was met in the hallway by Charlotte's father who managed to tell him in a broken voice that Charlotte had died from her injuries less than half an hour before.

Following the funeral Sir Samuel returned to his home and was seldom seen. His many friends paid visits but his door remained bolted and their concerned letters of friendship and comfort went unanswered. By the end of November, the local police were persuaded that something was amiss and broke into his home where they discovered his body, the pistol with which he had ended his life still clutched in his hand.

One year later, on the anniversary of Charlotte's death, shopkeepers on Chipping Bevington High Street reported being awoken in the early hours of the morning by loud noises as though a carriage had clattered through the streets at enormous speed. One witness reported seeing 'a jet black carriage' drawn by 'a fiery horse' heading in the direction of the Dunnetts' farm and local legend claims to this day that on the night before Halloween, the ghost of Sir Samuel Lagthorpe races through Chipping Bevington, desperately trying to reach his beloved Charlotte.

Neither of us spoke for a few moments; the only sounds were the crackle of the fire, the soft ticking of the hall clock and the tapping of the wind-blown rain against the windows. The shutters were still open and I'd not yet drawn the curtains.

There was a sudden blinding flash of lightning as it struck a tree a little way down the lane, and the almost simultaneous explosion of thunder gave us both such a start that I dropped the book and we both yelped in surprise. A gust of wind blew sparks from the fire.

And then, of course, came the inevitable laughter.

'Gracious!' said Lady Hardcastle. 'That was a close one.'

'It'll be the ghost of Sir Samuel, cursing you for not believing in him,' I said.

'Without a doubt,' she said, still laughing. 'I recant my sceptical ways and shall hie me to a séance at the earliest possible opportunity.'

'It's funny you should say that, my lady.'

'No,' she said firmly.

'You don't know what I was going to say.'

'Yes, I do. You saw your pal Daisy putting up a poster for a séance this morning and you think it would be fun.'

'Oh, go on,' I said. 'Daisy does so want us to go.'

'I refuse to sit around a table at the Dog and Duck in the pitch black while some charlatan talks to her spirit guide in a silly voice and rattles the china.'

'Spoilsport,' I said.

'Seriously? You really want to go? You grew up in a circus. Surely you've seen all this before.'

'I've seen some . . . "performers", yes. I know a few of the tricks the fakers pull. But Mamgu had the sight. She really did. They're not all frauds. There are more things in heaven and earth, my lady, than are dreamt of in your philosophy.'

'I wouldn't dream of casting nasturtiums on your grandmother's gifts, Flo, you know that. But I'd wager she never charged a fee.'

'You're always saying we should involve ourselves more in village life,' I persisted.

She looked at me thoughtfully for a moment. 'Oh, I suppose it couldn't hurt,' she said at length. 'And we could do with an evening out.'

I grinned. 'Daisy claims Madame Eugénie is one of the best. Clairvoyant, too, she said. She'll do a private reading for a shilling.'

'A shilling!' said Lady Hardcastle. 'I'm in the wrong line of business.'

'Give her the shilling and she'll be able to tell you what line of business you should be in.'

She laughed. 'All right, then, I'll strike a bargain with you. If Madame Eugénie can tell me a single thing about me that she couldn't have picked up from the newspapers or from village gossip, I'll give you a shilling as well.'

'Done,' I said.

'But if I get even a trace of ectoplasm on my new dress, you can clean it up and I'm taking the money back.'

'It has occurred to you that I'd be cleaning it anyway?' I said.

She harrumphed and we returned to our books.

9

Sunday saw no end to the storms, just brief interludes when we would look out of the windows and optimistically suggest that it might finally be over. The resumption of meteorological hostilities was met with weary resignation and I returned to my moping.

With Edna and Miss Jones sensibly staying away, there was even more to do about the house. Somehow, though, being trapped indoors made time hang heavy and I looked for ever more industrious ways of passing it. Things were tidied, mended, cleaned and polished whether they needed it or not, and cake production reached an almost industrial level.

Lady Hardcastle came into the kitchen to cadge a cup of tea. 'Are we opening a cake shop?' she asked when she saw what was cooling on every available surface.

'I got a bit bored, my lady,' I said, piping some whipped cream into a choux bun.

'So it would appear,' she said. 'Let's hope someone drops in unexpectedly for tea. Several people.'

'We'll get through it, my lady. Be brave.'

'Woman cannot live by cake alone, Flo.'

'I can give it a bloomin' good try.'

'Are we being fed tonight?' she asked.

'At the pub?' I said. 'There was talk of a tray of sandwiches, but I wouldn't get your hopes up. Joe does his best, but he'd not be well reviewed in the society pages for the soaring quality of his cuisine.'

'So perhaps we should eat a decent lunch?'

'I am, as is so often the case in matters domestic, at least one step ahead of you,' I said. 'If my lady would care to ready herself for luncheon, I have prepared a delicious pie.'

Lunch came and went, followed by tea where we made a reasonable dent in the cake supply. Eventually it was time to get ready for our evening at the Dog and Duck.

A séance works best in the dead of night 'when the spirits are abroad', so it was actually quite late by the time we left. I realized that I was no longer concerned about the quality of Joe's sandwiches – I would happily eat anything.

We had been granted a brief respite from the viciousness of the storms and we walked into the village through what seemed, by comparison, a very pleasant gusty drizzle. By the time we reached the door of the Dog and Duck less than ten minutes later, we were wet through. Somehow, though, it still seemed less disagreeable than having battled through the tempest.

I tried the door but it was locked. I was forced to hammer upon it quite vigorously before we heard the bolts being drawn on the other side.

'Welcome to the Dog and Duck, ladies,' said Daisy Spratt as she opened the door. 'Please join us.' She was wearing a long, black, old-fashioned dress that I'd not seen before. She was attempting a breathy, would-be mysterious tone which would have fitted the mood perfectly had I not found it so funny.

I tried not to laugh. I also gave Lady Hardcastle my most threatening stare as we walked in, just to make sure she knew to behave herself.

The tables and chairs in the public bar had been pushed against the walls. A large circular table now filled the centre of the room where the other guests were already seated. The room was lit only by a lamp in the centre of the table. The rest of the guests looked up at us through the gloom as we took off our coats.

'I'm so sorry,' said Lady Hardcastle, hanging up her hat. 'We seem to be the last to arrive. I do hope we haven't kept everybody waiting too long.'

There was a cheerful murmur of assurance from the small group.

'Madame Eugénie isn't quite ready yet,' said Daisy, 'so we were just having a little tipple and a gossip. Come and sit down. I've put you on that side of the table, either side of Madame Eugénie. I hope that'll be all right. Can I get you a drink?'

'Brandy for me, please,' said Lady Hardcastle enthusiastically.

'And for me, please,' I said. 'That would be lovely.'

We sat in our allotted places while Daisy poured two generous measures of brandy behind the bar.

'I think we all know each other,' she said as she came back to the table and handed us our drinks. She moved to her own chair and sat down. 'Let's see,' she said. 'Lady Hardcastle most of you know. Then there's Mr Snelson.'

The smartly dressed man to Lady Hardcastle's right inclined his head in greeting.

'Our Ma, I think you knows her an' all.'

Mrs Spratt smiled self-consciously.

'This is Mr Holman from the bakery. I'm Daisy, as I reckon you knows. Dr Fitzsimmons everyone knows. And then my pal Miss Armstrong who works for Lady Hardcastle.'

I nodded my own greeting.

There was a momentary flutter of excitement when the door to the back room opened, but it was just the landlord, Joe Arnold, bearing the promised tray of sandwiches.

'I'll just leave these on the bar,' he said toothlessly.

'Not joining us, Joe?' asked Lady Hardcastle.

'No, m'lady. T''i'n't right, messin' with t'other side.' He gave a little shudder. 'I'll just provide the refreshment and keep out of the way if you don't mind.'

And pocket a decent slice of the entrance money, too, I entirely failed to say out loud.

He shuffled back out towards the kitchen and left us to wait for Madame Eugénie to arrive. I was just about to get up and help everyone to sandwiches when the door opened again and a tall, willowy woman wafted in. She was clad entirely in black, from the gauzy veil thrown back over her black hair and the darkly tinted spectacles perched on her long nose, all the way to her black boots. Even her earrings, necklace and rings were of jet.

'Good evening, ladies and gentlemen,' she said in a faraway voice. 'My apologies for my late arrival, but I am bound to the rhythms of the other realm and oftentimes the spirits forget that I have appointments to keep in this world.' She glided to the empty chair and sat down. 'Daisy, my dear, have you made the introductions?'

'I have, Madame Eugénie,' said Daisy with an eager nod. 'Would you like me to—'

'No, my dear,' interrupted the medium in her dreamy voice. 'I prefer to let the spirits guide me.'

'Yes, Madame Eugénie,' said Daisy, a good deal more respectfully than I'd ever heard her speak to anyone before.

'So, dear friends,' said Madame Eugénie, 'let us begin. We are about to breach the barrier between this world and the next. Most of the spirits that loiter near the border seeking access to the world of the living are benign. They are merely curious to visit once more the world they have left behind. But there are those who are not so well intentioned, who would wish us ill. Alone we cannot fight them, but together we are too strong for them and they can do us no harm. Please take your left hand and hold tightly to the right wrist of your neighbour to form a circle of earthly power. Only then can our psychic strength combine to protect us.'

After a moment's puzzled hand waving, we managed collectively to work out what she had in mind. Mr Holman clasped my right wrist with his left hand while I took Madame Eugénie's slender right wrist in my own left hand. The chain formed around the table.

'There,' she said, with satisfaction. 'Now we are protected. Remember, we must not break the circle, no matter what might happen.'

There were nods and murmurs of agreement from around the table.

'Daisy, would you be so kind as to extinguish the lamp, my dear? The spirits prefer the darkness.'

Daisy freed her right hand from Dr Fitzsimmons's grasp and turned down the wick on the lamp until it was extinguished. In the darkness, I could hear the tiny sounds of movement as the doctor tried to find Daisy's wrist once more. They soon settled and the room fell into silence.

Suddenly, Madame Eugénie broke my grip on her wrist and leaned back in her chair. She gave the loudest and most forceful sneeze I have ever heard.

'Oh, my dears, I am most dreadfully sorry,' she said through a slightly blocked nose. 'I think I must have picked up a chill in this awful weather. Do please excuse me.'

After a moment's rustling, she blew her nose with a sound like an inexpertly played euphonium. There was more rustling while the handkerchief was put away. She grasped my wrist again.

'Can you find my hand, my dear?' she said.

'Yes,' said Lady Hardcastle. 'I have it now, thank you.'

The room was quiet again save for the steadily increasing rain outside, and for a few moments everything was perfectly still. Then, starting with the smallest movement, but with slowly growing strength, Madame Eugénie began to sway back and forth.

'Come, spirits,' she said in her faraway voice. 'Join us. Join us in our—' I could feel that she had stopped moving. Her grip on my wrist relaxed slightly. Then there was a knocking which sounded for all the world like someone rapping on the table, but with everyone's hand held firmly by their neighbour's, it couldn't possibly be anyone at the table.

'Is it you, Madame Eugénie?' she said in a deeper, foreign-sounding growl. 'You have been gone far too long. I have many here waiting for your call.'

There were questioning murmurs around the table.

'That's Monsieur Diderot,' whispered Daisy, who had clearly done her research. 'Her spirit guide.'

The murmurers seemed satisfied.

'There is someone here who wishes to communicate with Dr Fitzsimmons,' said Madame Eugénie – or Monsieur Diderot, I should say. 'Her name is . . . her name is Jane . . . Jennifer . . .'

There was no reaction.

'Juliet? Or is it June?' 'he' said.

'My late wife was June,' said Dr Fitzsimmons sadly.

'She says she is happy, and that you must be, too,' said Madame Eugénie's growly voice.

'That's nice,' said the doctor quietly. 'Thank you.'

'Is there anyone else there?' said Madame Eugénie in her normal voice.

'There are many,' said the growly voice. 'I have John here.'

'Mum?' said Daisy excitedly. 'Wasn't Grandad's brother called John?'

'Ohh,' said Mrs Spratt. 'He was. Is that you, Uncle John?'

'He says that the matter that has been concerning you will be settled soon and that all shall be well,' said Madame Eugénie's growly voice.

'Oh, thank goodness for that,' said Mrs Spratt. 'I'd been worrying myself silly.'

Suddenly, Madame Eugénie began to convulse.

'There is someone trying to get through,' said the spirit guide. 'He is angry! I cannot hold him!'

I heard the scrape of a chair near the window and turned to try to see what was happening. There was a sudden draught, the coldest of breezes. From the opposite side of the table, a man gasped. Mr Snelson. 'Something touched me,' he said in a terrified voice. 'Freezing cold.'

Daisy and her mother screamed together. A flash of lightning. Something moved in the shadows. Another flash, and there, standing behind Dr Fitzsimmons was a man. A ghastly white face. A ghostly white suit. His arm outstretched and pointing directly at Mr Snelson. All visible in an instant and then gone. A terrifying crash of thunder. Then in the silence that followed, a hoarse, ghostly whisper said, 'Murderer!'

There was uproar. Mrs Spratt screamed again. Daisy, who had seen nothing of the ghost, screamed anyway. Mr Holman yelled in alarm and there was a rustle of movement around the table.

'Do not break the circle!' shouted Madame Eugénie above the hubbub. 'We shall be perfectly safe as long as we do not break the circle. If the lady to my right will join hands with the lady to my left, I shall relight the lamp. I shall be perfectly safe with my spirit guide to protect me and the circle will be broken for a mere moment. Not time enough for us to come to harm.'

She released my hand and I scrabbled around trying to locate Lady Hardcastle's hand. I felt her grip my wrist as Madame Eugénie stood and leaned forwards towards the lamp at the centre of the table.

A rattle of bangles. A clink of glass. A match flared. And suddenly the gloom was gone. She lit the lamp and refitted the chimney. We were once more in what seemed a bright and welcoming room.

'The spirits will not trouble us while there is light. Not with so many of the living in the room,' said Madame Eugénie. 'Daisy, my dear, would you be so kind as to bring the sandwiches over? And some more drinks? I think we could all do with a bit of a break.'

Daisy did as she was asked. With the tension broken, the room erupted into nervously excited chatter.

The apparition was discussed at some length as the sandwiches were devoured. Madame Eugénie took several bookings for private consultations on the next day. I had felt somewhat cheated that the séance had lasted only a few minutes, but the others were abuzz, having expected nothing so exciting as a full-blown apparition, still less one that made such an extraordinary accusation.

Mr Snelson was questioned at length. Although he was clearly shaken, he was adamant that he had no idea what the spirit had meant when it had pointed at him and called him a murderer. Nevertheless, Daisy avoided him for the rest of the night, casting suspicious sidelong glances his way, and refused to say goodnight to him when she had eventually shown us all to the door.

We arrived home late and both slept in. I had made breakfast and we were sitting together in the morning room, wearing our dressing gowns. We ate scrambled eggs in companionable silence. Once the second pot of tea had begun to revive us, I ventured a question.

'What did you think, then, my lady? Are you still sceptical?'

'I'm curious, certainly,' she said, sipping her tea.

'Curious?'

'Of course. Either we witnessed a genuine psychic event last night, in which case I should like to know more. Or Madame

Eugénie is a fraud, in which case I should very much like to know how she did it.'

'If she's a fraud, my lady, I can tell you half a dozen ways she might have done it. But she'd have to be very skilled. I've seen more than my fair share of fake séances. I took part in quite a few. But none so good as that one. That apparition. It touched Mr Snelson from the other side of the table. With its hand. Deathly cold. I do honestly wonder if we might have witnessed the genuine article.'

'We certainly witnessed all of those things,' she said. 'But what did we really see? If it were real, it was quite the most astonishing thing I've ever seen, and I've seen some pretty astonishing things in my time, I can tell you.'

'Daisy was convinced. She was all of a pother.'

'Daisy's always in a state about something,' she said. 'She does so love to be the centre of attention, that girl.'

'You're not wrong,' I said. 'But I thought it was an extraordinary experience. I'm only sorry it was so short.'

'Yes, I did feel a little cheated. We were seated for, what, five minutes? I do hope you didn't pay a lot for the tickets. You must let me pay for mine.'

'No, my lady, it was my treat. I have a spare shilling, too, if you fancy a private reading. You could find out what the future holds for you . . .'

She laughed, and the smile lit her face. 'No, dear, you save your money. I'll take my chances and let life unfold as it may.'

I smiled. 'As you wish, my lady.'

I began to tidy away the breakfast things. 'Do you have any plans for today, my lady?'

'Oh, I don't know,' she said impishly. 'I was thinking that maybe we could go back to the pub. There's still no word from the blessed police surgeon on what might have killed Spencer Caradine and I've no idea yet how we're going to get poor Lofty off the hook. So it might be nice to have a bit of a poke about at the Dog and Duck instead. See if we can't find out a little more about our visitation of last night. Let's nip over there at lunchtime and see what's what.'

'Right you are, my lady. In the meantime, would you care for some cake?'

She laughed. 'We've only just had breakfast.'

'Yes. But. There's cake,' I said, with the tiniest hint of desperation as I remembered the pastry-filled kitchen.

'Perhaps we should take some with us to the pub. We might persuade Joe to make us a pot of tea.'

The storm had finally blown itself out, and now that it was light we were able to see some of the havoc it had wrought. The tree that had been struck by lightning had been all but completely destroyed. Its massive trunk had been split almost in two and stripped of all its bark, while its charred limbs lay scattered in the field. There was more debris in the lane and the village green resembled nothing so much as a swamp. As we rounded the green we could see that there were slates missing from a couple of shop roofs, and at least one chimney pot lay smashed in the road.

'They don't muck about when they have storms down here, do they?' said Lady Hardcastle as we opened the door to the pub and stepped in.

'No, my lady. Nothing like the quality of a decent Welsh storm, of course, but they try their best.'

'They do, they do,' she said. 'I say,' she said slightly more loudly. 'Anyone at home?'

Unusually, the pub was deserted.

'That's odd, my lady,' I said, opening the door to the public bar and looking through. 'There's no one here, either.'

'Joe?' shouted Lady Hardcastle.

'Daisy?' I thought I might try a bit of shouting, too.

There were clomping footsteps on the stairs behind us and Joe appeared in the doorway.

'What's all the racket?' he grumbled. 'Who the devil . . . Oh, it's you, m'lady.'

'It is, Joe, it is,' she said. 'Are you all right? We were beginning to get worried about you.'

'Oh, I'm fine, m'lady. I was just upstairs checking on Madame Eugénie. Locked herself in her room, she has.'

'Oh, dear. Why?'

'There was a bit of a to-do in the night. We had to get her out of bed to deal with it.'

'A "to-do"?' said Lady Hardcastle with more than a hint of a mischievous twinkle in her eyes.

'A right old to-do,' he said, 'and no mistake.'

'Were the spirits getting rowdy on your beer and cider?' she said.

'They didn't need no booze to get 'em goin',' he said. 'There was bangin' and crashin' and carrying on. I got up to see what the matter was, saw the mess and went straight up to get Madame Eugénie. She come down and waved her hands and swayed a bit. She muttered some stuff and it all calmed down. Then she went back into her room and I a'n't seen her since.'

'How extraordinary,' said Lady Hardcastle. 'Did she say what had caused it?'

'She reckons 'twere that ghost you summoned up last night. I said no good would come of it. I told our Ma. I said, "You shouldn't go messing with t'other side." She just laughed and said, "Let Daisy have her fun, Joe." But I were right, weren't I?'

We had never met, nor even seen Mrs Arnold. I always assumed, given his own old age, that 'our Ma' was his wife rather than his mother, but other than speculation we had nothing to go on.

'It certainly seems as though strange things are happening,' said Lady Hardcastle. 'Was there any damage?'

'Damage? Couple of chairs knocked over, couple of glasses broke. But come with me, m'lady. Let me show you the strangest thing.'

He led us through the public bar to the skittle alley. The scores were kept on a small chalkboard screwed to the wall, which he indicated with the flourish of a stage magician revealing his latest illusion. Written in chalk in a shaky hand were the words 'NELSON MURDERED ME'. It was signed in an equally shaky hand with what looked like 'Mummy Bear', but I couldn't be sure.

'"Mummy Bear"?' said Lady Hardcastle. 'How odd. I thought it was "Mama Bear" in the Goldilocks story.'

'I should be surprised if this has anything to do with Goldilocks, my lady,' I said. 'More importantly, who's Nelson? Anyone we know?'

'Mr Snelson what's rentin' the old Cooper house up the way,' said Joe.

'A sloppy ghost, then,' said Lady Hardcastle.

'Beg pardon, m'lady?' he said.

'Missing off the S.'

'Oh, I get you. No, it's his first name, i'n't it?'

'Oh, how precious,' she said delightedly. 'Nelson Snelson. That's altogether too wonderful. Flo, dear, can we change your surname to Lawrence? You shall be Florence Lawrence.'

'Only if you agree to be Emily Demerly, my lady,' I said with a frown.

She laughed, still tickled by the whimsical mischief exhibited by Mr Snelson's parents. 'But who is this Bear? Whose mummy is she? And what's this about murder?' she said.

'Don't know nothing about it, m'lady,' he said. 'But Daisy said as how that ghost you saw last night had accused him o' murder – I reckon it must be he.'

'Hmmm,' said Lady Hardcastle.

'Ghosts are unquiet spirits,' I said. 'They most often have something on this side that they need to finish. Seeing his murderer brought to justice would fit the bill.'

'But "Mummy Bear"?' she said, still unconvinced. 'The "ghost" we saw was a man.'

'It's not an especially clear signature,' I said. 'Perhaps it's not Mummy Bear at all.'

'Hmmm,' she said again. 'Perhaps.'

I decided a change of subject was in order. 'It's quiet in here this morning, Joe. We were expecting you to be busier.'

'They all be clearin' up after the storm, miss,' he said. 'They'll be in later I reckons.'

'Oh,' I said. 'We brought some cakes and pastries.' I offered him the basket which I had packed with some of the surplus from our kitchen.

'That's very kind of you, miss,' he said, looking a little nonplussed.

'Perhaps we might buy a pot of tea?' asked Lady Hardcastle.

This seemed to amuse Joe. 'Tea, m'lady?' he said with a grin. 'In a pub? Whatever next?'

'Well, we don't have a tea room and despite my frequent protestations it sometimes can be too early for brandy. I thought a nice pot of tea and a bun in convivial surroundings might be pleasant. You have a kitchen, you have tables and chairs – I thought it might be a nice little money-spinner for you.'

He looked thoughtful for a moment, and then made up his mind. 'You know,' he said with another toothless grin, 'I reckons you might be right at that. I'll fetch our Ma's teapot and you can have your elevenses here in the snug.'

He trudged off in the direction of the stairs.

'Do you have an explanation for all this, my lady?' I asked once he was out of earshot.

'Not yet, no,' she said, looking around. 'There don't seem to be any signs of a burglary. All the residents were apparently in bed: Joe had to get up to see what the matter was; Madame Eugénie had to be roused from her slumbers; and Mrs Arnold has, to my knowledge, never ventured from their private rooms. And yet there's a small amount of mess and a message on a blackboard. It's a mystery, Flo dear. A mystery.'

'Or it's the ghost of Mummy Bear,' I said.

'Getting up to make porridge? It's a starting point, I suppose.'

We could hear Joe in the pub's kitchen clattering about with what I hoped wasn't 'our Ma's' best china – it would be returning to her dresser in pieces if it were.

After a little more clattering and at least one extremely colourful toothless oath, Joe emerged from the kitchen with a tea tray.

'Blow me, but 'tis harder work than pourin' a pint or makin' a round of sandwiches,' he said. 'I might have to talk to Daisy about makin' the tea when she gets in.'

We thanked him and he lumbered off again to make good the ghost's mess.

'I say, Mr Arnold,' said Lady Hardcastle as he picked up a chair. 'What do you know about this Mr Nelson Snelson?' She seemed to be taking great pleasure in the poor man's name. 'We met him once or twice before the séance but no one has told us much about him.'

'I don't know so much m'self, m'lady,' he said, sweeping up a few fragments of broken glass with a dustpan and brush. 'He rented the old Cooper house a couple of months back. Come from Gloucester, they say, had a company up there. Timber, I think they said. Sold up and come down here for a quiet life in the country is what I heard.'

'There's a lot of that about,' she said. 'No rumours that he was a murderer?'

Joe laughed. 'No, m'lady, nothin' like that. But seems as there should have been, eh?'

'If the ghost of Mummy Bear is to be believed, then perhaps there should,' she said. 'Perhaps she was seeking revenge from the timber merchants for chopping down her forest home.'

She was clearly determined to mock the ghost idea so I decided not to remind her yet again that the ghost had been a man.

'When are you expecting Daisy?' she said after munching a slice of lemon cake.

'Not till lunchtime, m'lady,' said Joe. 'She helps her dad in the mornings, then comes over here for the lunchtime rush.'

'Ah, yes, of course. Armstrong did tell me. I'm keen to find out more about the mysterious Madame Eugénie, you see,' she said. 'I thought she might be able to tell me a little more about her.'

'Reckon she'd be the one to ask, yes,' said Joe, setting the last table straight. 'There we goes. Fit for a king now. Can I get you ladies anything else?'

'Would you be a poppet and refresh the pot, please, Mr Arnold?' said Lady Hardcastle with a smile. 'We'll have a little more tea and then we'll biff off and see what adventures the day holds in store.'

'Right you are, m'lady,' said Joe, picking up the teapot. 'I'll have to look into getting some crockery for the bar. You reckon this'll catch on?'

'Bound to,' she said. 'People love a cup of tea and a gossip in the morning. Think of the extra trade.'

Having finished our tea and cakes, I retrieved the now empty basket from Joe and we went out into the weak sunshine.

'Come on, Flo,' said Lady Hardcastle. She strode off down a side road towards the houses behind the shops. 'Let's go and pay a call on Mr Nelson Snelson.'

'As you wish, my lady,' I said, though I confess I didn't really think it was such a terrific idea.

We navigated as much by instinct as knowledge, up the hill towards the only house that we judged grand enough to be the new home of a retired merchant. It was a moderately sized, square Georgian house, painted dazzling white. We approached the dark-green door and tugged firmly on the bell-pull.

An elderly man in a slightly dated butler's uniform opened the door and looked imperiously down at us.

'Yes?' he said, managing to draw the word out to much more than its natural length. 'How may I help you?'

'Good morning,' said Lady Hardcastle breezily. 'Is Mr Snelson at home?'

'I'm afraid the master is not at home, madam, no.'

'No matter,' she said, delving into her handbag for her silver card case. After a considerable amount of rummaging and some impatient muttering, she managed to find the silver case and triumphantly presented the ageing butler with her card.

'Would you be so kind as to tell him I called?' she said. 'Perhaps I could call again? When might be convenient?'

He looked at the card and there was a slightly more deferential tone in his voice as he said, 'I'm afraid I don't know, my lady. He is . . . otherwise engaged and may be so for some time. I shall endeavour to encourage him to send you a note should he . . . return.'

'Thank you,' she said with a warm smile. 'That would be most kind. Good day.'

He bowed slightly and closed the door.

We had already walked a little way down the road when we heard the butler's voice again. 'Pardon me, my lady,' he called loudly.

We stopped.

Lady Hardcastle turned and said, 'Yes?'

Leaving the door open, he hurried towards us. 'Mr Snelson appears to have returned without my noticing, my lady. He asks if you would care to join him for coffee.'

'That would be most agreeable,' said Lady Hardcastle, giving me a wink. 'Lead on.'

Mr Snelson was waiting for us in the drawing room. It was furnished in an old-fashioned style, as rented houses so often are. He had obviously tried to introduce something of his own taste into the room, though. I saw not only the Union Jack steam engine from Pomphrey's on a shelf, but also a photograph of two smiling men standing outside what appeared to be a sawmill. It could have been anyone, of course, but I judged it more likely to have been Snelson and a friend than something belonging to the house's owner.

'Please forgive me, my lady,' he said.

'Think nothing of it, Mr Snelson. I'm not at all sure that I would have been "at home" either, had I had the same experience.'

'Thank you. Please, won't you sit down? Luckman will bring the coffee in just a moment. I'm sure cook would make your maid a drink if she were to go down to the kitchen.'

'Armstrong can certainly leave if you wish, Mr Snelson. If you can bear it, though, I'd rather she stays. We come as a pair for the most part.'

His brow furrowed for a moment but I sensed he was more bemused than disapproving. 'As you wish.'

'Thank you,' she said. 'And thank you for agreeing to see us. We were quite worried about you after last night.'

'That's very kind of you,' he said. 'But, really, it was nothing.'

'Nothing? You were accused of murder. By a ghost, no less.'

He laughed. 'It certainly seemed like it, didn't it?'

'You must forgive me for being so blunt, Mr Snelson, but sometimes curiosity has a tendency to overrule discretion. Can you think of a reason why a ghost might accuse you of such a thing?'

'None whatsoever,' he said.

'Of course not,' she said. 'That would be ridiculous. Other than spectral accusations, how are you settling in?'

'Quite well, actually. It seems like a fine and friendly village. I've decided to stay. I've made some enquiries about buying this place as a matter of fact. But there's also the possibility of buying a farm. Time will tell, time will tell. I do find I get my own way eventually, one way or another.'

'How very splendid,' she said. 'It's a charming little village, isn't it? Where have you come from?'

'Gloucester most recently. I had a timber business there.'

'That's right,' she said. 'I'm sorry, I should have remembered. The gossip had told us that much. You don't sound like a Gloucester man, though.'

'No, I don't suppose I do. I'm from Birmingham originally.'

'Ah, yes of course. I can hear it now. I do so love accents. Don't you?'

He smiled. 'I never really give it much thought, to be honest.'

Luckman, the butler, came in with a tray of coffee. Lady Hardcastle and Mr Snelson stopped talking while he poured them each a cup. For a short while, the only sound in the room apart from the clattering of cups was the ticking of a preternaturally ugly clock on the mantel. The butler left without so much as glancing in my direction.

'Other than to offer you cook's indifferent coffee,' said Mr Snelson as the door clicked shut, 'I have another reason for getting Luckman to call you back.'

'How very intriguing,' she said. 'Is there something we can do for you?'

'Well, yes, actually, there is. We've both mentioned the power of the local gossip network. Among the many complimentary things I heard about you and Miss Armstrong were stories about you solving a handful of murders last year. And a jewel theft. Some folk round here think there's more to you even than that.'

Lady Hardcastle smiled. 'Yes, we did have something to do with clearing all that up. As for the other speculations, well, you know how people tattle.'

'I know only too well. That's why I was hoping to be able to ask for your help. Ghost or otherwise, it does a man no good at all to be slandered like that. I've killed no one and I should very much appreciate any assistance you can give in making certain that the slander doesn't take hold. Mud sticks.'

'It does, indeed,' she said. She paused a moment in thought. 'Can we offer the tattlers no crumbs? Is there something, perhaps, that might give someone – ghost or otherwise – cause to imagine you to be a murderer?'

He took a lengthy pause of his own. 'No,' he said at length. 'Not a thing.'

It was clear that despite his desire for our help, he wasn't prepared to say anything more.

'I do so hate false accusations, Mr Snelson. We're already trying to do something about one of those in another matter we're looking into. Armstrong and I shall do our utmost to find out what's going on at the Dog and Duck and you can rest assured that we shall make every effort to stamp out any slanderous rumours we hear.'

'You can't say any fairer than that, my lady,' said Snelson. 'Would you care for a biscuit?'

10

We ate a light lunch and I was just contemplating which chore I should undertake next, when the doorbell rang. To my immense surprise, it was Sergeant Dobson.

'Good afternoon, Sergeant,' I said as I opened the door. 'How lovely to see you. To what do we owe the pleasure?'

'Afternoon, miss,' he said, touching the brim of his helmet with his forefinger. 'Sorry to trouble you. Is your mistress at home?'

'To you, Sergeant,' I said, 'she is always at home. Please come in.' I stood aside and let him into the hall where he removed his helmet and I placed it on the table for him. I led him through to the drawing room and invited him to sit while I fetched Lady Hardcastle from her study.

I knocked on the study door and poked my head round.

'Sergeant Dobson to see you, my lady,' I said.

She was sitting with her feet on her desk, reading a large, thick book. She took off her spectacles and sat up straight in her chair, swinging her legs off the desk as she did so.

'I'm sorry, dear,' she said. 'I didn't even hear the bell. Did he say what he wanted?'

'No, my lady. I just put him in the drawing room and came to fetch you.'

'Right you are. Let's go and find out, shall we?'

We walked through and I opened the door for her, following her in. The sergeant rose to his feet and inclined his head in greeting.

'Good afternoon, Sergeant,' said Lady Hardcastle, sitting down and motioning that he should also seat himself. 'A pleasure as always.'

'Afternoon, m'lady,' said the sergeant with a smile.

'What can we do for you? Is anything the matter?'

'I'm not entirely sure, m'lady,' he said, tugging thoughtfully on his impressive moustache. 'See the thing is, I've been getting reports all day about certain events last night, and a number of enquiries as to what exactly we intends to do about it. And to tell the truth, I doesn't have the first idea what to say, let alone what to do. I wondered if you might be able to shed some light on it, as 'twere. I gathers you were both there last night.'

'At the Dog and Duck? Yes, we were. I hadn't been keen, but Armstrong persuaded me. I'm rather glad she did now.'

'Right,' said the sergeant. 'So what exactly went on? The things I've heard don't make no sense. No sense at all.'

Between us we recounted the events of the previous evening and our visit to the pub that morning.

The sergeant sat for a while, frowning. 'I'm still not sure it makes sense, m'lady,' he said at length.

'Nor to me, Sergeant,' said Lady Hardcastle. 'But that's what we saw and heard. Have we left anything out do you think, Armstrong?'

'No, my lady, that's it, exactly as it happened,' I said.

'Well, now, you see, that puts me in rather a quandary,' he said. 'On the one hand, a most serious accusation has been made against Mr Snelson. On t'other, it's been made by a ghost. I don't pretend to know a great deal about the workings of the legal system, but I'd lay ten bob there i'n't a court in the land as would prosecute a man on the say-so of a spirit.'

'I think you're right, Sergeant,' she said. 'Have you tried talking to Mr Snelson?'

'I just come from there, m'lady. He weren't at home.'

'Just not at home to the rozzers, I'm afraid. He was there earlier.'

'You called on him?'

'Yes, before lunch. His butler turned us away at first but then called us back.'

'Typical,' said the sergeant. 'I couldn't get nothing out of the butler 'cept to be politely told to sling my hook.'

Lady Hardcastle laughed. 'A butler of the old school, that one,' she said. 'Do you want our help again? We're still looking for the missing trophy, but we're closing in. I'm sure we can spare a little time for another mystery.'

'I'd not want to divert you from anything important, m'lady. This one's sommat and nothin' as far as I can see. If it's going to keep you from findin' the trophy, I'd rather you were concentratin' on that. Lofty's makin' a right old fuss. Swears blind he a'n't done nothin'.'

'Well, he would, Sergeant. I rather think he's telling the truth, too. But we can work on both. I know we're not getting anywhere with investigating Mr Caradine's death, but that's more Inspector Sunderland's problem really. Or, rather, the police surgeon's problem. Until he comes up with a cause of death there's not a lot we can do. I'm sure the inspector will be in touch if he wants us to do anything further.'

'He's not said nothin' to me, m'lady,' said the sergeant.

'As I thought. What say we join forces again, then? Armstrong and I can do a little snooping for you. We'll try to dig up whatever we can about the mysterious Mr Nelson Snelson and you can reassure a worried public that the police have matters well in hand. They can sleep easy once more knowing that you're doing all you can to get to the bottom of it. I'd like to find out a little more about our mysterious medium, too. Do you know anything about Madame Eugénie?'

'Not a thing, m'lady. She arrived a couple of days ago in a trap from the station, installed herself in the Dog and Duck and a'n't been seen much since 'cept for last night's doings.'

'Hmm,' said Lady Hardcastle. 'Well, we'll have to see what we can rootle out about her, too.'

'Right you are, m'lady,' said the sergeant, standing up. 'I appreciates your help, I really does.'

'Think nothing of it, Sergeant,' she said, with another of her room-illuminating smiles. 'It really is rather fun.'

I returned to the dining room and flopped into a chair.

'How on earth are we supposed to deal with this one?' I said with a sigh.

'What do you mean?' asked Lady Hardcastle.

'Well, we usually start by talking to witnesses and likely suspects and asking a few pertinent questions,' I said.

'Impertinent questions sometimes,' she said.

'Quite. But our best witness is a ghost.'

She laughed. 'A ghost, yes. But . . .'

'But you don't believe in ghosts, my lady, I know.'

'Which means that I think there must be a more down-to-earth explanation for it all. Someone or something that very much resembled the traditional idea of a ghost quite definitely appeared in the room.'

'It did,' I said.

'You of all people know that these things can be faked, though.'

'I said I'd never seen anything that convincing. Remember?'

'Very well. I don't yet doubt that Mr Snelson – wouldn't it be too, too wonderful if his middle name were Kelsen – that Mr Snelson was touched by the cold hand of . . . of something or other. We know that everyone's hands were on the table because we were all grasping each other's wrists. We know that the "spirit" was too far away to do that. That's what we know, at any rate.'

'Others might know differently?' I suggested.

'You said yourself that we can't very well question the ghost—'

'We could hold another séance,' I interrupted.

'We could let Madame Eugénie fleece us for another séance, yes.'

I said nothing.

'But,' she continued, 'we can talk to one or two of the others to see if their stories match ours. And I'd very much like to find out a little more about this Eugénie character. What's her story? How did Daisy find her?'

'Daisy's very interested in spiritualism,' I said. 'It's what got us chatting in the first place. When you were indisposed.'

'Interested enough to know who the big names in the spiritualist world are?'

'I should think so,' I said. 'She's talked about seeing them in theatres and the like.'

'Do you have plans to meet her again soon?'

'Nothing definite, my lady.'

'In that case why not drop in on her at the butcher's tomorrow. You could subtly persuade her to blow the gaff on the secret world of spiritualism.'

'Or just ask her what she knows about Madame Eugénie.'

She raised an eyebrow. 'Or that, of course.'

'Right you are, my lady,' I said.

'Splendid,' she said. 'Oh, I say, you can nip to the butcher's early tomorrow for some urgent hogget. You can catch her then.'

'Oooh, hogget,' I said. 'What an admirable idea. Hot pot, do you think? Or something more exotic?'

'I rather fancy a curry,' she said. 'Memories of Bengal.'

'Right you are, my lady,' I said. 'I brought a tin of curry powder from the London flat. It should still be all right. What shall you be doing?'

'I thought I might pay a call on Dr Fitzsimmons. He wanted to look over the old war wound so I shall drop in and let him peruse the scar with a clinical eye. Meanwhile, I shall engage him in conversation about our shared evening of terror.'

The evening had ended with me winning six thousand, two hundred and thirty-seven pounds at piquet and Lady Hardcastle vowing never to play me again. We entered my winnings into our cards ledger. After a few minutes' tipsy efforts at calculation we worked out that I now owed her three shillings and sixpence ha'penny. I slept well.

The following dawn saw neither larks nor robins, but it did see yours truly mending yet another rip in Lady Hardcastle's overalls. After breakfast, we went our separate ways, with Lady Hardcastle heading to one side of the green to see the doctor and me turning right to go to the shop of F. Spratt, Butcher.

The bell tinkled welcomingly as I opened the door. There was sawdust on the floor and a familiar smell in the air. I find myself unable to describe it, that smell of meat and sawdust, but it's the smell of a butcher's shop. Mr Spratt was sharpening his knives behind the counter. Daisy sat on a high stool in the corner, poring over a ledger. Mrs Spratt was on her way out of the shop in the company of a woman I'd not seen before. She was, as always, talking.

'. . . and so I says, "I can't see what she ever saw in that Lofty anyway. Clever girl like her. She could make somethin' of herself,

that one, 'stead of mooning about after some lanky burglin' baker."
And she says . . .'

The door closed behind them.

'Morning, Miss Armstrong,' said Mr Spratt with a smile. He
was a large man, not quite fat, but meaty, as befits a butcher. The
white stripes of his blue apron were stained with blood. 'What can
I do for you today?' he said, putting down his knife and steel and
coming forward to the counter. 'I've got some lovely sausages. Made
fresh this morning. How about some lovely pork chops?'

'Good morning, Mr Spratt. I was actually after some hogget.'

'Hogget, eh? I've got just the thing. Nice bit of shoulder?'

'Just what I'm looking for, thank you.'

'I'll be two shakes of a hogget's tail, miss,' he said, and he
disappeared into the back room.

I sidled over to the other end of the counter and leaned on it.
'*Bora da*, Daisy, *fach*,' I said.

She looked up from her adding. 'Oh, hello, love. How's Lady
Hardcastle getting on? Did you enjoy the séance t'other night?
Wasn't it amazing? Madame Eugénie is an extraordinary woman,
isn't she? To be able to do all that.' It all tumbled out of her like
someone had upended a bucket of words.

'We're both all right, thank you,' I said. 'We loved the séance.
Astonishing. Where on earth did you find her?'

'Loads of people has been asking me that,' she said proudly. 'I
knows this woman in Woodworthy, see. I goes to see her for readings
once a month if I can afford it. She does the cards and palms as well
as contacting t'other side. She put me on to Madame Eugénie, said
she was well known among the Birmingham spiritualists. Came
highly recommended, she did. And they was right, weren't they?
She's amazing. And who would have thought old Snelson was a
murderer? Well, o' course, I knew something was up with him the
moment I saw him. He's got beady eyes, see. You can always tell.

And our Ma reckons I've got the gift meself so o' course I'd be able to see something in him, wouldn't I?'

'Birmingham, eh?' I said, trying to limit her to one subject at a time.

''S right,' she said. 'She's a regular at spiritualist meetings up there.'

'Well, she certainly has the gift, doesn't she?' I said.

'I can introduce you if you like. She was quite taken with me, she was. Said I was one of the best hostesses of a meeting she'd ever come across. Said I should be managing a theatre or something, she did.'

'Did she? Blimey. Have you seen much of her?'

'No, she keeps herself to herself, she does. Sensitive, see? Gots to rest. Takes it out of you, talking to t'other side.'

'I dare say it does,' I said.

Mr Spratt reappeared with my joint of meat neatly wrapped. 'There you go, m'dear. What have you got planned for that?'

'I was thinking of a nice curry, Mr Spratt. We got a taste for them on our travels.'

'I could never get on with curries,' he said. 'We did try 'em, didn't we, Dais? Sir Hector's cook says they loves 'em up at The Grange. So we got her to give us some of their curry powder.'

Daisy nodded.

'The missus is a lovely cook, but I never quite liked the taste. I prefers my food plain and simple, like my women.' He laughed, but then looked worried. 'Don't tell Mrs Spratt I said that. She'd skin me.'

'Your secret is safe with me, Mr Spratt,' I said with a wink.

'You too, Dais,' he said, looking over at his daughter.

'Right you are, Dad. I won't tell our Ma you said she was simple and plain.'

Amid more teasing and laughter, I paid for the meat and bade my farewells.

After a few more calls I had everything we needed for our curry. As I came out of the greengrocer's I saw Lady Hardcastle on the far side of the green, on her way home from visiting Dr Fitzsimmons. I waved but she didn't see me so I trotted round the green to meet her.

'What ho, Flo,' she said when she finally noticed me hurrying towards her. 'All done?'

'As much as I could manage without seeming odd,' I said.

'You, dear? Odd? Never.'

'You're most kind, my lady. I wanted to keep it natural and casual, and not at all as though I were quizzing her.'

'Tell all, tiny servant. What did you learn?'

I recounted my conversation with Daisy as closely as I could.

'Birmingham is plenty to be getting on with,' she said when I had finished. 'I'd wager the spiritualist community is a small one, even in a city that large. She should be easy enough to track down now. Good work.'

'Thank you, my lady. And what did the doctor have to say?'

'The good doctor was a tad shaken up, I feel,' she said.

'Oh?' I said. 'How so?'

'He had never spoken to Madame Eugénie before and yet, he said, she knew his late wife's name. Even against all his better judgement he's convinced that he really has had a message from her from the Great Beyond.'

'He's convinced, then?'

'He very much is,' she said. 'I think it's comforted him. I expected a scientific man to be a bit more sceptical, but he was utterly convinced that he had been given a message from his late wife. He was rather euphoric about the whole thing. She died in childbirth, you know. Over thirty years ago. He said that not a day passes that he doesn't think of her and feel at least a twinge of guilt for having brought her death upon her.'

'Poor man,' I said. 'I've always liked Dr Fitzsimmons.'

'Indeed,' said Lady Hardcastle distractedly. 'But some good might come of it. It seems the poor dear has been racked with guilt of late because he's rather fallen for a widow from Woodworthy. He feels that to pursue the subject of marriage would be a betrayal of his late wife. Now that he's been given June's blessing to "be happy" he feels finally free to plight his troth. Or further his amorous advances, at least.'

'That's charming,' I said.

'Yes, I think it rather is,' she said.

'It's just . . .'

'What is it?' she said.

'Well, we shouldn't say anything to him. And I know that I've been trying to build a case in support of Madame Eugénie's gifts . . .'

'But?'

'But the business with the names is as old as the hills. She eventually gave him a message from "June" but she tried a handful of other names before he agreed on her name. I'm not sure how she might have seized upon the letter J, but that technique – trying guesses until you get a reaction – is tried and trusted.'

'Hmm,' she said thoughtfully. 'We'll keep that under our hats for now, I think.'

'Right you are, my lady. So what's next?' I said.

'Lunch, I think, don't you?'

'No, silly, I meant with our investigations. We've an alleged murderer in our midst. Possibly more than one if Caradine was poisoned as well.'

'So they say,' she said, still rather distracted. 'I wish that blessed telephone had been installed. I should rather like to speak to Inspector Sunderland. I'm sure he'd be able to find out all about Mr Snelson in a jiffy.'

'Perhaps we could telephone from the police station,' I said helpfully.

'I really rather think we should,' she said. 'The inspector is bound to have all the particulars. The police are good at that. They always take down a chap's particulars.'

'I say!' I said. 'How very forward of them.'

Constable Hancock was only too happy to allow Lady Hardcastle to telephone Inspector Sunderland at Bristol CID.

We were just about to leave when Sergeant Dobson emerged from the back room.

'Ah,' he said, 'Lady Hardcastle. We was just talking about you.'

'You were?' she said. 'Nothing slanderous, I hope.'

The older policeman laughed. 'Nothing like that, m'lady,' he said. 'We still got Lofty Trevellian in the cell. Had him here all week like. Can't see the magistrate till the middle of next week so we's holdin' him here. He was askin' about how he come to be locked up here in the first place. I told him about your discoveries, like.'

'Oh dear,' she said. 'Would it be terribly against protocol for me to speak to him?'

'I should think we could bend the rules for you, m'lady, even if 't were.'

He led us to the back of the cottage where the prisoner sat in the 'cell'. It was a bare room with a bed, a chair, a stout door and bars on the window, but it still resembled the back parlour of a cottage more than a gaol cell.

Trevellian was sitting forlornly on the edge of the bed as Lady Hardcastle and I entered. He made to stand up, but Lady Hardcastle waved him back down and sat in the chair. I stood in the corner of the room and the sergeant lurked in the doorway, listening intently.

'Good morning, Mr Trevellian,' she said. 'Are they treating you well?'

'Well enough,' he said, without resentment. 'I've been in worse cells.'

'The sergeant tells us you're a little baffled by your arrest.'

'Sommat to do with a pair of me old boots.'

'Old boots?' I said.

'Yes,' he said, lifting his legs to show off the handsome pair of work boots he was wearing. 'I ain't worn they old 'uns for months. I used to wear 'em to walk to trainin', save gettin' these new 'uns scuffed up on the path, like, but they disappeared one week and I ain't seen 'em since.'

'Disappeared?' said Lady Hardcastle.

'That's right,' he said. 'The lads used to take the mickey sommat rotten, said they was a disgrace, said they was going to chuck 'em. So one day when they wasn't there after trainin' I assumed they'd got rid of 'em and went home in me rugby boots. Truth is I didn't need 'em no more since I got the new ones, so I thought I'd just go along with the joke, like.'

The sergeant snorted disbelievingly from the doorway.

'It's the truth, Mr Dobson, I swears. I ain't seen they boots since February.'

'Hmm,' said Lady Hardcastle. 'Well this puts a whole new complexion on things. Wouldn't you agree, Armstrong?'

'Certainly, my lady,' I said.

'Don't worry, Mr Trevellian. We'll get to the bottom of this,' said Lady Hardcastle. With that, she rose and swept towards the door. The sergeant stepped aside and I followed her.

After locking the cell door, the sergeant and the constable joined us in the main office.

'Beggin' your pardon, m'lady,' said Dobson. 'But what's goin' on? We got this fella damn near red-handed. Red-booted, at least. Are you sayin' he didn't do it?'

'It just doesn't make any sense, Sergeant,' she said. 'As I was about to say when we found the boots in the first place: why would a man use his own old boots to commit a burglary and then hide them where he could be sure they'd eventually be found? What would he gain from it? Why not wear his ordinary boots? If he were using his old boots to throw us off the scent – "No, look here, my boots are oil-free" – why hide them? Why not take them home? No, I think there's more going on here. I think someone is trying to pull the wool over our eyes on this one.'

'You're sayin' someone else wore his boots?' said Sergeant Dobson. 'Someone's tryin' to make it look like Lofty pinched the trophies?'

'Or at least to make it less obvious who really did it,' she said.

'Well, 't wouldn't be the first time we've been led down a false trail,' he said, thoughtfully. 'But I can't just let him go.'

'No, I suppose not. But be kind to him. I really don't think he did it.'

'Right you are, m'lady,' he said. 'But please be quick. It'd be nice to get this one sorted before the Gloucester detectives change their minds and come sniffin' around. I don't like them, not one bit.'

'We shall move heaven and earth, my dear Sergeant,' she said.

11

We were settling down to elevenses in the morning room the next day, about to tuck in to freshly brewed coffee and some ever-so-slightly stale cake, when Edna bustled in.

'Beggin' your pardon, m'lady,' she said. 'I thought you was elsewhere. I was just comin' in to do me dustin'.'

'Don't worry, Edna. We'll be done soon. Is all well with you?'

'Quite well, thank you, m'lady,' she said. She was hovering at the door.

'Is there something the matter?' asked Lady Hardcastle.

'Just a bit of news, m'lady,' said Edna.

'Ooh, excellent,' said Lady Hardcastle. 'I do love news.'

'It's the pub, m'lady. I was walking past there this mornin' on my way here. Old Joe was out in his yard, like, sortin' his barrels or some such. And I says, "Mornin', Joe." We've known Joe since we was kids, me and our Dan. I reckon he was old even then. So he says, "Mornin', Edna." I always thank the Lord I a'n't got no S's in me name – he's a lovely bloke but he don't half spray when he talks. I keeps tellin' him to get some false teeth but he don't listen.'

'He wouldn't be Joe with a head full of Hampsteads,' I said.

She looked at me blankly.

'Hampstead Heath,' I said. 'Teeth.'

'If you says so, m'dear,' she said. 'Anyway, I asks him how he is and he says, "Not so bad, my lover, but come in and see what I've got to put up with lately." So he takes me in the public bar and there's something scrawled on the blackboard.'

'Aha, yes, we saw that the other day,' said Lady Hardcastle.

'No, m'lady. He said as how you'd seen one similar, but he said this un's new. He asked me to tell you about it, like.'

'What did it say?' I asked.

'It was all shaky like, but it said "Nelson – murderer". And it was signed. I couldn't make it out but Joe reckons it says "Mummy Bear".'

'Well, well, well,' said Lady Hardcastle. 'Mummy Bear is getting quite insistent. Did he see or hear anything in the night?'

'He didn't say so, m'lady,' said Edna. 'But he asked if you wouldn't mind popping round and taking a look. If it's not too much trouble, like. He's all of a pother.'

'Of course we shall. You didn't have any plans, Flo?'

'Nothing that can't wait, my lady,' I said.

'I think we should drop in on the sergeant, too. I'd like him to contact Inspector Sunderland again. I know I spoke to him about the Caradine case the other day but someone needs to start knocking heads together down at the police surgeon's office.'

'We can take some cakes,' I suggested. 'We need to get rid of them somehow. Do please take cake with you when you go home today, Edna. As much as you can carry.'

The pub was open. There was no one in the saloon save Joe, but we could hear voices in the public bar.

'Mornin', m'lady, Miss Armstrong,' said Joe from behind the bar.

'I hear you've had a spot more bother, Joe,' said Lady Hardcastle amiably.

174

'I shan't lie to you, m'lady,' he said, 'it's fair shook me up, it has. I told that Daisy there'd be trouble if she started meddlin' with t'other side. And now look.'

We looked. I could see no real evidence of any supernatural activity, but then again it was almost lunchtime and Joe would certainly have cleared up by now.

'May we see the message?' I said, gesturing in the direction of the skittle alley.

'Course you may, m'dear,' he said. 'I left it there so's you could take a look.'

We went through to the other bar, where a couple of young farmhands were sitting at a table in the corner, tucking into great slabs of bread and cheese as they discussed one of the local girls in the most indelicate terms. They stopped mid-sentence when they noticed us. Grinning at each other, they sipped their ciders.

Dick Ackley and Noah Lock were sitting together at another table.

'Good morning, gentlemen,' said Lady Hardcastle.

'Good morning to you, Lady Hardcastle,' said Lock, standing.

'I trust we find you both well,' she said. 'Is Mr Tribley not with you? I thought you all came in here together. Isn't that right, Armstrong?'

I nodded.

'No, m'lady,' said Ackley. 'He usually comes over after the mornin's work, but he's busy this mornin'. Sommat to do with gettin' a ring from a jewellers in Chipping.'

'For his lady love?' she asked.

'Actually, that's what we were just wondering,' said Lock. 'It seems the logical conclusion, but I've never seen him so much as talk to a lady, much less be smitten enough to be proposing.'

I coughed to express my impatience with this distraction from Joe's urgent blackboard-related business.

'You'll have to excuse us, gentlemen,' said Lady Hardcastle. 'Duty calls.'

We crossed to the skittle alley. There on the blackboard, in the same untidy hand, was the message that Edna had described.

'Whoever or whatever it is is quite determined to get this message across, aren't they?' said Lady Hardcastle as we examined the scoreboard more closely. 'I just wish we knew who this Mummy Bear was. A Sioux spirit guide, perhaps?'

I frowned thoughtfully. 'Perhaps,' I said at length. 'Would you mind awfully distracting Joe somehow, my lady? I'd like to have a poke around and it would be most helpful to have him out of the way.'

'Of course, dear,' she said. 'You're on to something, do you think?'

'Perhaps,' I said.

'Excellent. I'll go and have a little chat.' She went back to the other bar.

I could still see them as I began my examination of the bar.

''T'i'n't much different to t'other one, is it?' said Joe as Lady Hardcastle joined him for a chat.

I was looking for signs of fakery. There are many, many ways to produce the effects of spirit world activity so I wasn't looking for anything specific. I just knew I'd know when I found something.

'Very similar,' said Lady Hardcastle. 'What about the activities in the night? Did you hear or see anything this time?'

'No, nothin', m'lady. I got up this mornin' same as usual and come down here to get ready for openin' up. There was a couple of chairs knocked about but nothing broken. I hadn't heard a thing in the night.'

'How did you know the chairs had been moved?'

'They was on their sides in the middle of the floor,' he said. 'I always stacks everything up neat before I goes up to bed. Makes it easier to sweep up in the morning, see.'

'Ah, yes, of course. But nothing broken this time.'

'No, m'lady, not this time. But what do you reckon it could be?'

'We're keeping an open mind, Joe. It seems unscientific at this point to rule out the possibility of it being an unquiet spirit come to settle some unfinished business with Mr Snelson. By the same token, it would also be negligent to dismiss the idea that mortal hands are responsible.'

'Ar, righto,' he said disappointedly. He had clearly been hoping for something a little less equivocal. My fussing about beneath the window caught his eye. 'Are you all right there, miss?' he said when he realized it was me.

I was on my knees, examining the chair legs. 'Fine, thank you, Joe,' I said. 'Don't mind me.'

'Floor's been swept, miss, but you'll get yourself filthy down there even so. Is there anything I can do?'

'No, no, I'm fine,' I said, standing up. 'All done now. And look, it brushes off.'

I patted at the knees of my now dusty black dress, making no difference to its cleanliness whatsoever. 'Well, it will, at any rate,' I said. 'I'll work some of my mysterious magic on it later.'

'Find anything, miss?' he asked.

'I've an idea or two bubbling away,' I said.

'Anything you can share?' asked Lady Hardcastle.

'Not at the moment, my lady, no. I think it's my turn to be enigmatic.'

'Right you are, dear,' she said. 'We're working on it, Joe.'

'We are indeed,' I said.

'Shall we pop along to the police station and see what the fine gentlemen of the Gloucester Constabulary have got to say for themselves?' she said. 'They must have replied to Constable Hancock by now.'

'I appreciates all your help, m'lady, Miss Armstrong,' said Joe.

'It's entirely our pleasure,' she said. 'Oh, one more thing before we go: have you seen anything of your guest lately?'

'Madame Eugénie?'

'The same.'

'No, m'lady. Same as I told Wally – she stays locked in her room and only opens the door to take in her meals and pass out the dirty plates. She's paid till the end of the week, mind, so if it weren't for all these goings-on I'd be happy enough to leave her be.'

'But you'd rather she came out to help?' I said.

'Well, seems a shame to have an expert on the occult livin' under your roof while there's mysterious goings on afoot and then have her stay in her room all the time. She don't even talk to no one.'

'At least she's a quiet guest, though, eh?' said Lady Hardcastle. 'No trouble.'

'No, m'lady, she i'n't no trouble. I hears her mutterin' to herself sometimes when I goes past the door, but she don't cause no trouble. Somethin' to be grateful for, I s'pose.'

'That's the spirit,' said Lady Hardcastle bracingly. 'We'll be on our way, but we'll keep working on your little puzzle and we'll tell you the instant we know anything. Toodle-pip.'

'Cheerio, m'lady, Miss Armstrong,' he said, and we stepped out into the daylight.

'Did you find what you were looking for?' asked Lady Hardcastle as we strolled along the street to the police station.

'I think I did, yes,' I said.

'And . . . ?' she said, slightly frustrated by my uncharacteristic reticence.

'All in good time, my lady. All in good time.'

She harrumphed.

'You can huff and puff all you like, my lady. I'll tell all when I'm good and ready.'

She harrumphed again, but we'd reached the police station so her continued disgruntlement went unanswered. We were saved from further conflict when we were hallooed by Lady Farley-Stroud from across the green.

'You don't really need me to come in, do you? I don't expect Gertie wants anything more than a chat, but it seems rude to ignore her.'

'Not at all, my lady. You pop off and do whatever it is you nobs do when the serfs aren't around. I'll see you at home.'

'Splendid,' she said, and we parted.

The police station was housed in one of a pair of cottages facing the village green. Sergeant Dobson lived above the station office while Constable Hancock lived in the much smaller cottage next door. We teased them about their extensive accommodation, but they paid no heed. They were doing an important job, they said, policing villages and hamlets for miles around. They needed their police station and their convenient quarters.

There was no one in the small front office so I picked up the little bell from the counter and tinkled it in what I hoped was a polite way.

Sergeant Dobson emerged from a back room bearing a fat manila folder.

'Ah, there you are, miss. I was just about to come over the pub looking for you. Is Lady Hardcastle not with you?'

'She sends her apologies, Sergeant, but she has urgent business elsewhere.'

'Not to worry, miss, I'm sure you'll be more than able to convey the news to her.'

'What news?' I said.

'Look what the Gloucester boys sent down by one o' they motorcycle messengers this morning.' He brandished the file.

'Crikey,' I said. 'They must think it important if they've gone to that much trouble.'

'Unsolved case,' said the sergeant, importantly. 'Would you like to come through to the back? There's more room at the kitchen table and I've just put the kettle on for a nice cup of tea.'

'That sounds splendid, Sergeant,' I said. 'Lead on.'

I returned home to find that Lady Hardcastle had retired to her study to make some notes, so I prepared an early dinner and we then sat together in the dining room, eating fried Dover sole.

'What did the good sergeant have to say for himself, then?' she said once we were settled and the wine had been poured.

'He was rather excited,' I said. 'A file had been sent by messenger from Gloucester and we spent a while going through it together.'

'Gracious,' she said. 'What was in this file? Treasures?'

'Of a sort, my lady. It was an account of the investigation of a fire. It seems that our Mr Snelson was in business with one Emmanuel Bean—'

'Oh,' interrupted Lady Hardcastle.

'"Oh", my lady?'

'Yes, oh. We've been so silly,' she said.

'Silly?'

'Yes, Emmanuel Bean. Manny Bean. It wasn't Mummy Bear at all. I was so very much hoping that Goldilocks would become involved at some point, but it was just poor handwriting and wishful thinking.'

'Quite so, my lady,' I said. 'Snelson and Bean owned a timber business in Hardwicke, just along the canal from Gloucester, which they called – disappointingly unimaginatively, I feel – Hardwicke Timber Limited.'

'That will be the photograph we saw in his drawing room. Do you remember?'

'I do, my lady. They looked every inch the successful business-men, didn't they?'

'Quite the entrepreneurs,' she said. 'Builders of a wooden empire.'

'It wasn't all beer and skittles, though. A year ago, almost to the day, there was a fire at the yard. It completely destroyed the office, the stores and all the stock. When they were finally able to search through the devastation, they found a body. It was badly burnt, but they identified it as belonging to Emmanuel Bean by the distinctive signet ring he wore.'

'And they suspected arson?' she said.

'They most certainly did. There was a surprisingly thorough investigation, but they could prove nothing. The insurers were reluctant to pay at first, but there wasn't enough evidence to prevent them. There were stories that the company was in financial difficulties, but the accounts were destroyed so no one could say for sure.'

'And poor old Bean was killed in the fire as well,' she said.

'Indeed he was. Obviously there was some speculation that he'd set the fire himself and had been trapped, but it was little more than speculation. They investigated Snelson but they couldn't pin anything on him, either. Not for certain. He had apparently been in Birmingham on business – they found witnesses to corroborate. But there were gaps in the story and it might have been possible for him to get back to Gloucester and do the deed without anyone being any the wiser.'

'Snelson certainly seems a steely sort,' she said. 'I wonder if he's quite ruthless enough to kill his best friend for an insurance settlement, though.'

'It would take more than a little steel,' I said. 'But one never knows.'

'One never does. And now,' she said dramatically, 'the ghost of Mummy Bear has come back to seek earthly redress for his untimely demise.'

'That's one interpretation, my lady,' I said.

'The other, of course, is that it might be someone who wants to tell us something about the case.'

'What else should we try? We could go up to Gloucester now we have the motor car. They're bound to have back issues of the local newspaper in the library.'

'If we can find the library,' she said. 'I know where the Bristol library is. But it's an excellent notion. Newspaper reports so often flesh out the more lurid aspects of the story that a dry old police report tends to leave out.'

'Perhaps we could go to Bristol first. It's six of one and half a dozen of the other, really, now that you have the infernal machine.'

'A trip for tomorrow, then, if the weather holds,' she said.

'Very well, my lady,' I said.

'And while we're at it, we might be able to find out once and for all if Madame Eugénie is the genuine article or an absolute old fraud.'

'Which would be good,' I said.

'You're less convinced than you were?'

'A little bit,' I said.

'How's that?' she asked.

'I have one or two, shall we say, suspicions about her methods. I'll need to speak to a couple of people before I can fully make up my mind, but I'm afraid the evidence is stacking up against her. I think our Madame Eugénie is just another charlatan.'

'If anyone could spot it, dear,' she said, 'it would be you.'

'That's not to say that I'm prepared to declare that everyone who claims to have the sight is a fake, mind you. Mamgu was the real thing, for one. She genuinely had a gift. And so did her mother. And her mother. Back for generations. It's a Celtic thing. But I'm almost sure that Eugénie isn't quite all she would have us believe.'

'All the more reason to pop down to the city tomorrow and try to track down an explanation,' she said.

'Can we drop in at the Dog and Duck on our way? I'd like to ask Joe Arnold if I can stay the night.'

'On your own?'

'Yes, please. I'd like to be there in case the ghost comes back again.'

'Not afraid, then?' she said with a grin. 'I know that only cows have the power to frighten my Florence.'

'I'm wary of cattle, my lady. Respectfully wary.'

'Ah, yes,' she said. 'What about a cow ghost, though?'

'A bovine *bodach*, my lady?'

'A *bodach*, by George. No wonder you're such a whizz at crosswords.'

'It's a Scottish ghost, my lady,' I said.

'I surmised as much,' she said. 'But fear not, dear heart. We are attempting to pin down a human spirit. Even if it's real, your night shall be entirely cattle free.'

'That's what I'm counting on.'

'And my evening appears to be entirely sweet-free. What's for pudding, chef?'

'Cake,' I said sadly.

'Ah,' she said. 'In that case, might I respectfully suggest that we skip pudding and move straight to brandy and the piano? Is there cheese?'

'There's cheese, my lady, and some cream crackers. I might be able to rootle out some chutney. I think Miss Jones was making some the other day.'

'Cheese and biscuits it is, then,' she said. She wiped her mouth with her napkin and stood. 'I shall go and find something fun to play, and you bring the coagulated curds. Any requests?'

'Something fun, I think,' I said. 'A little more ragtime? I could fetch my banjo.'

'That's settled then. I shall see you presently.'

Getting ready for the drive into Bristol had been something of a palaver. Unlike the motor cars we had been used to recently, Lady Hardcastle's new transport was a tad . . . open. To be sure, it had a hinged folding 'roof', such as one might find on a perambulator, and a substantial windscreen. But there was not much by way of what one might call 'doors'. There were half-doors (presumably to conceal our sinful ankles) but precious little protection from the elements as the wind whipped through from the sides.

'We're going to have to get some proper driving togs, Flo,' said Lady Hardcastle as I did my best to secure her hat with a broad ribbon. 'And some gauntlets.'

'Gauntlets, my lady?' I said. 'In case we need to challenge someone to a duel?'

'Goggles for warmer days, too.'

I was beginning to wonder if the new motor car might be more trouble than it was worth.

As the younger, stronger member of the team, I had been charged with the task of turning the starting handle. After only three goes, we were on our way into the village.

The car itself drew a small amount of attention. A bright scarlet motor car always does. What really caught people's eye, though, was the sight of Lady Hardcastle at the wheel. This sort of scrutiny was nothing new. I'd been working for her for almost fifteen years and I had grown accustomed to the censorious stares and mutters of those people (mostly men, it must be said) who thought that a woman just shouldn't be doing that (where 'that' was pretty much whatever Lady Hardcastle happened to be doing at the time). But a motoring lady was a new source of disapproval and I felt a childlike glee in their collective dismay.

We pulled up outside the Dog and Duck. I hopped out while Lady Hardcastle stayed at the wheel with the engine running and the handbrake yanked firmly on. The pub door was still locked so I rapped loudly on it with my gloved fist. Joe eventually opened it.

'Oh, mornin', m'dear,' he said when he saw who I was. 'What can I be doin' for you?'

'Good morning, Joe,' I said. 'Might I come in for a moment? I have a favour to ask.'

He stood aside. 'Certainly, miss. In you come. 'Scuse the mess, I'm just moppin' the floor.'

I stepped inside and he shut and bolted the door behind me.

'Just in case anyone thinks we's open,' he said. 'Leave the door open and they'll all be in here demanding morning refreshment.'

'We did say that morning tea would be a big seller,' I said.

'Oh, I'm sure it will once we gets started on it, miss,' he said. 'Soon as we gots our new china, I'll be startin' that. I already got old Sep Holman ready to make us rolls and pastries. But no, 's not that, it's they farmers – they sees a pub door open and they'll be in and suppin' cider 'fore you can say, "Sorry, gents, we're closed." I'd never get any cleaning done.'

I laughed. 'Well, I shan't hold you up,' I said. 'I just wanted to ask a favour.'

'Anything for you, miss, you knows that. Just name it.'

'I wonder if I might have a room for tonight.'

He looked concerned. 'A room, miss? Here?'

'Yes, please,' I said. 'I'll pay the full rate, of course.'

'There'll be no need for that, miss, not for you. But what's wrong? Has Lady Hardcastle kicked you out?'

I laughed again. 'Oh, I see what you mean. No, nothing like that,' I said. 'Although, in a way, perhaps she has. She wants me to spend the night in the pub to get a first-hand view of your haunting.'

Realization dawned. 'Ohhhhh,' he said. 'Well, to be honest, m'dear, I'd quite like a witness to it meself. It were quiet last night, but I'd like to get another opinion on it all 'fore Madame Eugénie leaves at the weekend.'

'She's still here, then?' I said.

'Ar,' he said with a nod. 'She been doin' readin's and private consultations these past two days. Up in 'er room. All sorts of folk come in, people you'd-a never thought. They comes in, and I sends 'em up. Then they comes down again a little while later. I don't know what they does.'

'Do they seem pleased?'

'Ar,' he said. 'They all says they's pleased they went, but they none of 'em looks like it was a calmin' experience.'

'I promised Lady Hardcastle I'd arrange a reading for her,' I said. 'But I'm not so sure it would be a good idea if that's the effect it has on people. She's had a difficult time of it these past few months, I shouldn't want to expose her to more unpleasantness.'

'If you asks me, I'd say you was absolutely right. She's best off out of it.'

'I agree, Mr Arnold, I agree. And so I shall be her eyes and ears here tonight, if that's agreeable.'

'It will be a delight to have you here, miss,' he said. 'You can have our second-best room and I'll make you a nice big breakfast an' all.'

'How wonderfully generous of you, thank you.'

'It'll be like a little holiday for you.'

'With added ghosts,' I said.

'Don't remind me,' he said.

We said our goodbyes and I left him to his mopping.

Back outside, I hopped back into the motor car and we sped off towards the Gloucester Road. Well, I say 'sped' but it was more of a sedate potter, if I'm honest. Still, it was quicker than walking.

We clattered our way into the city and parked the car near the city library. The architects had done a fine job of making the new library fit into its surroundings. It looked almost as though it were part of the cathedral, but still it was the cathedral itself that caught my eye.

'That's a magnificent old building, isn't it, my lady?' I said as we passed the front of the cathedral.

'The towers aren't terribly old, actually,' she said. 'Built in the 1880s, I think.'

'That's a magnificent new building, isn't it?' I said. We carried on to the library.

We went inside and after a brief, hushed conversation with the librarian at the front desk, weaved our way past shelves and shelves of books to the periodicals section. We found the Gloucester newspapers for early 1908 and began our research.

By lunchtime, I was bored almost beyond endurance. I love to read, and am ordinarily fascinated by the lives of others, but provincial newspapers have a peculiar knack of turning even the most interesting story into something turgid and dull. I was glad when Lady Hardcastle finally passed me a note that read, 'Shhhhh. I've had quite enough of this. Lunch?'

I nodded my hearty agreement and we put away our newspapers and returned to the world of chatter and noise.

'Did you find anything?' she asked as we walked back to the motor car.

'Nothing to contradict anything in the police report,' I said. 'How about you?'

'No, not really. There was some speculation about financial difficulties at the company and a concerted attempt at discrediting Snelson and painting him as the villain of the piece. It stopped short of libellous accusation but it was obvious what the journalist thought.'

'I did find one account which mentioned what good friends the two owners were. Inseparable, apparently. It makes the claims of murder seem all the more unlikely.'

'Quite so,' she said. 'Although it's odd that he made no mention of it when he spoke to us. He was very keen that we might help him stamp out any slanderous rumours, but he didn't speak of his partner's death at all. Quite an oversight, wouldn't you say? One might have thought he'd mention that his best friend had actually died in a terrible fire.'

'Unless he thought that mentioning the fire would just be providing the gossips with more ammunition,' I suggested.

'No point in stoking the fire,' she said.

'Must you, my lady? Of course . . .'

'Of course what, dear?'

'It might be that he's not actually dead.'

She stopped in her tracks. 'What?' she said.

'Well, he'd not be upset at all if his friend wasn't dead. Just a thought.'

'What a splendid thought. I say, I've an idea. I think we should leave the motor here, and take a stroll to that hotel that Gertie loves. My solicitors' office is on the way. I'll get them to do some digging for me.'

'Then home for tea?' I said.

'Then home for tea and to prepare you for a night in the haunted pub.'

'Right you are, then, my lady, let's go. You do remember where the hotel is, I take it.'

'Of course I do,' she said, entirely unconvincingly. 'It's . . . this way.'

12

There were a few chores to take care of at home while Lady Hardcastle retired to her study. We ate a light supper at around eight o'clock and then I packed some overnight essentials into my trusty Gladstone bag. I slipped out into the chilly spring night to walk to the pub.

After a couple of days of calm, the weather was becoming boisterous again, and there were a few spots of rain in the strengthening wind as I skirted the green. The pub was full and there was a lively sing-song in progress around the battered, poorly tuned piano in the corner. I could hear the clonk and rattle of the wooden ball in the skittle alley in the other bar, and the roars and raucous laughter of the players.

The air was thick with tobacco smoke; its aroma mixed with the beer and cider to produce a smell that instantly took me back to dodgy back-street pubs in the East End of London. It wasn't so long ago that Lady Hardcastle and I, dressed down for the occasion, had been to places like that to meet weasel-willed informants, flat-nosed thugs, cocksure villains and assorted other ne'er-do-wells for the good of King and country.

As I looked around for Joe, I caught sight of Lock and Tribley leaning against the bar. I considered hailing them but they appeared deep in conversation.

'. . . but she's sweet on Lofty Trevellian,' said Lock.

'Not for long,' said Tribley. 'That lanky troublemaker will be behind bars soon.'

'For the theft from the clubhouse? It hardly seems to warrant a lengthy sentence.'

'Ah, but he has form. He came up here from Cornwall to avoid a gaol sentence. To think I gave that bounder a chance. I knew he was a wrong un, but I let him join the club anyway. Second chances and all that. And look how he repays us. You mark my words, she'll be free of him soon enough, and then our way will be clear. And once the farm is sold, we can get away from this blessed place together.'

So Winnie Marsh was the mystery woman, I thought. How odd. She was a bright girl, perhaps a little too bright for Lofty, but she didn't seem like the sort to give Tribley the time of day. Much less run off with him.

Joe broke into my reverie. 'Evenin', miss. Can I get you a drink 'fore you goes up?'

'Oh, good evening, Joe. I'm sorry, I was miles away. A brandy would be most welcome, please. May I take it up to my room?'

'Course you may, m'dear. I'll just show you where 'tis and I'll bring it up to you. On the house, of course.'

'You're most kind, Joe, thank you.'

'Come with me,' he said. 'Let's get you out of this madhouse.'

He led me through the bar to the door at the back and then up the stairs to the first floor. There were four doors off the landing.

'Here you goes, m'dear,' said Joe, indicating the door to our right. 'This un's yours. Bathroom is there at the end, and Madame Eugénie is in the room opposite.'

'Thank you, Joe. And the door next to hers?'

'That's the stairs up to mine and our Ma's rooms up in the attic. We keeps it closed, give ourselves a bit of privacy like.'

'Lovely, thank you,' I said with a smile. 'Just getting the lie of the land, you know how it is.'

'Oh, ah, miss, yes. They say you done a fair bit of the old cloak-and-dagger stuff in your time.'

'People say a lot of things, Mr Arnold,' I said, still smiling. 'I should take no notice.'

He looked at me shrewdly. 'Right you are, miss. Mum's the word.' He winked and then opened the door to my room and gestured me inside.

The room was slightly larger than I was expecting, with a comfortable-looking bed, a nightstand with a drawer, a wash-stand with jug and basin, a chair, and a small wardrobe. It was plainly decorated, but clean, and the bedlinen looked crisp and fresh. The lamp was already lit and there was a candlestick beside the bed.

'I hope it's all right for you,' he said tentatively. 'There's more candles in the nightstand if you needs 'em.'

'Oh, Joe, it's marvellous,' I said.

He beamed. 'Not quite what you're used to, I don't s'pose, but I'm glad you likes it.'

'It will do splendidly,' I said. I looked back at the door. 'Is there a key?'

'On the nightstand, m'dear.'

'Ah, yes, so it is. Well, I'm sure I'll be very comfortable. Let's just hope our ghost puts in an appearance.'

'Yes,' said Joe doubtfully. 'Let's just hope.' He turned to go. 'I'll leave you to get settled, then, m'dear, but I'll be back in two shakes with that brandy.'

He left, shutting the door behind him.

I sat on the bed and pondered my plan. Or, rather, pondered the sudden realization that I had no plan whatsoever. Why was I spending the night 'away from home', less than a mile from home? What was I intending to do? Should I try to stay awake all night, listening for ghosts? What was I going to do if I heard one? Was I there to observe? Or to attempt to deal with the situation? How does one 'deal with' a ghost anyway?

I was still sitting there in bewildered contemplation when there was a knock at the door.

'Yes?' I said loudly.

'It's me, miss,' said Joe.

'Come on in, Joe,' I said.

The door opened and in came Joe with a tray bearing a large glass of brandy and one of his celebrated doorstop sandwiches.

'Thought you might like a little somethin' to eat, miss,' he said, setting the tray down on the nightstand.

'You're very kind, Joe. Thank you.'

'My pleasure, miss,' he said. 'I'll leave you to it now, then. You just come up and get me if you needs anything.'

'Thank you, I shall.'

He left again. After a few moments' more thought, I made up my mind what to do. There was no point in exhausting myself in an attempt to remain awake for a ghost that might never come, so the best course was surely to get ready for bed, settle down with a book, nod off to sleep when I needed to, and then to 'deal with' whatever situation might arise if it happened to awaken me. Even if it didn't wake me, at least I'd be one of the first on the spot in the morning to see the results first hand.

So I did just that. With the door locked and the key returned to the nightstand, the lamp extinguished and a candle lit in its stead, I changed into my nightgown and crept under the covers with *The Man Who Was Thursday*. I munched a little of the surprisingly pleasant cheese sandwich and sipped at the indifferent but no less welcome brandy as I read. It wasn't long before the words began to swim on the page and I found myself reading things that Chesterton had never written. I snuffed out the candle and settled down to sleep.

I didn't own a watch and there was no clock in the room, so I had no idea what time I was awoken by a metallic click and the creak of a floorboard. Whatever the hour, I was awake at once. I wrapped a shawl around me and picked up the key from the nightstand. As silently as I could manage, I made my way towards the door. I pushed the key into the lock. Or I tried, at least – something was blocking the keyhole. I got to my knees and tried to look through it, but I could see nothing in the gloom. I was shut in.

Closing my eyes and concentrating hard, I could hear sounds of movement downstairs in the bar. I heard chairs fall and the scrape of table legs on the flagstone floor. There was a crash as a bottle or jug broke, and then silence.

I moved back towards the bed and hunted around in the darkness for the matches so that I could light the candle. With it finally lit, I examined the keyhole once more and thought I could see something glint within it. It appeared that someone had put a key in the lock from the other side. I briefly considered hammering on the door and calling for help, but I couldn't see that that would accomplish very much. Any miscreant – spectral or human – would hear the commotion and flee. They'd either go back to the other realm or out into the night, never to be seen again.

Instead, I found my brooch and its concealed picklocks. I worked at the key for a few minutes but it was stuck fast.

Giving up, I dressed as quickly and quietly as I could, concentrating all the while for sounds from below. I thought I could hear movement, but the Dog and Duck was a substantial old building with thick walls and heavy oaken floors, and I couldn't be sure. What sounds I could hear were soon entirely masked by the clomping of boots on stairs as Joe came down from his attic rooms. The sound seemed to have woken Madame Eugénie, too, and I heard her door open just as Joe clumped through the door to the stairs and onto the landing.

'Are you all right, ma'am?' he said blearily.

'Quite all right, Mr Arnold, thank you,' said Madame Eugénie in her dreamy, breathy voice. 'I became aware of a strong spiritual presence in this place. I wondered if I might be able to help in some way.'

'P'raps you might, ma'am,' said Joe. 'I'd quite like Miss Armstrong to come with us, too, if you don't mind. I'd like her opinion of things.'

There was a pause. 'If you think that's wise,' she said dubiously.

'Ar,' he said. There was a knock on my door. 'Miss Armstrong?' he said in a louder voice. 'Miss Armstrong? Are you awake?'

'Awake and dressed, Joe,' I said. 'But I can't get out. There's something in the lock.'

I heard the sound of a key being rattled in the lock. 'So there is, miss,' he said. 'Looks like . . . looks like the key from the bathroom door. Can you unlock yourself now?'

I tried my key in the lock, which opened at once. I lifted the latch and opened the door to find Joe and Madame Eugénie on the landing, each in their night attire and holding a candle. Joe's long nightshirt was set off most entertainingly by a pair of large, unlaced boots.

I nodded a greeting to Madame Eugénie. 'Good morning,' I said. 'Shall we go down?'

'I shall lead the way,' she said. 'I know how to deal with unquiet spirits.'

'As you wish,' I said. 'Joe, was anyone else up here after I retired?'

We made our way down the stairs.

'Not so far as I knows, miss,' he said.

'Hmmm,' I said as Madame Eugénie opened the door into the snug. 'Then I wonder how that key came to be placed in my door.'

Madame Eugénie stopped and turned, her face illuminated by her candle. 'I'm certain it was the ghost, my dear,' she said. 'They can be quite ingenious.'

'Can they, indeed?' I said. To be truthful, for all my belief in the mysteries of the supernatural, jamming a key into a lock and turning it so that it couldn't easily be pushed out from the other side seemed altogether too human an action for blame to fall upon the ghost of Emmanuel Bean. I held my peace for the moment, though.

'This way,' said Madame Eugénie, leading us through the snug, past the obvious signs of disruption and into the public bar. She went straight to the skittle alley and held her candle up to the score board. There was a new message.

'Strongbox. Old Barn. Long Lane Farm. I will be avenged. Manny Bean.'

'Another message,' said Madame Eugénie.

'So it would appear,' I said. 'Do you know Long Lane Farm, Joe?'

'Not round here, m'dear. Could be up Gloucester way, maybe?'

'Could be. Does it mean anything to you, Madame Eugénie?'

'No, nothing,' she said. 'But it was obviously most important to the spirit for him to have gone to this much trouble.'

'Joe, light the lamps, please,' I said. 'Let's have a good look round.'

He did as I asked and we quickly searched both bars, revealing nothing of any interest. The chairs and tables I had heard moving and falling were quickly righted, and the remains of the shattered water jug were swept up, but we could see nothing else to indicate what the cause might have been.

The clock behind the bar said it was already a quarter past five so I made my excuses and returned to my room to collect my bag. Madame Eugénie's door was still open and I took the opportunity to have a quick look inside. The room was very similar to the one I had slept in, with the same assortment of mismatched furniture. I was about to step in and take a look in the wardrobe when I heard footsteps on the stairs. Trying to appear as nonchalant as possible, I turned away from the door and towards the top of the stairs as though I had just stepped out of my own room. It was Joe.

'Just checkin' you's all right, m'dear,' he said. 'Not too shook up?'

'I'm fine, Joe, thank you. It's just that it'll be dawn soon and I want to report back to Lady Hardcastle as soon as I can. Are you all right?'

'Right as rain, miss,' he said with a toothless grin. 'I's just glad someone else was here to see it all. Thought I was going mad for a while.'

'No, Joe, not mad at all. There's something going on here, that's for certain. I just wish I knew what.'

'What we goin' to do about the new message?' he asked.

'I think we should let Sergeant Dobson know. He should be able to get in touch with the Gloucester police and see if they know anything about Long Lane Farm. In the meantime, I think Lady Hardcastle has a few things she wants to look into, so between us we should get to the bottom of all this very soon.'

'Right you are, miss,' he said, standing aside so I could get down the stairs.

The morning air was crisp and chill, but the skies were clear and I sensed a beautiful spring day in the offing.

Lady Hardcastle was still fast asleep when I let myself in. Edna and Miss Jones had only just arrived, so I pitched in with the preparations for breakfast. Although they tried to pretend otherwise, they were more than a little interested in what had happened at the haunted pub. I told the tale, hamming up the more exciting moments.

'Well I never,' said Miss Jones. 'We never has no excitement like that. Daisy'll want to hear about that. We needs to get together again. Seems we never manages to see each other all at the same time these days. It's either you and her or me and her. We needs a night out and a good gossip.'

'We do, Blodwen, we do,' I said.

''Course, Morris'll be ticked off,' said Edna.

'Morris Caradine?' I said. 'Ticked off about me and the girls having a cider or two?'

'No,' she said with a laugh. 'About Mr Snelson bein' a murderer. If he's banged up waiting to be hanged, he's not going to be able to buy Top Farm, is he?'

'He's buying Top Farm?' I said.

'Wants to stay in the area, he says. Made Morris an offer. He won't be able to make good on it if he's in gaol.'

'But I thought Morris had another offer,' I said.

'So he did, my love, so he did. But then Snelson came along and topped it. Be foolish not to take the better offer, wouldn't it?'

'I suppose it would, yes. Still, a sale's a sale at the end of the day. He'll get to art school.'

As we busied ourselves in the kitchen I was struck with the sudden realization that I had been most foolish in my haste to get home: Joe had promised me a nice big country breakfast. Heigh ho, it couldn't be helped. He got his bacon, eggs, bread, tomatoes and mushrooms from the same places we did, after all, so it's not as though he was going to be giving me any local delicacies that I wouldn't have at home. And he wasn't the world's most gifted chef, either, so it was unlikely to be a great luxury. Except, of course, that the real luxury would be someone else doing all the work, no matter how inexpertly, and serving it to me on a huge platter while I sat at a table in the snug and sipped strongly brewed tea from a great big mug. Harrumph.

With a cup of tea and a round of buttered toast on the tray I went upstairs and knocked on the bedroom door. There was no answer, so I opened it and went in. She stirred a little at the sound of the teacup rattling in its saucer as I negotiated the pile of discarded clothes on the floor.

'Is that you, Flo?' she said blearily.

'Let's hope so, eh?' I said. 'Although a burglar who made you tea and toast wouldn't be entirely unwelcome.'

'Not entirely, no. What are you doing here? I thought you'd still be at the pub, living it up on bacon and eggs and grilled mushrooms.'

'That was the plan, my lady,' I said. 'But we were awakened early and by the time all was done, I thought I may as well come home. Good thing I did, by the look of it – you seem to have had some poltergeist activity of your own while I was away.'

'What do you mean?' she said, sitting up.

'There are clothes everywhere,' I said.

'Oh pish and fiddlesticks. Not everywhere. Just in that pile there. I didn't think I should pick them up. I've been poorly. I have to take it easy.'

'Take it easy, my lady? If you took it any easier you'd be back in your coma.'

'Oh, let's not make a fuss about a few clothes on the floor. What got you up in the middle of the night? Ghoulies and ghosties and long-leggedy beasties?'

'And things that smash jugs in the night, yes.'

'Tell all,' she said.

I sat on the bed and gave her a brief outline of the morning's events. She listened attentively while she munched on the toast and when I was done, she sat in quiet contemplation for a few moments.

'Was Joe going to tell Sergeant Dobson about the new message?' she said at length.

'I didn't ask him to specifically,' I said. 'But you know what those two are like. We can pop up to the police station later, but I'd lay five bob the sergeant already knows by the time we get there.'

'A safe bet, I'd say. But I'd still like to trot up there after lunch just to make certain.'

'Of course, my lady,' I said. I stood and picked up the tray from her lap. 'If you can find your way out of the room through the trail of devastation you've left behind, breakfast proper will be in about fifteen minutes.'

'Thank you, dear,' she said. 'Of course you could always pick it all up for me.'

'And I shall, of course. But after breakfast,' I said and I returned to the kitchen to leave her to gather herself.

'To be perfectly truthful,' I said, 'I was a tiny bit disappointed.'

'How so?' she said, spearing another sausage with her fork.

'Well, it was just more bumping and clattering and a fresh message in the skittle alley. I was expecting something fresh and a little more ingenious, I suppose.'

'It does sound a little anticlimactic,' she said. 'Although being locked in your room was a new twist.'

'It was, but it lacked subtlety. I expected something with a little more panache.'

'Needs must, I suppose,' she said.

'I suppose. But it does rather put the tin hat on the possibility of it being a real haunting.'

'It does?' she asked.

'I'm afraid so. I'm not wholly surprised, either. I know that there are charlatans—'

'And mountebanks—'

'And humbugs galore. My mam and dad worked with a few over the years. One swindler doesn't make it all a lie, mind you.'

'No, indeed,' she said. 'How did she work the séance, though?'

'I have one or two ideas,' I said. 'I'd like to ask a couple of questions of an old friend of my parents. I'll write to him. I have his agent's address somewhere.'

'Meanwhile I'm waiting for a reply from the solicitors so it will be a day or two before we can move.'

'Move, my lady?' I said.

'Oh, yes. We'll definitely be making our move.'

'Will we have time? What if Madame Eugénie does a moonlight flit before we can confront her?'

'If we're right, she'll be lurking about for a few days yet. We've plenty of time.'

'Right you are, my lady,' I said. 'Another crumpet?'

'Tempting, but I think not. Have a few things to catch up with.'

'Jolly good. I'll get this lot tidied away. Then I'll write that letter. Then sort out the chaos you left on the floor last night.'

'Already done, dear girl. You shamed me into it.'

13

The next day, I was helping in the kitchen while Miss Jones prepared a tray for Lady Hardcastle's elevenses. There was a knock on the kitchen door.

'Daisy,' I said as I saw our friend standing there. 'Come on in, *fach*. What can we do for you?'

'I thought you and Blodwen might want to know,' she said. 'They've arrested Mr Snelson.'

'For murder?' asked Miss Jones.

'That's right. Sergeant Dobson marched him through the village in handcuffs this morning.'

This was not promising news.

'Tell me you found out more,' I said.

'I had a word with Sam Hancock,' she said. 'Constables is always keen to gossip – makes 'em feel more important like. He says they got a telephone call from Gloucester this morning. He reckons the Gloucester police went to Long Lane Farm and searched the place for the strongbox. You know, the one in the message. They found it, he says. And when they opened it, it had stuff in it what implicated Snelson in the murder.'

'What sort of "stuff"?' I asked.

'He didn't say.'

'I'm sorry, Daisy, *fach*, but I've got to tell Lady Hardcastle. She'll not be pleased about this. Make her a cup of tea, Blod, and I'll see you both later.'

I hurried out to the morning room with the tray.

Lady Hardcastle, as I had predicted, was not impressed.

'Whatever did he go and do that for?' she asked. 'This will never do, never do at all. I do adore the pair of them but, I mean, really. It's like a compulsion with them, arresting the wrong person. I only hope we can set things straight before it all gets too out of hand.'

I was about to pursue it further but I was interrupted by the clatter of the post on the mat.

'Go and fetch that for me, would you, dear,' she said. 'We might have our replies.'

I went out to the hall and returned with four letters.

'Hand them over, Flo, quick sticks,' said Lady Hardcastle impatiently. She immediately discarded two, muttering, 'Bills.' The next she passed to me.

'Here's one for you,' she said. 'From your old family friend?'

She opened the fourth and read it intently. It was a lengthy missive and it took her quite a few minutes.

'That makes things a great deal clearer,' she said at last. 'How about yours, dear? Anything helpful?'

'Just a short one, my lady. He says it's all a little complex and he'd prefer to speak to me in person.'

'Oh, that's a shame.'

'It would be rather a blow, my lady,' I said. 'But he's playing in Bristol, at the Empire. He says he'd be delighted to see me any time.'

'I say, that's excellent news. We need our driving togs. It seems you have an appointment in the city.'

We got up from the table and I cleared the cups and plates away.

'Would you like to drive?' she said from the door.

'Do you know, my lady, I rather think I would. Can I have a peaked cap?'

She laughed. 'We shall visit a milliner at the earliest opportunity. But don't get used to it, I rather enjoy driving. We'll have to share.'

After a couple of failed attempts to start the Rover, we were on our way into Bristol.

I'd driven the car around the lanes a few times when it had first been delivered, but this was my first proper journey. I loved it. Being in control of such a powerful and sophisticated machine was a thrill beyond imagining as we puttered down the Gloucester Road and into the heart of the city. Lady Hardcastle was navigating. Somehow she managed to get us to Old Market where I pulled up outside the Empire, Bristol's most famous music hall.

'I'm so sorry, my lady, but I have to leave you out here,' I said as I got out of the motor car and adjusted my coat. 'He has agreed to see me only on the condition that I come alone.'

She smiled. 'Think nothing of it, Flo dear,' she said. 'A chap like that must have his secrets. I shall just wait here. I can pretend to be a chauffeuse. I could polish the car or something. Isn't that what they do?'

I spent a very enjoyable hour in the company of my old family friend. By the time I returned to the Rover and started the engine, Lady Hardcastle was fast asleep.

'All done, my lady,' I said, climbing back into the driving seat.

'What?' she said as she struggled to wakefulness. 'Oh, yes, splendid. Jolly good.'

'Where to now, my lady?' I said.

'Home, I think.'

'Right you are, my lady. Via the Dog and Duck, if you don't mind. And the police station.'

'Certainly, dear girl. You have a plan?'

'I do, my lady.'

I resisted all Lady Hardcastle's attempts to prise further information from me during the afternoon. Meanwhile, the weather had slowly deteriorated and another storm was brewing.

I was forced to reveal at least the beginning of my plan when I laid out a black evening dress for her.

'So we're going out, then?' she said.

'Only to the Dog and Duck, my lady,' I said. 'But I thought it would be nice to dress up. We're going to another séance. You said we should make our move. Are you ready with your part?'

'All I need is for you to give the lie to the haunting. Leave the explanations to me.'

By the time we had eaten supper and changed for the pub, the storm was well and truly under way, with rain once more lashing the windows and the sound of distant thunder rumbling in across the hills.

We were drenched when we reached the pub, and I was glad that Daisy didn't keep us waiting too long at the door before letting us in. The room was laid out exactly as it had been for the first séance. I was pleased to see that Mr Snelson was there, along with the rest of the original guests who were all in their original seats.

Lady Hardcastle raised a questioning eyebrow, but I shook my head. We sat down, but I indicated that she should sit in the seat that I had occupied the week before.

Sergeant Dobson was behind the bar with his friend Joe Arnold, but he was still in uniform and obviously still on duty, whatever the pint of cider in his hand might have suggested. My instructions earlier in the day hadn't said anything about not supping with his old pal, so I left them to it.

'Thank you all for coming,' I said. 'I know it was horribly short notice and you've all probably got much better things to be getting on with on a Saturday night so I'm very grateful that you were able to attend. We just need to make one more attempt to communicate with the spirits before we can finally see justice done.'

There were murmurs and nods of acknowledgement from around the table.

'Daisy, do you think Madame Eugénie might be ready now?' I said.

'I'll just go and see,' said Daisy, but before she reached the door, it opened and in swept Madame Eugénie in her lacy black dress.

'Good evening, my dears,' she said dreamily as she wafted to the table and sat in her chair. 'I can feel that the spirits are anxious to commune with us this night. Is everyone ready?'

There were more murmurs, which she took as assent.

'Very well,' she said. 'Let us begin. You remember the procedure from last time, I trust? Grasp your neighbour's right wrist with your left hand and under no circumstances break the circle. Once we begin, that circle will be our only protection.'

We managed to link hands much more easily this time. Once again, Madame Eugénie asked Daisy to turn down the lamp. In the darkness, Dr Fitzsimmons once again found her wrist and we waited in silence. There was a flash of lightning so bright that it could be seen even though the windows were tightly shuttered. It was followed by a booming crash of thunder so loud and so sudden that there were screams and gasps from around the table and a flutter of movement as several people raised their hands in shock.

'Calm, please, my dears,' said Madame Eugénie's ethereal voice. 'Re-form the circle and we shall begin.'

There was more rustling and fidgeting as everyone made fresh contact with their neighbour's wrist. After a few moments the room fell silent once more with only the hammering of the rain on the windows to break the peace.

'Spirits, we implore you, join us. Join us and share your knowledge and wisdom that we might see justice done,' said Madame Eugénie.

As before, there was a knock on the table but this time, there was an answering, lighter knock. Once more the louder knock, as though the spirit were testing, and once more, the lighter reply.

'Who calls me at this hour?' said Madame Eugénie. The gravelly voice we now knew to be her spirit guide, Monsieur Diderot, was less confident than before. 'Is that you, Madame Eugénie?'

'It is I, Monsieur Diderot,' she said in her usual voice. 'We seek answers in the matter we spoke of last time. We have been troubled by an unquiet spirit. Is it Emmanuel Bean? Is he there? Does he have anything else to tell us?'

'He is here,' said the gravelly voice. 'He is greatly troubled. He craves one more chance to avenge himself by revealing the truth of his death.'

'Let him come forth,' she said. 'Let him cross over.'

There was a chilly gust. Suddenly, the ghostly white figure that had appeared last time was among us. He raised his chalk-white arm and pointed once again at Mr Snelson. His mouth opened to speak, but instead I said, 'Now, Sergeant Dobson, if you please.'

With that, a lamp flared by the bar and the room was suddenly illuminated.

The scene that greeted us was at once shocking, astonishing and comically disappointing. Around the table, everyone's hands were joined as instructed, except for those of Madame Eugénie and me. We each had our left hands free.

Mr Snelson was grasping my right wrist as instructed. But I had used the shock of the thunderclap to break my grip on Madame Eugénie's right wrist. When we had remade the circle I had used my right hand to grasp Madame Eugénie's wrist, leaving my left hand free.

I waved at Lady Hardcastle with my free hand.

Madame Eugénie, meanwhile, had pulled the same trick and was glaring menacingly at me. In her left hand was a short fishing rod. Hanging from the end of the line was a white leather glove, stuffed to make it appear fleshy and full. I caught it and pulled it towards me.

In the light of the lamps it was comically fake. It was wet and chilled, though – it had obviously been left outside. I knew that in the dark, with everyone in the right mood, it would be surprisingly convincing. A cold clammy finger from the beyond, poking the accused in the chops.

Daisy turned up the lamp on the table. We all saw that what we had taken to be the ghost of Emmanuel Bean was actually a small young woman in a white suit, wearing ghoulishly white makeup on her otherwise rather pretty face. She made to scamper for the door to the stairs, but Constable Hancock appeared in the doorway to block her escape.

'Ladies and gentlemen,' I said once chatter had died down a little. 'I'm sorry to spoil the show, but I really don't like being humbugged. Even by an accomplished expert.'

Madame Eugénie placed the fishing rod carefully on the table but said nothing, continuing to glare murderously at me.

'Madame Eugénie, you see,' I continued, 'is more properly known as Queenie Huggins from Birmingham. I had a most marvellously illuminating conversation this morning with an old friend of my parents. He makes his living now as a stage magician.'

'A blinkin' magician?' said Daisy, clearly bitterly disappointed.

'Sorry, Dais,' I said. 'My old friend let me in on a few of the tricks of the trade, as it were. The thing with the circle really is quite clever. I'll give you that, Queenie.'

'Madame Eugénie,' she said aggressively.

'As you wish,' I continued. 'It seems Queenie Huggins here worked for a few years as a magician's assistant on the music hall circuit. She picked up a few of the magician's secrets and realized that she could make a much better living for herself gulling the lonely and vulnerable by pretending to put them in touch with their departed loved ones. She recruited an assistant, Miss Lizzie Bean – that's her by the door in her ghostly garb – and together they travel the land, rooking the desperate and bereft with their thoroughly convincing spiritualist show.'

'But she spoke to my uncle John,' said Mrs Spratt. 'No one here knew I had an uncle John 'cept our Daisy.'

'Did she?' I said. 'Do you remember what she said? She said she had someone with her called John. John's the most common man's name in England. It was Daisy who suggested that it was your uncle.'

'But what about Dr Fitzsimmons's wife,' said Mrs Spratt defensively. 'She said his June wanted to speak to him.'

'She did indeed,' I said. 'In the end. That's a trick I already knew from the circus fortune tellers. It's part of something they call cold reading. You throw out a few names and wait for a reaction.'

'But she got it spot on. In one go,' said Mrs Spratt.

'Actually, no, she didn't,' said Lady Hardcastle. 'She tried several names before she hit upon June. There was Jane, Jennifer and Juliet before June ever appeared.'

'But the spirits is sometimes hard to hear,' said Mrs Spratt, with somewhat less conviction. 'All she could make out was the J.'

'The J, yes,' said Lady Hardcastle who was already a step ahead. 'Have you ever glanced at the signet ring that Dr Fitzsimmons wears on his wedding finger, Mrs Spratt?'

'Can't say as I have, no.'

'It's a rather beautiful thing. I asked him about it a few days ago. It's rather unusual for a man to wear a wedding ring, but he wears his as a reminder of his lost love. If you look carefully you can see the letters C and J entwined on the face. Charles and June. A good charlatan pays attention to such things. A man she had been told was a widower, the initial J on his ring. It's not a massive leap to work out that J was probably his late wife. Then all she had to do was to try a few names and see which one worked. We all wanted to believe, so we all forgot the three wrong guesses.'

There were frowns and scowls around the table.

'How did you get your hands free?' asked Mr Holman, the baker.

'When the lightning struck and we broke the circle in shock,' I said. 'We simply rejoined our hands in the manner you saw, leaving us free to rap on the table and for Queenie here to manipulate her fishing rod.'

'But there weren't no lightning last time,' said Mrs Spratt, still desperate to cling to the possibility that it might be true, despite the props on the table and the embarrassed accomplice standing before her.

'That's true,' I said. 'That was a lucky opportunity for me, to tell the truth. I'd planned to slip off my chair, but the thunder gave me much more convincing cover. No, last time, if you remember, Queenie sneezed and blew her nose once the lamp was out. That was her chance.'

'That's all very well and good,' said Mr Holman. 'But what's all that got to do with Mr Snelson here?'

'Ah, now that's altogether more convoluted,' said Lady Hardcastle. 'Perhaps Mr Arnold would be good enough to pour us all a drink while I tell you the tale.'

While Joe poured fresh drinks for everyone, Constable Hancock led the ghost to a chair and sat her down. Madame Eugénie still hadn't said anything, but she had made no move to flee and so

Sergeant Hancock seemed content to leave her be. If anything, she seemed resigned to her fate, as though this sort of thing were an occupational hazard.

Once we were all settled and had taken a sip or two of our tipples, Lady Hardcastle motioned for silence.

'Thank you,' she said once we were all paying attention. 'I can't take credit for all the information I'm about to share, much of the hard work was done by my solicitors who scoured company records, birth records, and probate records.'

I wasn't the only one keeping secrets. That had clearly been what was in the long letter she had received.

'Now, the more attentive of you might have noticed that the young lady so ably playing the part of the ghost here, shares a surname with the ghost she has been portraying. It's not a spooky coincidence, though. She's his daughter. Mrs Bean left her husband twenty years ago, taking young Lizzie with her, and neither of them ever saw him again. Lizzie is Emmanuel Bean's "estranged daughter" as the press so melodramatically say.

'When Mrs Bean knew him, Emmanuel was a rather lacklustre businessman, with a string of failed ventures behind him. She brought her daughter up to believe that he was an abject failure. It was with some surprise, then, I should imagine, that when she heard of her father's unfortunate death, she learned that he was a partner in a successful timber business in Gloucester. A business that was destroyed in a suspicious fire. She would have learned, also, that the beneficiary of the considerable insurance policies on the business was his business partner, Mr Nelson Snelson. There was a policy on her father's life, too, upon which Mr Snelson collected.

'There wasn't a penny in the late Mr Bean's will for his former wife, nor for the daughter he hadn't seen in all those years. He left his considerable personal fortune to Mr Snelson as well.

'Now the next part is pure speculation on my part, but I imagine that events proceeded thusly. Miss Bean approached her employer, Mrs Huggins, with news that she had missed out on a substantial inheritance, and between them they hatched a plan to try to get the money for themselves. They reasoned that if they could implicate Mr Snelson in the torching of the factory and the manslaughter of Mr Bean, that he would no longer be entitled to the insurance money. Once Bean's rightful heir had come forward, the rest of Mr Bean's estate would be theirs.

'Our dear friend Daisy gave them just the opportunity they needed to sow the seeds of suspicion when she booked Madame Eugénie to appear in the very village where they had learned that Mr Snelson now lived. Madame Eugénie duly arrived and booked in to her room at the pub, never letting on that she was accompanied by her assistant. Lizzie was smuggled in through the back door, I imagine. With no one ever entering the room, no one would know that there were two women staying there. If needs be, she's small enough to hide in the wardrobe.

'So they put on their show, which, as Armstrong has so ably demonstrated, was pure theatre. Over the ensuing nights, Lizzie would sneak downstairs, wreak a little havoc, and reinforce the accusation of murder by leaving messages on the skittle alley scoreboard. They nearly came unstuck three nights ago when Armstrong spent the night in the pub.

'Queenie is nothing if not quick-thinking, though. She used a spare key to leave Armstrong locked in her room. When it was time for Lizzie to hide away again, Queenie kept everyone busy and out of the way while Lizzie crept back to their room. This time they were able to leave their message, the one that led the Gloucester police to the evidence on the farm. I have no idea what that evidence was – letters, perhaps, spelling out the plan, or a forged confession – but whatever it was, it was enough to convince the Gloucester detectives that Mr Snelson should be arrested and that they should investigate further.

'So far, so good, and their plan was proceeding well. Mr Snelson was arrested, there was fresh evidence that might secure his conviction, and it was only a matter of time before they were "in the money" as the saying goes.'

'Even if a word of that were true,' said Queenie Huggins, a harsh, Black Country twang replacing the dreamy voice we were used to, 'we ain't done nothink illegal. Snelson still set that fire, and he still murdered Lizzie's pa. All we done is help out by speaking the truth.'

'Ah, well, I'm afraid there's one extra little part of the story that you don't know, and which a rather excellent investigator employed by my solicitors managed to dig up for me when I suggested what I thought might have happened. You see, Mr Snelson can't have killed Mr Bean, because Mr Emmanuel Bean is alive and well and living in Manchester under the name Isaac Goldstein.'

There was a minor uproar. Mr Snelson, who had up to that point been looking rather relieved that things were finally going his way, slumped in his chair and held his head in his hands.

'Not dead?' said Queenie. 'But there was a body in the timber yard. Of course he's dead.'

'No, Mrs Huggins, I'm afraid not. The whole thing was another fraud. A pleasing little touch, don't you think?'

Queenie didn't appear in the least bit pleased.

'Of course, the popular suspicion might have been true. Mr Snelson might somehow have managed to get to Gloucester to torch the timber yard with his partner still in it and still get back to Birmingham in time to give himself an alibi. But it's all rather unlikely, don't you think? Much more likely was that he had been in Birmingham the whole time.

'So it was either an accidental fire, or an arson attempt by Bean himself that went tragically wrong. But what if it wasn't either of those things? The only thing that identified Bean's burnt body was his signet ring. What if that wasn't Bean at all? What if they had chanced upon the body of some unfortunate derelict and had come up with the idea of using his poor body to fake Bean's death?'

Mr Snelson made to protest, but a glare from Lady Hardcastle cut him short.

'The business, we know, was in difficulties, but the insurance premiums were up to date. Bean had been salting away money and had a substantial policy on his own life. What an opportunity this would be to rid themselves of the failing business, to claim on the insurance policies and live a comfortable retirement. So Snelson was sent to Birmingham to make sure he couldn't be implicated in any wrongdoing, while Bean put his ring on the tramp's corpse and set the fire that destroyed everything. All Bean had to do then was disappear and wait for Snelson to give him his half share of the proceeds.'

'Well I never,' said Mrs Spratt.

'You still ain't got nothink on us,' said Queenie belligerently.

'Oh, I don't know,' said Lady Hardcastle. 'I'm sure there's taking money under false pretences, not paying for a room for Lizzie, some criminal damage to Joe's pub. My solicitors also tell me about a rather splendid piece of eighteenth-century legislation. They tell me that under the Witchcraft Act of 1735, it's an offence to claim that one can produce spirits. I gather that the two of you can look forward to at least a year in gaol if convicted. And' – she indicated the assembled throng – 'we're not exactly short of witnesses.'

'You can't. It ain't our fault. It weren't even our idea.'

'Right,' said Sergeant Dobson, taking this as his cue for action. 'Mr Nelson Snelson, I am arresting you on suspicion of making fraudulent insurance claims and of . . . well, I'm sure there's some offence of falsifying someone's death and of not properly disposing of a body, too. Meanwhile, Mrs Queenie Huggins and Miss Lizzie Bean, I am arresting you two under the . . . what was it, m'lady?'

'The Witchcraft Act of 1735, Sergeant, dear.'

'Under the Witchcraft Act of 1735, for making false claims of being able to produce spirits. I'd also like a word about you roughing up Joe's bar.'

14

'Bother,' said Lady Hardcastle over Sunday lunch. 'A note from Hector.'

'Not your usual reaction to notes from The Grange,' I said, helping myself to another slice of pie.

'Guilt, dear, that's all. Gertie's away and he's invited us to tea. Which is lovely. But I'll wager he wants to talk about the blessed trophies. In all the excitement I've not given them another thought. Nor a thought for poor old Lofty Trevellian. He'll be up before the magistrate this week.'

'Am I invited?' I asked.

'It's Hector, dear. Of course you're invited. He's taken quite a shine to you.'

We made our own way to The Grange, with Lady Hardcastle weaving the little motor car at alarming speeds through the still-damp lanes.

Sir Hector asked Jenkins to bring us tea and cake in the library and we settled ourselves in comfortable chairs clustered around a small occasional table. He seemed pleased to have company and had been chattering almost continuously since we got there. As the refreshments arrived, he finished his account of the replanting of the rose beds and switched the points to divert his train of thought towards the rugby club.

'Still reelin' from the goings-on at the rugby club,' he said as Jenkins poured three cups of tea. 'Bad business, what? We got the fella, but not the loot. Need the loot back. Damn shame. Were the diaries any help the other week? Any clues in the background?'

'They were fascinating, Sir Hector,' I said before Lady Hardcastle could reply. 'It seems to have been a lively place in the past.'

'It's a lively place now, m'dear,' he said with a grin. 'Quite the liveliest.'

'But you can't have any characters to rival Jester Dunleavy,' I said. 'He seemed to have been quite a card.'

'Dear old Jester,' he said wistfully. 'No, I don't think we'll see his like again. He'll be sadly missed.'

'He's no longer with us?' I said.

'No, poor chap was working at the Hackney Empire. Slipped on something an elephant had deposited on the stage and fell headfirst into the orchestra pit. Head stuck in a euphonium. They rushed him to the hospital, of course, but he'd broken his neck in the fall.'

Lady Hardcastle struggled to contain herself but let out such a bark of laughter that she set me off. Soon all three of us were guffawing fit to burst.

'I'm so sorry, Hector,' she said. 'I meant no discourtesy.'

'Nonsense, m'dear,' he said kindly. 'It's exactly the reaction he would have wanted. Very fitting that a man who filled the club with so many practical jokes should still be making people laugh even after he's passed. The inventor of the disappearing cash box and the self-pouring beer tap should be remembered with a laugh or two.'

'He was quite the inventor, then?'

'Certainly, certainly. It's how he made his living. Invented . . . "gags" he called them . . . invented gags for stage conjurors. Magic cabinets and whatnot. Jolly clever chap. Best scrum half the club ever had, too.'

'Magic cabinets?' I said, my interest suddenly piqued. 'Of the sort that might make things disappear?'

'Exactly that sort,' he said enthusiastically. 'Once saw him make a lady vanish – vanish completely, mind you – right before me eyes. Man was a genius.'

'Are you thinking what I think you're thinking, Flo, dear?' said Lady Hardcastle.

'Probably not, my lady,' I said. 'I was thinking that I could do with a cabinet like that from time to time.'

It was Sir Hector's turn to guffaw. 'Me too, m'dear, what?'

I winked.

'What I was thinking,' she continued, affecting to ignore us, 'was that we ought to get back to the committee room and let Flo have another look round.'

'Truthfully,' I said. 'That's what I was thinking, too.'

'I say,' said Sir Hector. 'Would you like to go now? We could go together. I'll ring for Bert.'

'We should make our own way,' said Lady Hardcastle. 'We came up in the Rover. I'd offer you a lift but it's a bit of a squeeze for two as it is.'

'Nonsense, m'dear. That's what Bert's for.'

'We're not dragging you away from anything?' she asked.

'Bored witless here,' he said. 'Nothin' to do and no one to talk to with Gertie away for the day. Love to get m'teeth into one of your mysteries, what?'

'What are you lookin' for?' asked Sir Hector as I peered closely at the trophy cabinet.

'I'm not entirely sure,' I said, running my hands over the frame. 'I'm afraid it's one of those things I'll only know when I've found it.'

Sir Hector had accompanied us to the committee room, barely able to contain his curiosity. He bobbed about, trying to see what I was up to. I opened the cabinet, closed it, opened it again, examined the shelves, studied the hinges and the lock. I pressed firmly on one of the abstract decorations carved on the front. It seemed to move inwards, but nothing else happened.

Then I had an idea. I got to my knees and lay on my stomach in front of the cabinet, trying to look underneath it. With an 'Ah-ha!' of triumph, I got up again and stood once more in front of the cabinet with one hand on the moving decoration, and the toe of my boot in the gap between the cabinet and the floor. I pushed the ornament and moved my foot to one side. With a click and a rattle, the panels at the back of the cabinet began to slide up and out of sight. As they did so, the shelves concealed behind the panels began to slide forwards. There, exactly as I had imagined them from the descriptions, were the shield, jersey, penny and cup. Not stolen, but hidden from view.

'Well, I'll be blowed,' said Sir Hector. 'Fancy that. Not missin'' at all. Here all the time, what?'

'So it would appear,' said Lady Hardcastle with a grin of what I hoped might be pride.

'How on earth did you know it was there?' asked Sir Hector, pulling his reading glasses from his pocket and examining the cabinet for himself.

'To be absolutely honest,' I said, 'I didn't. Not for certain, at least.'

'When we first saw that the footprints led back into the store-room,' said Lady Hardcastle, 'I'd expected to find the loot hidden in there somewhere, but all we found were Lofty's boots.'

'But what on earth would he do that for?' said Sir Hector. 'Don't make sense.'

Lady Hardcastle fiddled with the mechanism and once again made the trophies disappear into the wall. 'It doesn't, does it?'

'So now we've got Trevellian, and we've got the loot back,' said Sir Hector. 'Sergeant Dobson tells me Trevellian the villain is up before the beak tomorrow. This should seal his fate, what?'

'His fate? I'm not sure hiding things is a crime, dear. We'll have to let the sergeant know so that he can release Trevellian.'

'Release him?' roared Sir Hector. 'But—'

'But nothing, Hector. What happened here is a matter for the club, not the law.'

Sir Hector scowled.

It seemed almost everything had been settled. Queenie had been caught, Snelson had been caught, and now the loot had been recovered. Two matters remained unresolved: who hid the trophy and what really happened to Spencer Caradine?

On Monday morning I was up with the robin. I had decided by then that not only did I have no idea when larks rose, but that I shouldn't know a lark if it perched on my shoulder and sang in my ear. But the robin was an entirely different proposition. Even I could spot our neighbourhood robin as he hopped proprietorially around the walled garden.

So Mr Red Breast and I rose together and went about our business. He was digging about in the grass for worms and insects and I had vanquished many a chore before Edna and Miss Jones arrived.

By ten o'clock Lady Hardcastle was up and dressed, we had eaten a substantial breakfast and had moved to the dining room with fresh coffee to examine the crime board. During our first investigation the previous summer, Lady Hardcastle had hit upon the idea of using a large blackboard to help us keep track of all the information relating to the apparent suicide of a man in the woods. She drew sketches of the people involved, which she pinned to the board, and then we made notes, attempting to make connections, see patterns and, eventually, solve the mystery. Our friend Inspector Sunderland ribbed her mercilessly about it. He told me privately that he thought it was an excellent idea and that he had begun using something similar with his colleagues in Bristol CID.

It seemed Lady Hardcastle was troubled by our lack of progress on the Caradine case as well.

At the centre of the board was Lady Hardcastle's sketch of Spencer Caradine. Under it we had written, 'Grumpy, argumentative, universally disliked.' Around the rest of the board were sketches of other people we had met or knew about. There was Audrey Caradine, Spencer's long-suffering and devout widow. His son, Morris, the bullied artist. Their neighbour, Noah Lock, in love with the beautiful Audrey. Caradine's rival, Dick Ackley, with whom he was locked in a perpetual battle of one-upmanship. All of them might have had reason to do the old man to death.

Lady Hardcastle put the finishing touches to a sketch of Lancelot Tribley. I pinned it up for her.

'What would Mr Tribley's motive be, my lady?' I asked.

'Aside from the fact that almost anyone who met Spencer Caradine would happily have killed him?' she said.

'Aside from that, my lady. If that were motive enough there wouldn't be room on the board for all the people who might have done him in.'

'Jealousy,' she said.

'Of what?'

'Morris Caradine seems to have a buyer lined up for Top Farm. Maybe Tribley found out about it and killed the old chap out of spite. He said he was having a devil of a job selling his own place.' She gazed at the board. 'So where are we now? Everyone has a motive, no matter how slender. Several people might have had the means to kill him, though we have no idea what the poison was, nor even if it was poison at all. And almost everyone seems to have had some sort of opportunity to administer the putative poison. Perhaps we should call Inspector Sunderland. The police surgeon must know something by now and a professional detective might have a better idea of how to proceed. Or would it profit us to visit The Hayrick and speak to the landlord there, I wonder?'

'Towels, my lady. "Call me Ronnie".'

'I say, what a memory you have.'

'It's a gift, my lady. And sometimes a curse. I remember, for instance, every time I've had to save your silly skin when you've put yourself in danger for King and country. I remember every cad, scoundrel and bounder I've had to outwit. Every ruffian, thug and bruiser I've had to "neutralize". Every—'

'Oh, pish and fiddlesticks, you make it sound like we never have any fun.' She flicked through the pages, looking at the notes she'd made over the past few days. 'Ah, look, there he is. Ronnie. You're so clever. Would it help to talk to him, I wonder?'

'We could. But what would we ask him?'

'That's the thing, isn't it? We could—'

The doorbell prevented me from finding out what it was that we could do. I left her leafing through her notes and went to answer the door.

'Good morning, Miss Armstrong,' said Inspector Sunderland with a smile.

'And good morning to you, Inspector,' I said, stepping aside. 'Won't you come in. We were just talking about you.'

'Nothing defamatory, I hope,' he said, stepping inside and removing his bowler hat.

I took the hat and put it on the hall table along with a leather document case he was carrying, then helped him off with his overcoat. 'No, sir, it's just that we're a little stuck and we thought you might be able to help us. Point us in a new direction as it were.'

'What have you managed so far?' he asked, picking up the case.

I led him to the dining room and ushered him in. 'I'll let Lady Hardcastle explain,' I said. 'Inspector Sunderland, my lady.'

'Oh, I say, what a treat. Do come in and sit down, Inspector,' she said.

'Thank you, my lady,' he said, sitting in one of the dining chairs.

'The inspector was wondering how we were getting on, my lady,' I said.

'Then we must give him chapter and verse. Why don't I bring him up to date while you make us all a fresh pot of coffee?'

'Very good, my lady,' I said with a smile, and I went to the kitchen.

It took only a short while to brew a pot of coffee and cut a few slices of the Madeira cake I'd made earlier that morning, but by the time I returned with the tray, their discussion had already moved on to other things.

'. . . and she bought this awful elephant's-foot umbrella stand,' Lady Hardcastle was saying. 'It's a replica, of course. Looks just like the real thing, and she was so taken with it that I couldn't bring myself to tell her what I really thought. Ah, there you are, Flo, thank you. Come and sit down. I was telling the inspector about our visit to the junk shop in Chipping Bevington with Gertie and Maude.'

'Pomphrey's Bric-a-Brac Emporium, my lady,' I said, sitting down.

'That's the place,' she said. 'She has a marvellous memory, Inspector. Pomphrey's. Yes.'

'I know of it, my lady,' said the inspector with a smile. 'Mr Pomphrey helped us out a few years ago with a case involving smuggled Egyptian mummified cats.'

'I think I read about that,' she said. 'That was you? Well I never.'

'I have my moments, my lady,' he said.

I poured the coffee and passed round the cake. When we were all settled, the inspector picked up the leather document case from the floor beside him and opened it. 'Now that Miss Armstrong is back,' he said, 'I can share my own news.'

He took out a manila folder and placed it on the table in front of him. From inside he produced a sheet of paper headed with the badge of the Bristol Police.

'At long last,' he said, tapping the paper with his finger, 'we have the report from the police surgeon. The cause of death was, indeed, poison. And unless Mr Caradine ingested it by accident, I should say it's murder.'

'By accident, Inspector?' I said. 'Is that common?'

'Not so as you'd notice, miss, no, but the surgeon is insistent that we don't rule it out.'

'And why's that?' said Lady Hardcastle.

'Because in spite of his painstaking efforts, using the entirety of the baffling array of chemical tests available to him, he has no idea what the poison was.'

'Oh,' I said dejectedly.

'Quite, miss, quite. And without knowing exactly what poisoned Mr Caradine, the surgeon refuses to discount the possibility that he might have unknowingly ingested something deadly without any skulduggery or mischief being involved.'

'Oh.' Lady Hardcastle echoed my dejection.

'"Oh", indeed, my lady,' said the inspector. 'Looking on the bright side, at least he's ruled out the common poisons: arsenic, strychnine, even cyanide. And the reports from the laboratory say that there was nothing untoward in his pie or his cider. Although they're not completely convinced that the meat was beef as advertised.'

'Oh,' said Lady Hardcastle again. 'We were rather counting on the poison pointing us to the killer. We've been asking the local farmers what poisons they keep.'

'Excellent work, my lady,' he said. 'Exactly what I would have done. But no interview is ever wasted. Impressions and feelings can take you just as far as facts in the quest for the truth.'

'I don't disagree, Inspector,' she said. 'But we can't take our impressions to a magistrate. Facts are so much more compelling, wouldn't you say?'

He chuckled. 'I do like a nice cold fact, my lady, yes. But they seem a bit thin on the ground in this case.'

'Quite,' she said.

'What do you suggest we do next?' I asked, trying to buck them both up. 'We were thinking of going into Chipping Bevington to interview the staff at The Hayrick.'

'Well, I'd not stop you if your hearts are set on it,' he said. 'But I went over there myself when I had a spare afternoon on Saturday.' He took another sheet from the folder and passed it to me.

I read it through quickly. 'Oh,' I said. 'They saw nothing, they heard nothing, they know nothing. It might be something of a wasted journey, my lady.' I passed her the report.

'Well, pish and the fiddliest of sticks,' she said. 'I'm stumped.'

'For the moment, my lady,' said the inspector, 'so am I. Unless a witness comes forward and tells us exactly what happened, I'm rather afraid to say that this might have to remain unsolved.'

'That will never do, Inspector,' said Lady Hardcastle with sudden passion. 'Never do at all. I refuse to be beaten. I'm going to assume that Mr Caradine was poisoned by person or persons unknown and I'm going to make it my business to know them. We owe his widow and son that, if no one else.'

'Unless it turns out that they were the ones that killed him, my lady,' said the inspector sagely.

'Oh,' she said. 'That would be doing them a disservice after all. But no.' Her resolve returned. 'If they did him in then they must be brought to justice. This is England. We don't just ignore the law when it suits us or when we find that we like the criminal more than we like his victim.'

'Hear hear,' said the inspector with a smile. 'I just wanted you to consider the consequences, that's all. More often than not in a case like this, it's the wife's doing.'

'We must let things unfold as they may, Inspector,' she said. 'We shall solve this.'

'I'm pleased to hear it,' he said. 'May I have another slice of that cake, please, Miss Armstrong? It's quite delicious.'

I helped him to another slice of Madeira and poured more coffee for all of us.

'How's Mrs Sunderland?' said Lady Hardcastle while I poured. 'Is she well?'

'Very well indeed, thank you, my lady. She sends her regards.'

'Thank you, dear. And you must pass my best wishes on to her, too. We haven't seen her since the circus.'

'No, my lady, and she was quite taken with you. With both of you. I'm sure we promised to invite you round for dinner. I'm sorry we haven't managed it.'

'It seems we all do nothing but make apologies of that sort, dear, I shouldn't worry about it. We're still trying to arrange to host Sir Hector and Lady Farley-Stroud for supper but that seems trickier than one would have imagined. I say, you wouldn't care to join us? Make a bit more of a party of it?'

'It's a lovely offer, my lady, but I should need to ask Mrs Sunderland first. I shouldn't like to impose Lady Farley-Stroud on her without at least a warning.'

Lady Hardcastle laughed. 'Gertie's a sweetie. They'd rub along splendidly. But don't fret. I say, how about we treat you to supper in Bristol? There must be a restaurant in town that you've been dying to go to. It would save poor Mrs Sunderland from having to cater for two extra mouths and it would give us the chance to get together, away from murderers and ne'er-do-wells.'

'That's very generous of you, my lady, I shall consult Mrs Sunderland. But I should expect that she'll still insist on having you round at some point. She's a fine cook and she does like to entertain.'

'That's agreed, then,' said Lady Hardcastle delightedly. 'We shall do both. Flo, dear, make a note.'

I sighed and rolled my eyes. 'My lady, I should love to. But . . .'

'Oh, I know, I know,' she said exasperatedly. 'I have the blessed notebook.' She began hunting through the confusion of drawing paper and pencils on the table beside her.

'It was a gift from Inspector Sunderland, my lady,' I said. 'One would have thought you'd at least pretend to take better care of it while the poor man is in the room.'

'I much preferred her when I was ill, Inspector,' she said. 'She wasn't nearly so impertinent when she was having to feign concern for me.'

'You weren't ill, my lady,' I said. 'You were injured. And I was just as impertinent as ever, it's just that the laudanum made you too doolally to notice.'

The inspector laughed. 'I have missed you two,' he said. 'It's good to have you properly back among us, my lady.'

'It was the good friends I've made here that gave me the strength to recover, Inspector. Thank you,' she said. 'I say, look at the time. Do you have to dash off? Or can you stay for lunch?'

'I'm not expected back at the station until much later, my lady,' he said. 'If it wouldn't be an imposition, lunch would be most welcome.'

15

The road to Tuesday is paved with good intentions. We had intended that Monday should be a busy day, a productive day, and had begun that day suffused with a resolve to crack the case. But coffee with Inspector Sunderland turned into lunch with Inspector Sunderland, which turned into an afternoon of chatter and gossip with Inspector Sunderland, which turned into a piano recital from Lady Hardcastle. This was where we also discovered that the inspector was a rather accomplished baritone who had sung in the Bristol Cathedral choir as a boy. By the time he left to walk into the village to find someone to give him a lift to the station in Chipping Bevington, it was too late to do anything very much but prepare supper and sing more silly songs until bedtime.

Tuesday morning saw us both up with the blackbird (there being no sign of my newfound friend, the robin). Up, dressed, breakfasted and inactive. Now that we had learned that the poison was unknown and that not even an experienced professional policeman had any idea how to proceed with the case, we were once again at a loss for something to do.

'There was a don when I was up at Girton,' said Lady Hardcastle, looking out of the window at the bright spring morning. 'Taught me physics. He used to say, "Miss Featherstonhaugh, whenever I find a problem intractable, I like to go for a long walk. Hills are best. Or forests. A forested hill is absolutely ideal. It's a shame our founders saw fit to build the university in Cambridgeshire. Very short on hills and forests. But the lanes suffice. Walk, Miss Featherstonhaugh. It will clear your mind and the solution will come." And over the years, his advice has repeatedly been proven sound. What do you say, Flo? Combe Woods? We haven't ever properly explored there. Perhaps the fresh air will inspire us.'

'Perhaps it will at that, my lady. Would you like to go now?'

'Why not? We're just going to mope about here otherwise. Let us find appropriate foot coverings and vestments and hie us to the forest.'

'Boots and coats, my lady. Right you are.'

'And my stick.'

'Really, my lady? You're sticking with the stick?'

'Possibly not in the long term,' she said. 'But a stick is always handy on a sylvan perambulation.'

As we walked into the village we were greeted by the postman. Moments later, Hilda Pantry waved to us from across the green as she gave the windows of her grocer's shop a wipe down with a piece of damp scrim.

We set out on the other road, up towards the woods, and found our way into the clearing where we had found Mr Pickering hanging from the oak tree the previous summer. Then, instead of heading back down the familiar path towards Toby Thompson's dairy farm, we took the path on the other side of the clearing, which we imagined would take us deeper into the woods.

'I say,' said Lady Hardcastle as we tramped along the still-muddy path. 'This is more like it, eh, Flo? I've missed our little walks.'

'Me too, my lady,' I said. 'I think I've learned a few things, too. Is that a beech tree?'

'No, dear, that's a sycamore.'

'I was close though, eh?' I said with a grin.

'No, dear, not really. But you get marks for trying.'

We laughed and strolled on.

After a few more minutes we came to another, smaller clearing and had a choice of paths. We took the left one and I soon saw something that would definitely improve my standing as a nature spotter. With birds and trees I stood no chance, but I prided myself that I knew a thing or two about food. When I saw a clump of mushrooms growing in the shade of an unidentified tree I strode boldly forwards and said, 'Chanterelles.'

Lady Hardcastle laughed delightedly. I was bending down to gather some when I was stopped in my tracks by a booming parade-ground voice yelling, 'Stop!'

Startled, we both turned to see who had shouted. A small, trim, elderly man was striding towards us. His clothes and cap were worn but meticulously well maintained, and his lined face was red with rage.

'What the blue blazes do you think you're doing?' he barked. 'Don't you stupid people know nothing?'

'I don't think we've met,' said Lady Hardcastle calmly. 'I'm Lady Hardcastle and this is my maid, Armstrong.'

'One more step and she'll be your former maid, the late Miss Armstrong,' he said, moving to grab my arm.

I stepped to one side and grasped his wrist, pulling it up and back into one of the pleasingly effective holds I'd learned during our time in China.

'Please don't do that, sir,' I said, just as calmly as Lady Hardcastle. 'It makes me anxious when people do that.'

He relaxed a little. 'It's all right, Miss Armstrong,' he said. 'You can put me down. I were trying to stop you harming yourselves, that's all.'

I released the hold and stepped away, alert for retaliation.

'That's quite a talent you have there, miss,' he said, rubbing his shoulder. 'Quite a talent.'

'Thank you,' I said. 'Would you care to explain yourself, Mr . . . ?'

'Halfpenny,' he said with a nod. 'Jedediah Halfpenny. Folk round here call me Old Jed. Can't say I care for it overmuch, but it seems to please 'em.'

'How do you do, Mr Halfpenny,' I said. 'And how were you saving us from harm?'

'Thy's the second damn fool I've seen round here pickin' them damn mushrooms,' he said. 'They're deadly webcap, Miss Armstrong, not blessed chanterelles. If thy wants chanterelles get to a fancy bloomin' greengrocer, or learn the difference.'

I was stunned. 'I take it from the name that deadly webcap aren't terribly good for you.'

'No, miss, clue's in't name, just as you say.'

'I say,' said Lady Hardcastle. 'Oh, I say!' she said again more forcefully.

'What, my lady?' I said.

'Mushrooms, dear, don't you see? Poisonous mushrooms.'

Realization dawned on me slightly more slowly, but I got there. 'An unidentified, deadly poison,' I said. 'Do you think this is it?'

'Do you know who it was that was picking the mushrooms, Mr Halfpenny?' said Lady Hardcastle.

'Can't say I know many of the folk round here by name,' he said. 'I try to keep meself to meself.'

'But could you describe him?'

'Can't say as how I could, no,' he said thoughtfully. 'He were over here, helpin' 'imself, then he were off 'fore I could get a proper look or even say owt. Stupid beggar.'

'He harvested some of these?' she said.

'Aye. Took a few by the look,' he said, frowning slightly.

'Are they dangerous to touch?' I said.

'Touching them won't do you no harm, but if you get even a tiny bit on your fingers and then it gets into your mouth from there, you've 'ad it.'

'Instantly?' asked Lady Hardcastle.

'What? No, takes a while. Up to a week sometimes.'

'Up to a week, Flo. Don't you see what this means?' she said, turning to me.

'Not entirely, my lady, no.'

'It means we've been idiots,' she said. 'We've been looking for fast-acting poisons that someone could have given him on the day he was killed, or the day before. What if he was poisoned with these deadly webwhatsits a whole week before?'

'On market day . . .' I said.

'. . . at The Hayrick . . .' she said.

'. . . in the beef and mushroom pie!' I finished. 'Gracious. Do you really think so?'

'Well, it's better than anything we've come up with so far. We need to talk to whatshisname at the pub.'

'Ronnie, my lady.'

'That's the chap. He cooked the pies.'

'But he didn't serve them; he was behind the bar. It was "the girl" who brought them out.'

'Plump woman with no teeth? Yes, she'd have to be in on it. Make sure the right man got the deadly pie,' she said.

'Now it's all terribly far-fetched again. Now it's a conspiracy,' I said dejectedly.

'Pardon me, ladies,' said Halfpenny politely.

'Yes, Mr Halfpenny?' said Lady Hardcastle.

'To tell t' truth, I prefer Jed, missus. But that i'n't it. Are you saying someone's been poisoned wi' these mushrooms?'

'It certainly looks that way, Jed,' she said, and she briefly recounted the events of the previous week.

231

'I see,' he said when she had finished. 'Well, it weren't a woman, I can tell thee that.'

'Could you even see if he were young or old?' she said.

'No, just saw a figure over here in t' woods. By the time I got here, he were gone and so were t' mushrooms.'

'If nothing else, it does give us a new poison to investigate,' I said.

'Quite so,' said Lady Hardcastle. 'Jed, it was a genuine pleasure to meet you. Is there a way we can contact you if we or the police need to talk to you again?'

'Police? Aye, I reckon they knows where to find me.'

'Oh?' she said.

'I'm "known" t' police,' he said. 'They reckon I'm a poacher.'

'And are you?'

He chuckled. 'Never been convicted, so I don't reckon so, no.'

She smiled. 'But they know where to find you.'

'Aye, they do. Old caravan over there a way.' He pointed deeper into the woods.

'Thank you, Jed, you've helped more than you know.'

'P'raps you could explain it to me some time.'

'I promise. Over there, you say? We'll come and find you. But for now you will excuse us, won't you? I rather think we've got a few fresh things to ponder upon – I need tea and a blackboard.'

He chuckled and bowed. 'As you wish, ma'am.'

We turned and walked back the way we had come, while Jed vanished back into the woods behind us.

'Unusual man,' said Lady Hardcastle as we walked back towards the road, filled with a newfound enthusiasm for the case.

'I rather liked him,' I said.

'Oh, I was definitely warming to him,' she said. 'And he seems like a very reliable witness. Oh, Flo, we've been so dense.'

'Dense, my lady?'

'All that messing about with rat poisons and who'd popped round for a cuppa. We should have been thinking on a much grander scale.'

'We should?'

'Always, dear. Always.'

It seemed like no time at all before we reached the road.

'Most mysteries offer up a mundane solution in the end, you know,' said Lady Hardcastle as I locked the door and we walked to the motor car on Wednesday morning. Lady Hardcastle had decided to drive.

'Even the murder of Mr Caradine?' I said.

'Actually, that could turn out to be a little more out of the ordinary, but I'd wager you'll still say, "Oh", in a disappointed tone if I'm proven correct. Mysteries are at their most interesting while they remain mysterious.'

The Gloucester Road took us all the way into Bristol and we saw few people until we arrived in the heart of the city. There were a few more motors, carts and carriages about as we climbed the slight hill towards the Bristol Royal Infirmary on Marlborough Street, our first stop.

'This is a surprise,' I said as we drew up outside the entrance.

'Just a quick visit to that old university friend I mentioned, dear,' she said. 'I'm sure he won't mind helping us out.'

After a long walk down echoing corridors that smelled strongly of disinfectant, we finally arrived at a closed door the brass nameplate of which declared it to be the office of Dr Simeon Gosling. Lady Hardcastle knocked.

'Yes? What?' said an irritated voice from inside.

She opened the door and we both stepped tentatively into the cramped office.

A bespectacled man of about Lady Hardcastle's age was sitting behind a desk piled high with folders and papers. His expensive-looking suit was rumpled and his collar slightly askew. Without looking up, he said, 'Look, I really am most fearfully busy. Can you just leave whatever it is there and I'll deal with it presently.'

'Good morning to you too, Sim, dear,' said Lady Hardcastle cheerfully.

He looked up and his weary face broke into a smile that made him look a great deal more handsome than I had at first thought. He stood, knocking a teetering pile of paper to the floor.

'Emily! What ho, my darling girl. How the devil are you? What a delight.'

'Uncommonly well, thank you, dear,' she said, leaning across the chaos of the desk to greet him with a kiss on the cheek.

'I heard you'd been in the wars, old girl,' he said, looking her up and down. 'But you're looking well on it, whatever it was. Sit down, do.'

'Thank you, dear. This is Armstrong.'

'I've heard only good things. Welcome to my lair, Miss Armstrong. My apologies for the mess; it's so hard to find decent help these days. Don't fancy a part-time job on the side, I suppose?'

'Full time if you like, sir,' I said, sitting down on one of the rickety bentwood chairs. 'I can start on Monday.'

Lady Hardcastle harrumphed.

'So what can I do for you, Emily?' he asked. 'I presume this isn't a purely social call.'

'I regret to have to admit that it isn't, darling, no. Though we really must have lunch soon.'

'Any time you like,' he said with a smile. 'We have a delightful canteen.'

'I'm sure that would be charming,' she said, and he laughed. 'But for now, dear, I need to pick your considerable brains. What do you know about poisonous fungi?'

'A little,' he said. 'Why? Planning to do someone in?'

'Not quite, but it might have something to do with a case we're working on.' Once again she ran succinctly through the events of the past month, this time starting with our trip to the cattle market with Lady Farley-Stroud and Maude Denton. When she had finished, she handed over the manila folder that Inspector Sunderland had given us.

'Well I never,' said Dr Gosling once he had finished skimming through the contents of the file. 'What a world you live in. I thought it was all country dancing and "Who's Got the Prettiest Pig?" competitions out there.'

'"Out there"?' said Lady Hardcastle with a laugh. 'We're about fifteen miles away. "Out there" indeed!'

'You know what I mean,' he said. 'It's scarcely the beating heart of modern civilization, is it?'

'Perhaps not, dear. But unfortunately they still find the time between all the country dancing and pig fancying to do each other to death over the slightest things.'

'And deadly webcap is a particularly nasty way to do it,' he said after a moment's consideration.

'You think it's possible?' she said. 'Could it be the mushrooms?'

'Well, the symptoms fit, certainly,' he said. 'We don't know much about the poison, but its effects are well documented.' He got up and reached down a thick book from the shelves beside his desk. 'If the mushrooms were in his pie on market day,' he said, riffling through the pages to find the reference he was after, 'then the timing is right, too. Here we are, Deadly Webcap, Cortinarius speciosissimus . . . He'd have started feeling poorly a few days later: stomach pains, headache, nausea and the like. It would have seemed like influenza or something similar. Then once the kidney damage started to show, he'd have had all sorts of problems with his waterworks that he'd most likely have kept to himself. Hang on . . .' He looked back at the file. 'Ah, yes, here it is. One of the witnesses says he looked a little "funny coloured". Jaundice is another sign. Convulsions and death usually come in about a week. I'm surprised he hadn't succumbed to the effects sooner, though. It says here victims usually slip into a coma.'

'Strong as oxen, these farming types. It's all the country dancing,' said Lady Hardcastle thoughtfully. 'But you think it's possible?'

'I'd have to run a few tests of my own on the body to be certain,' he said. 'But the police surgeon's report is very thorough and he has taken great pains to rule out most other possible causes. He's definitely of the opinion that it's some sort of poison rather than illness or infection. So, yes, on balance I'd say it's extremely possible. Is that what you wanted to hear?'

'One always likes to have one's hypotheses validated, so, yes, it is,' she said. 'The world would be a much nicer place if he had died of natural causes, I suppose, but if it has to be murder, I'd rather be right about the method than not.'

'Do you have a suspect?' he asked.

'As a matter of fact,' she said, 'I do. But I need to confirm another matter before I'm certain. That's our next stop.'

'How exciting. Will you let me know how you get on?'

'Of course, darling. The Crown might need an expert witness when it gets to trial.'

'Not sure that's me, old girl,' he said modestly. 'But I can put you in touch with a chap at Bart's – he's quite utterly utter when it comes to organic poisons.'

'Thank you, darling. And thank you for letting us interrupt you this morning. You look frightfully busy.'

He looked ruefully at the paper-strewn desk. 'Trying to prepare a report for the Board on post-operative infection rates.'

'Well, that sounds rather important,' she said, standing. 'We shall leave you to it. Are you still at the same address in Clifton?'

'I am, yes.'

'Then expect my invitation to lunch very soon,' she said, leaning across the desk to kiss him goodbye.

'I shall look forward to it.'

He was already writing as I shut the door behind us.

'That was very encouraging,' said Lady Hardcastle as we navigated our way back through the maze of hospital corridors to the entrance.

'It was?' I said, still somewhat nonplussed.

'Yes, very much so. There's been something nagging at me since we started all this, something I only confirmed when I looked at my notes yesterday, and having Simeon confirm that it could easily have been the mushrooms makes my latest hypothesis possible.'

'You're not going to tell me, are you?' I said as we emerged into the spring sunshine.

'No, dear. Poor Emily needs to be indulged.' She clutched her side. 'I've been poorly.'

I frowned. 'You know you're not going to be able to get away with that for much longer, don't you, my lady.'

'Just a little longer,' she said with a mischievous smile.

'Hmmm,' I said. I started the engine.

'Where to now, my lady?'

'Into the middle of the city,' she said. 'First I shall drop you off at the police station. Then I shall pop round to my solicitors' offices in Small Street.'

'Righto, my lady. Finally turning me in, eh?'

'It's not before time, is it, dear?' she said, waving a casual apology to the delivery boy she'd nearly run down. 'You're a menace to society.'

'I've been led astray,' I said.

'Quite so, quite so. I'll be along later to turn myself in as well. An accomplice at the very least. But seriously. I shall be asking my solicitor to look into a few matters for me. While I'm doing that you're to visit dear Inspector Sunderland and make him fully acquainted with the latest developments. Then I want you to invite him to lunch at The Hayrick tomorrow.'

'Market day,' I said.

'Market day, yes. And tell him to bring a couple of friends. The burlier the better.'

'You expect him to be able to make an arrest, my lady?' I said.

'If all goes according to plan, we shall prevent another tragedy and he should be able to cart the villain away with him.'

'I shall advise him of the possible need for a black maria, my lady.'

'Good girl.'

'And then lunch?'

'I say,' she said. 'What a good idea. We should have invited Sim.'

'I'm not sure he could spare the time, my lady. He looked snowed under.'

'Good point, dear, good point.'

We pulled up outside the police station on Bridewell Street. 'This is your stop, dear,' she said. 'I shall be around the corner on Small Street. The offices of Pentelow, Paddock, Playfair & Pugh, Solicitors. Green door. Can't miss it.'

I hopped out.

'I'll see you there, my lady.'

'Right you are,' she said. 'Tell Inspector Sunderland anything he wants to know and blame me for any gaps in your knowledge.'

At police headquarters, I stood at the front desk waiting patiently for the extravagantly bearded sergeant to notice me. After half a minute I cleared my throat.

The sergeant looked up briefly from his ledger, took in my driving coat and hat, and returned at once to his columns of figures. 'Be with you in a moment, miss,' he said distractedly.

I waited another minute, watching the time pass on the large clock on the wall above the sergeant's head. I cleared my throat again.

The sergeant looked up impatiently. 'I said I would be with you in a moment, miss.'

'You did, Sergeant,' I said calmly. 'And several moments have passed. I shan't take up much of your time. I just wish to see Inspector Sunderland.'

'Do you, indeed?' he said. 'Well, I dare say the inspector's a very busy man. And so am I. Please wait a moment.' He returned to the ledger once more.

'The thing is, you see, that I'm really rather busy myself,' I said, still calmly and politely. 'I see there's a bell beside you there. I would wager that all you need do is to ring it and an eager young messenger will appear. You might then instruct him to carry word to Inspector Sunderland that Miss Armstrong wishes to speak to him. It would have taken you less time to do that than it has so far taken you to play this silly game of "I'm More Important Than You".'

I smiled sweetly.

'Now listen here, you impertinent—'

There were footsteps on the stairs to my right and two men came into view, chatting amiably. One of them was Inspector Sunderland.

'Miss Armstrong!' he said with evident surprise. 'Fancy seeing you here. I thought you were going to telephone.'

I turned my back on the still-fuming desk sergeant. 'Good morning, Inspector,' I said. 'I believe there might have been some talk of telephones but Lady Hardcastle happened to be in the area so I've come to bring our news in person.'

'There's news?' he said, raising one eyebrow.

'Some, sir. And a fair amount of infuriating winking and just-you-wait-and-see-ing.'

He laughed. 'Come upstairs. I'll find a room where we can talk privately.' He turned to the younger man who had accompanied him down the stairs. 'I'll leave it in your hands, Portman. And get some uniformed constables to check the sewers. They're getting in there somehow.'

The young man nodded his assent and marched briskly out of the station.

'This way, Miss Armstrong,' said Inspector Sunderland and he started walking back up the stairs. He turned back after a few steps. 'Tea for two, please, Sergeant. Interview Room Three, I think.'

The sergeant mumbled his resentful acknowledgement.

I followed the inspector up the stairs and along a linoleum-floored corridor to a door with a frosted-glass window upon which the words 'Interview Room 3' were written in black.

'Come on in,' said the inspector, opening the door. 'We'll not be interrupted in here.'

I followed him into the bare room and we sat at opposite sides of the table.

'It's not quite as comfortable as your dining room,' he said, pulling his notebook from his jacket pocket. 'But it's all we have.'

'It's fine, Inspector,' I said with a smile. 'It's not the first police interview room I've been in.'

'No, miss, I don't expect it is. Though I don't suppose you've sat on that side of the table before.'

'Oh, you'd be surprised, Inspector,' I said. 'Not so often in England, but foreign police forces haven't always been quite as pleased to see us over the years as one might have hoped.'

He laughed. 'I dare say your particular brand of mischief doesn't go down too well with unfriendly foreign governments, no.'

'I can never understand why,' I said. 'We're just exhibiting a natural and exuberant curiosity for the most part.'

'By stealing their secrets.'

'Well, yes, I suppose when you put it like that . . .'

There was a knock at the door. In came Sergeant Massive Beard with a tray bearing a pot of tea, two cups, a small jug of milk and a few sugar cubes in a bowl. He looked at me sullenly, but said nothing.

'Thank you, Sergeant,' said the inspector and he waited for him to leave. 'He's a surly old cuss,' he said once the door was shut and we heard his boots clomping off down the corridor.

'There's always one,' I said.

'There is, but I don't properly understand why we have to put our one on the front desk where he can antagonize the public.'

I poured the tea.

'So, Miss Armstrong of Littleton Cotterell,' he said, picking up his pencil and preparing to make notes. 'What news of the murder of Spencer Caradine, late of Top Farm? Has much happened since Monday?'

'Not so very much, but I think it's turning out to be rather significant,' I said. I told him about the walk in the woods and our encounter with Jed Halfpenny.

'I think I remember that name,' said the inspector. 'Little chap? Very neat? North Country accent. Ex-Army, I think.'

'I say,' I said. 'I didn't realize he was famous. It sounds like the same man. He lives in a caravan in the woods.'

'Yes, yes, that's the chap,' he said, looking up at the smoke-stained ceiling as he tried to recall. 'He was staying up on the Downs for a while, minding his own business, but the locals took a dislike to him and drove him out. He helped us out with a tricky case involving a missing bank clerk, though, I think. Decent chap.'

'Quite so,' I said, returning to my narrative. 'He told us about the mushrooms, so this morning we visited an old friend of Lady Hardcastle's at the hospital. He agrees that it could well be deadly webcap that killed Mr Caradine. And because it can take up to a week, it means he was mostly likely poisoned much earlier than we all thought.'

'A week, eh? So that puts all sorts of new people in the frame. Including you, actually. Didn't you see him a week before he died?'

'We did, Inspector,' I said. 'And that brings me to the main reason for my visit.'

'You're going to confess? That would clear things up very neatly.'

'No, silly. If I'd done it, you'd never even find the body.'

He looked suddenly rather chilled. I had to smile to let him know that I was at least half joking.

'No,' I said, slightly more brightly. 'But Lady Hardcastle does think she's close to solving the case. She's paying a visit to her solicitor even as we speak to clear up some question or other, but please don't ask me what because that's one of the things she's being infuriatingly coy about.'

'When will we be allowed to know the results of her abductions?'

'Abductions?' I asked with a frown. 'Not deductions?'

'No, miss, definitely abductions.'

'I see,' I said. I had a vague memory of Lady Hardcastle making a fuss about it once before. 'Tomorrow. At twelve o'clock. At The Hayrick in Chipping Bevington. She said something about averting another tragedy. She also says you're to bring burly companions and a black maria and to expect to make an arrest.'

He chuckled his familiar throaty chuckle. 'Does she, indeed. Well, if it were anyone else I'd make them sweat for their impudence, but since it's her, I shall see what I can do.'

'Thank you, Inspector, you're an absolute poppet.'

'I am on the quiet, miss. But don't let on round here. I have a reputation as a stickler and a martinet to maintain.'

'Your secret is safe with me,' I said, finishing my tea. 'But I mustn't keep you. It seems you're hot on the trail of your bank robbers, too.'

'Not much gets past you, does it?' he said. 'Yes, I'm pretty sure it's got something to do with the sewers but my boys are on to them now. All I have to do is keep an eye on things.'

'How exciting,' I said, standing up and straightening my coat. 'Do you want to give me a black eye, just to make it look convincing?'

He laughed. 'I can't imagine many people managing to give you even a playful slap, Miss Armstrong. I'm not sure anyone would believe I'd blackened your eye.'

'Just thought I'd offer. Don't want your men thinking you're too soft on witnesses.'

'You're more by way of being "consulting detectives", miss,' he said. 'We don't beat up our consultants. Once one has that reputation it makes it very difficult to engage anyone else.'

'Consulting detectives,' I said. 'I like the sound of that. Like Sherlock Holmes.'

'I suppose so, miss, yes. But slightly easier to get along with, I'd wager.'

I smiled and offered my hand, which he shook warmly.

'Until tomorrow,' I said.

'I'm already looking forward to it,' he said. 'Here, I'll show you out.'

He led me back along the corridor and down the stairs. I gave Sergeant Massive Beard a cheery wave as I went out through the main door. He glared at me.

As I walked down the steps I could just about hear Inspector Sunderland barking a rebuke at Sergeant Massive Beard for being rude to members of the public.

I was still smiling as Lady Hardcastle came round the corner in the Rover.

'What splendid timing,' she said as I hopped in. 'It went well, I take it? You're terribly grinny.'

'Very well indeed, my lady. The inspector will join us for lunch tomorrow.'

'Splendid, splendid,' she said, crunching the gears. 'Mr Pentelow hopes to be able to send me a telegram by tomorrow morning to confirm my suspicions. After that we're all set for arrests and justice.'

'And you're still not going to tell me anything further,' I said as I slid in beside her.

'No, dear.' She clutched her side melodramatically. 'Poorly, remember? Need to be indulged.'

By the time we awoke on Thursday morning it was raining heavily.

'We're jinxed,' said Lady Hardcastle looking out of the kitchen window as we ate our breakfast. 'We should warn the farmers whenever we intend to attend the market so that they can make appropriate wet-weather arrangements.'

'We shall be attending often?' I said with ill-concealed dismay.

'Of course. Poor Gertie could do with the company.'

'But,' I said. 'Cows.'

She was still laughing at my disappointment when the doorbell rang.

It was the telegram boy, drenched to the skin but as cheeky as ever. I gave him a few coppers and he skipped off back down the lane with a cheery, 'Thanks, missus.'

I took the damp message through to Lady Hardcastle, who read it with satisfaction bordering on glee.

'It's all coming together nicely,' she said as I tidied away the breakfast things. 'And just in time, too. Bert will be here very soon with Gertie.'

I finished my tidying, and we went to the hall to put on hats, coats and galoshes in readiness for Bert's inevitably precise ten o'clock arrival. The clock began to chime. Just as it started to strike the hour, I opened the door to find a grinning Bert about to press the doorbell.

'Caught you,' I said.

He grinned even more broadly. 'Good morning, miss. Good morning, m'lady. Are you all set?'

'As ready as ready can be, Bert,' said Lady Hardcastle. 'To market, to market, to catch us a killer.'

'Home again, home again,' I said. 'Er . . . to drink to our wonderful success with the delicious produce of a fine French distiller.'

'Needs work, dear,' she said. 'But you can do it later. Let's go before Bert drowns.'

We bundled ourselves into the car and were greeted enthusiastically by Lady Farley-Stroud who seemed rather excited at the thought of being in the thick of things.

'Now, Gertie,' said Lady Hardcastle as we set off, 'you're not to get too giddy, darling. Inspector Sunderland and his men will be arriving at noon and I shall explain all then.'

'Oh, I say,' said Lady Farley-Stroud. 'How marvellous. A big theatrical dénouement like they do in the stories? Everyone gathered around and you explaining everything like a detective in a story?'

Lady Hardcastle laughed. 'I hadn't thought of doing it like that, dear, but it might be fun. What do you think, Flo?'

'I think you can't resist showing off, my lady, so I'm sure some sort of performance is inevitable. Though if you could avoid getting yourself wounded, that would be splendid.'

She and Lady Farley-Stroud laughed at this and Bert, sitting beside me, tried decorously to conceal his smile.

'We mustn't lose sight of the fact that we intend to apprehend a murderer, ladies,' said Lady Hardcastle.

'No, dear, quite,' said Lady Farley-Stroud. 'But you must admit that it is all rather exciting.'

'I confess I do get something of a thrill from it,' said Lady Hardcastle. 'But I think a more quiet and subtle approach might be more suitable this time.'

16

It took three-quarters of an hour to wind through the rain-soaked lanes to Chipping Bevington, and another ten minutes of tedious driving around trying to find somewhere to park amid the exuberant chaos of market day.

By the time we had disembarked and taken a stroll down the High Street and back (with some moments of mild terror occasioned by the ever-present bovine menace) it was almost time for our rendezvous with Inspector Sunderland at The Hayrick.

The rain had finally stopped by the time we walked round the corner and saw a damp Inspector Sunderland waiting outside the pub. There was no sign of the police wagon or of any other officers.

'Good morning, Inspector,' said Lady Hardcastle as we approached.

'Good morning, my lady. Oh, "my ladies", I do beg your pardon, Lady Farley-Stroud.'

'Good morning, Inspector,' said Lady Farley-Stroud brightly. 'May I wish you joy of the day, sir.'

'Yes, Inspector,' said Lady Hardcastle. 'Good hunting. Are your men here?'

'Yes, I thought it might be best to keep them out of sight. Since you've been reluctant to tell anyone who he or she might be, I didn't want to spook your suspect by having a load of coppers lounging about the place. But they're here, and so's the wagon. I'll have a couple round the front and a couple round the back once we go in. No one will get in or out without our knowing about it.'

'Splendid, splendid,' said Lady Hardcastle. 'Well, I think it's time we made our entrance, don't you? Are you ready, ladies?'

Lady Farley-Stroud and I both nodded and the four of us went into the pub.

As we'd seen before, the pub was bedlam on market day, filled with raucous laughter and oath-filled conversation. As we filed in, the noise lessened considerably. Heads turned towards us and the loud chatter became a suspicious murmur.

Noah Lock and Dick Ackley were sitting together in the far corner. Lancelot Tribley was making his way back from the bar with three pints of cider. He joined his friends.

Morris Caradine sat at another table with his mother. A last trip to the market before they were both free, perhaps.

Lofty Trevellian was sharing a joke with a similarly flour-covered friend.

Somehow our presence had frozen everyone. Food went uneaten, drinks undrunk.

We followed Lady Hardcastle to the bar where she leaned across to have a word with Ronnie, the landlord. He looked up, first at me, then at the inspector. He nodded and motioned us to follow him. We went through into the kitchen, with Lady Farley-Stroud bringing up the rear. After a moment we were joined by the toothless serving girl who had brought us our pies and cider the fortnight before.

'This is my sister Hilda, m'lady,' said Ronnie.

The woman eyed us nervously.

'Good morning, Hilda,' said Lady Hardcastle kindly. 'Ronnie tells me you've been worried about something.'

Hilda's eyes flicked anxiously to her brother and then back to the floor. Ronnie nodded his encouragement but she was still reluctant to speak.

'You think you might be in trouble?' said Lady Hardcastle.

'Stands to reason, don't it?' said Hilda.

'How's that, dear?'

'He was poisoned with food I brung him. They's all sayin' it. But I a'n't done nothin', I swears.'

'It wasn't you?'

'I swears it,' said Hilda, a tear slipping down her pock-marked cheek.

'So why are they saying it was you?'

'Weren't no one else in the kitchen that week. I told the coppers that. So now they all reckons I must-'a done sommat. They wouldn't say nothin' about our Ronnie. But it weren't 'im, neither.'

'And nor was it that week's pie that killed him,' said Lady Hardcastle.

'But he were killed right here in the pub that market day,' said Hilda. 'I saw him. Horrible, it was.'

'No,' said Lady Hardcastle, 'he died here that day. But he was murdered the week before. Everyone has been talking about the day he died, but I'd wager no one has asked you about the week before.'

'No, missus, they hasn't,' lisped Hilda through her missing teeth.

'And did anything odd happen the week before? Did anyone come into the kitchen?'

'Not as far as I . . . Oh,' said Hilda, clearly recalling something. 'There was someone here. I went out to take some orders to some of the lads from Oldbury, and when I come back there was—'

'No,' interrupted Lady Hardcastle, 'let me have my moment. The man you found in your kitchen on that fateful market day, Hilda, was Lancelot Tribley.'

'It was,' said Hilda. 'And he was here again today, too.'

'Today?' said Lady Hardcastle. 'Oh, my word, we're too late.'

'I presume you have a full explanation, my lady,' said the inspector.

'Full. Thorough. And rather too long-winded to trouble you with for the moment. We need to move quickly.'

Lady Hardcastle rushed back into the bar. Scanning about, she lit upon Lofty Trevellian about to tuck into his beef and mushroom pie.

She ran over to him. She snatched the fork from his hand. Pushed the plate across the table.

'I would strongly advise against eating the pie, Lofty, dear,' she said.

He looked blank.

'It's poisoned,' she said blandly.

Lofty gaped at her. Several other diners threw down their own forks.

'Don't worry,' she said, 'It's just his. Enjoy your lunches.'

There was a commotion near the door. Lofty was still gaping.

'I'll explain later,' she said. 'We have to arrest Mr Tribley. Inspector? Do hurry, dear, he's getting away.'

The inspector tutted but seemed otherwise unconcerned. 'Come on, then, ladies,' he said calmly. 'We'd better go and see.'

We trooped out after the inspector.

Lancelot Tribley was sitting on the pavement outside the pub sporting a split lip. He looked absolutely livid.

A uniformed constable was standing over him while another carried on watching the door. 'Caught this one trying to leg it, Inspector,' said the first. 'He . . . er . . . he resisted my attempts to reason with him. A bit. So I . . . er . . .'

'I can see what you, "er",' said Inspector Sunderland. 'Lancelot Tribley, I am arresting you on suspicion of the murder of Spencer Caradine. Anything you say may be taken down in writing and may be used against you at your trial. Constables, help him up and get him to the wagon.'

'You'll want to bring some other charges, too, Inspector,' said Lady Hardcastle. 'But I'm sure that can wait.'

The two uniformed policemen lifted the muscular farmer to his feet and started to lead him away. Some of The Hayrick's regulars were already out on the pavement and were parting to allow the constables through, while the rest looked out through the windows. Tribley turned his head and noticed that there was no one blocking the street behind him except two well-dressed ladies and a slightly built maid. I saw the decision flicker behind his eyes an instant before he broke free from the two constables and charged towards us, aiming directly for me.

His old rugby skills hadn't deserted him. He was head down, knees pumping, like a centre running for the try line. There was nothing on his mind except barging me aside and breaking for freedom. The boys back home in the valleys had taught me plenty of rugby skills as a girl, and I was briefly tempted simply to tackle him. But a Shaolin monk had taught me some infinitely more interesting tricks as we fled through China all those years ago and I had a childish desire to have a little fun.

I let him get close enough to think he was going to get away with it before stepping lightly to one side and following through with a move that would have made Chen Ping Bo beam proudly. I grabbed his coat as he passed me, shifted my balance and threw him, leaving him sprawling on the cobbles.

The assembled farmers cheered and were still laughing as the chagrined constables caught up with him, lifted him to his feet once more and led him away. I bowed to the crowd.

The inspector sighed. 'Perhaps you might try handcuffs, lads?'

The inspector began to lead us away to Bert and the waiting car, but the farmers were still milling around and began to bombard us with questions. He deftly deflected their entreaties for more information, telling them that there would be a full report in due course.

'Thank you for all your help,' he said as we finally reached the car and climbed in. 'Of course you'll be called upon for statements and the like, but for now I advise you to get yourselves home and leave the rest to us. If any newspaper reporters buttonhole you, say nothing and refer them to me.'

'Thank you, Inspector,' said Lady Hardcastle. 'That was fun.'

'I'll be in touch, my lady,' he said, and he banged on the roof of the car to signal Bert to leave.

We went straight back to The Grange where Lady Farley-Stroud exuberantly recounted the day's events to Sir Hector. She proclaimed that having Lady Hardcastle as a neighbour and friend was quite the most exciting thing to have happened to her for years. Sir Hector listened with affectionate patience and asked a few clarifying questions when his wife's commentary lapsed into hyperbole.

They invited us to stay for tea (which Sir Hector still endearingly referred to as 'tiffin') and we gratefully accepted, pleased to be able to enjoy Mrs Brown's celebrated sandwiches and cakes. We were just settling down to eat when Jenkins announced the arrival of Inspector Sunderland.

'Inspector,' said Lady Farley-Stroud expansively. 'Join us, do. We're celebrating Lady Hardcastle's brilliance.'

'Thank you, my lady,' said the inspector. 'Most kind. It was actually Lady Hardcastle that I came to see.' He sat in the chair that Jenkins had pulled out for him.

'Me, Inspector?' said Lady Hardcastle.

'You, my lady. I've had no involvement in this case whatsoever but now I shall be expected to take over. You said you had a full explanation.'

'Ah, yes, I did.'

'And there are other charges?' he said.

'Indeed there are. Actually, it was the other charges that put me on to Tribley in the end.'

'I'm all ears,' he said, tucking in to a slice of cake.

'You've heard, I presume, about the other goings-on in the village these past couple of weeks?'

'Some trophies stolen from the rugby club and a couple of hoaxers arrested for witchcraft, I believe.'

'Just so. Where to begin? Do you want the sequence of events or the explanation of our joint brilliance?'

'Start with the what and why, my lady, then move on to the how.'

'Very well,' she said. 'It begins with a very unhappy man. Tribley hated his farm and wanted more than anything to get away. He's a rather talented chef. He'd been working in a splendid hotel in the Midlands when his brother died, leaving him the farm. So he'd ended up there, against his will, having to keep the farm running while he looked for a buyer. All the while, desperate to return to the culinary life he loved.'

'No buyers were forthcoming, I suppose,' said the inspector.

'Not a one. Until one day he was approached by Messrs Ferwinkle and Papworth in Gloucester who were acting on behalf of a local property developer, with a view to acquiring his land to build new houses. My own solicitors did some digging for me and wired me the details. His prayers had very nearly been answered, but there was a snag. The developers' plans were entirely dependent upon also acquiring the land next door, owned by Spencer Caradine.'

'And Caradine being Caradine,' said Lady Farley-Stroud, 'refused to sell.'

'Exactly so,' said Lady Hardcastle. 'It would have set him up in a comfortable retirement, but it gave him much more satisfaction to deny Tribley his chance to escape. Tribley knew that if Caradine were suddenly to die, Audrey would give the farm to her son and marry Lock, and he knew that Morris would sell to the first person who offered him anything like the asking price so that he could move away. That, in turn, would mean that his own sale could go through. And the only person standing in the way was Spencer Caradine.'

'So Caradine died,' said the inspector.

'He did. By this time Tribley had refined his plan. Not only was he going to sell up and move away, he was also going to take the woman of his dreams, Winnie Marsh. And that presented another problem. Winnie Marsh was sweet on Lofty Trevellian. He needed to get Trevellian out of the way as well.'

'So the blighter made it look like poor Lofty had robbed the club,' said Sir Hector indignantly.

'That was the plan, yes. Tribley made it look like it was Trevellian to discredit the poor man. He must have thought that if Trevellian was disgraced, his own path to happiness with Winnie Marsh would be clear.'

'Good lord,' said Sir Hector. 'How on earth . . . ?'

'We'll get to that in a moment, dear,' she said. 'Poor old Tribley's problems didn't end there, you see. Shortly after Caradine died, the new chap in the village, Mr Nelson Snelson, decided he liked the area well enough to want to settle here. He made Morris Caradine an offer for his farm. Suddenly Morris had two offers and there was no guarantee that he would take the "right" one, so Snelson had to be got out of the way, too. He couldn't kill him – another death would be far too suspicious. The false accusation ploy had worked well with Trevellian, but two fake thefts would be just as suspicious as two murders. Notwithstanding the difficulty in arranging another fake theft.'

'Are you saying that he organized the haunting?' I asked.

'I think there was more than a little luck and opportunism in it,' she said. 'But, yes, I think we'll find that he knew Queenie and Lizzie from his days in the hotels of Birmingham.'

The inspector was scribbling notes as fast as he was able.

'That all sounds very plausible, my lady,' he said. 'I'll need some more details before I can take it before a magistrate, though.'

'Of course, Inspector. Of course.'

'I should very much like to hear it, too,' said Lady Farley-Stroud. 'Shall we retire to the library? I don't think it's too early for brandy, do you?'

Chairs were wrestled into place around one of the low tables in the library. Sir Hector poured us each a generous measure of brandy.

'Well, now,' said Lady Hardcastle, settling down. 'Let me see if I can explain it all. Shall we start with the poisoning?'

'Yes, please,' said Lady Farley-Stroud eagerly.

'At first, the most obvious suspects seemed to be Mrs Caradine and her would-be suitor. They were my definite favourites for a while. With the old man gone, their path to true love would be clear. But then we met Morris Caradine, the bullied son. We were told he was a wet lettuce, and against all my noblest intentions, his stammer made me think he wasn't quite the full shilling. But when we spoke to him we found that he was all there and halfway back, and I began wondering if he'd done away with his tyrannical father. Of course, Caradine's old "friend" Dick Ackley's rivalry might easily have turned deadly, so he had to be on the list, too.'

'Those were always my main suspects, too, my lady,' said the inspector.

'It was when Armstrong here tried to pick some mushrooms that things became a lot clearer. We were warned off them by . . . by . . .'

'Jed, my lady,' I prompted.

'Yes, by Jed, because although they looked ever so very much like delicious chanterelle mushrooms they were, in fact, an altogether less healthy variety called deadly webcap. I was immediately put in mind of your new umbrella stand, Gertie, dear.'

'My umbrella stand?' said Lady Farley-Stroud.

'Yes, dear. The one you bought from . . . from . . .'

'Pomphrey's, my lady,' I said, trying not to roll my eyes.

'Pomphrey's, yes. The elephant's-foot umbrella stand that looks just like the real thing. Those mushrooms in the woods looked just like chanterelles. Then I remembered that there were chanterelle mushrooms in the pies.'

'Ronnie told me that he'd been using chanterelles for a few weeks,' said Lady Farley-Stroud. 'Added a touch of class, he said.'

'Quite so,' said Lady Hardcastle. 'So, if someone hit upon the idea of committing murder using deadly webcap mushrooms, then the pies in The Hayrick would be an ideal place to hide them. But that's ridiculous. Who among his customers would even know that he used chanterelle mushrooms? Who would think of such a convoluted way of killing someone? It was altogether too far-fetched.'

'I've seen more convoluted plans in my line of work, my lady,' said the inspector.

'I'm sure you have. It was when we visited my dear old friend Dr Gosling at the BRI that I suddenly had the ideal suspect. Sim told us that deadly webcap can take up to a week to kill, you see. We needed to be looking for someone who was in the pub the week before Caradine died, and who would have known all about mushrooms and how best to serve them.'

'A frustrated chef,' I said.

'Just so. Tribley had positioned himself near the door to the kitchen that day. Do you remember, Gertie? He was at the end of the bar when you pointed him out to us.'

'I say,' said Lady Farley-Stroud. 'So he was.'

'He waited there until Caradine came to the bar to order his lunch. While Hilda was delivering someone else's order, he slipped into the kitchen and popped his deadly mushrooms into the next pie in line. It was risky – he might well have poisoned the wrong pie – but he was a desperate man and it was a gamble he was prepared to take. Hilda came back just as he was leaving, but didn't think anything of it. Then he slipped back to his place at the bar and stayed there supping and chatting until he was sure that his plan had worked.'

'It was very risky,' said the inspector. 'He could have killed anyone. He had no guarantee that Caradine would have eaten the pie.'

'No guarantee, no. As well as being somewhat desperate, though, he's also a very self-assured man. Arrogant, even. I'd wager he imagined that his planning was quite thorough. Even if he did consider the possibility of error he would have dismissed it as impossible. A man like him doesn't make mistakes.'

'Surely he'd never have got away with it,' said Lady Farley-Stroud.

'Why not? I expect it was Tribley who suggested the chanterelles to Ronnie. He'd been working on his plan for a while. And I'd wager he was confident that even if anyone worked out that it was mushroom poisoning, they would blame Ronnie anyway. "It's an easy but tragic mistake to make," people would say. "Poor old Ronnie accidentally picked poisonous mushrooms one day." He was building his own alibi.'

'Nasty piece of work,' said Sir Hector.

'Just so,' said Lady Hardcastle. 'And he made sure that he wasn't at the pub the day Caradine died, too.'

Inspector Sunderland finished his notes. 'That seems to be enough to be getting on with for the murder, then. I'll get some of the lads to search his farmhouse. We might find these deadly webcaps there.'

'You might, Inspector,' said Lady Hardcastle. 'Make certain that they wear gloves – the "deadly" part of the name "deadly webcap" isn't just poetic.'

'Duly noted, my lady,' he said. 'Now I've heard all about the fake hauntings from Dobson. I don't think we can get Tribley on any of that, but it's interesting to know that he was behind it. What's all this about the rugby club, though? I've not really had any details there.'

Lady Hardcastle briefly outlined our investigations and made a special point of playing up my involvement over the 'gimmicked' cabinet.

'Sterling work, Miss Armstrong. You've clearly a gift for uncovering tricks and chicanery.'

'Thank you, Inspector,' I said. 'Sooner or later my background was bound to come in useful.'

'She's a tiny Welsh marvel, Inspector, she really is,' said Lady Hardcastle.

'But how did the blasted chap do it?' asked Sir Hector.

'Let's start at the beginning,' she said. 'On the night of the rugby club dinner, we enjoyed a delicious meal at the Grey Goose. After the speeches, the ladies retired discreetly while you gentlemen returned here to the club to . . . to . . . whatever on earth is it that you do that makes you so ashamed that you can't bear to speak of it in front of ladies. No matter. You indulged yourselves with drink and carousing until shortly after dawn.'

'A fine night,' said Sir Hector.

'He was barely seen at all on Saturday except to demand water and aspirin,' said his wife affectionately.

'The last four to leave the club house were Donovan Trevellian, Jim Meaker, Lancelot Tribley and Dick Ackley. They walked home through the village while some unseen and unknown stranger entered the clubhouse through the unlocked storeroom door. He stepped in some oil and left a trail of bootprints as he ransacked the committee room and stole the Wessex Challenge Cup and a few other mementoes. The police were summoned by the caretaker in the morning and bafflement ensued.'

'That much I got from the sergeant,' said Inspector Sunderland.

'Yes,' she said, 'except that's not what happened. The robbery, if we can call it a robbery, took place earlier that night while everyone was still at the club. I may have some of the specifics a little wrong, but I believe I have the general outline of things. While the revels and roistering continued, Tribley slipped out to the storeroom and indulged in a little deception. He'd been planning it for some little while. Perhaps the idea had come to him when he saw Lofty Trevellian's old boots in the dressing room and decided to steal them. Perhaps he had formulated the plan much earlier and was just waiting for an opportunity to pinch the boots. Whatever the case, the boots were the key to his plan.'

'His plan to discredit his love rival?' said Lady Farley-Stroud.

'Indeed. On the night of the dinner, he retrieved those distinctively large old boots from their hiding place, put them on, and set about laying a trail. Knocking the oil can over was an inspired choice – oil cans are spilled all the time in tool sheds – but I suspect he had also considered whitewash or paint. Anything that would leave a clear trail of size-twelve bootprints would do. With the boots on and the oil spilt, he went straight to the committee room. He stood on tiptoes to look through that high window to check that no one was inside. Then he opened the door, used the secret mechanism to hide the booty and made good his escape back out through the store. I'm sure he would have preferred to go through to the bar to take whatever was in the cashbox, too. Only he couldn't because the bar was still full. He seemed a bit put out when we asked him about that. He was probably hoping no one would think of it.'

'He'd reckoned without you, what?' said Sir Hector.

'You're very kind,' she said. 'With the trophy hidden, he left a trail out onto the grass, with his footsteps leading off towards the lane. For all anyone would know, the burglar had headed back into the village.'

'Except he left more of a trail than he bargained for,' said Sir Hector.

'He did. When Armstrong and I took another look at those prints in the early morning light, we discovered that they turned around and led back into the shed. The thief had not made good his escape, but had instead returned to the club house. We searched the shed, where I confess I expected to find the loot hidden in some dark corner, but instead we found only the stolen boots. Clearly our thief had changed back into his own shoes, but why would he do that? Why return to the shed in his stolen boots? Why not get away and change the boots later? It seemed to me much more likely that if he had put his own shoes back on, he was returning to the party. He must have committed his theft during the festivities.'

'Well, I'll be blowed,' said Sir Hector.

'It was the absence of the loot from the shed that rang the alarm bells. If the thief had come back to the gathering and hidden his boots, surely he would have hidden the trophies in the store to be retrieved and sold later. A former petty criminal like Lofty Trevellian – or someone like Ackley trying to "put a few more bob in his pocket" – would want to be certain of being able to lay their hands on the valuables later. It would be no good hiding them outside – some passing vagabond might find them – so they would want to keep them hidden somewhere safe.'

'But they didn't hide them,' said the inspector. 'So you thought that maybe there was something else going on.'

'I did, but I confess I had no idea what. It was Armstrong who worked it all out.'

'It had been nagging at me for some time that the two sides of the fireplace are so very different,' I said. 'On the left, the bookshelves are deep – far too deep for the books they have on them. They've even got room to double some of them up. While over on the right, they have a trophy case with shallow shelves. There's barely enough room to hold the Wessex Cup. It seemed odd that the niches should be so different, so I wondered if there might be something behind the cabinet.'

'Something like a mechanism to make the shelves disappear,' said the inspector.

'Something very much like that, yes. I saw in the club diaries that Jester Dunleavy liked to pinch other clubs' trophies, and then when Sir Hector told us that Dunleavy was a designer for stage magicians, I just sort of put two and two together.'

'Brava,' said Sir Hector. 'These gels are remarkable, Gertie, m'dear, what?'

'Quite remarkable,' said Lady Farley-Stroud.

'What made you so certain it wasn't Trevellian, though?' asked the inspector.

'The footprints,' said Lady Hardcastle. 'Size twelve boots indicate a tall man. Lofty Trevellian is well over six feet tall, and we now know that those were his boots. Ackley is quite tall, too. I imagine the boots would be about his size, as well.'

'Which would seem to indicate that it was one of them,' said the inspector.

'It would,' she said. 'I was stuck on that for a good long time. I felt so utterly, utterly foolish when I realized that the most important clue had been on the floor outside the room all along. It was one of the first things we saw. The burglar stood on tiptoes to look through the window. We could see the prints most clearly on the passage floor where he had turned, raised himself up, and then doubled back to enter the room. He wasn't a tall man, at all. He was a short man wearing big boots.'

'So by that reasoning, it had to be Tribley or Meaker, the two shorter men,' he said.

'Exactly so. It was when I made the connection with Winnie Marsh that it all fell into place. Armstrong said the farmers had been talking about "Dennis Marsh's daughter" when she overheard them in the Dog and Duck one day.'

'It's all a bit circumstantial,' said the inspector as he wrote. 'I'm not sure there's anything we can charge him with, either. Still, it all fits together and it helps to paint a pretty good picture.'

'Well done, ladies,' said Lady Farley-Stroud. 'Hector! More brandy!'

It was early evening by the time we declined their kind offer of a lift home.

'It's fine, darling,' said Lady Hardcastle, kissing our hosts goodbye. 'It's a pleasant evening and the walk will do us good.'

We walked down the hill and back to the house. There was a small parcel on the doorstep.

'We ought to write to Jasper Laxton and ask him to name his house, you know,' said Lady Hardcastle as we removed our outerwear in the hall. 'We can't really go on calling it "The House" but since we're only renting the place it doesn't seem right to name it ourselves.'

'What would you call it, my lady?' I said, hanging up her coat.

'Oh, I don't know. "Dunspyin"?'

I laughed. 'I'm not sure Mr Laxton would approve.'

'No, dear, I don't suppose he would. Then again, he's in India so it would be simply ages before he found out.'

'I think "The House" will have to do for now, then, my lady. Will you be wanting any supper?'

'Oh, I hadn't thought. Perhaps some more sandwiches? Would you be a pet and make us some while I find out what's in this parcel?'

She followed me into the kitchen, picking at the string that fastened the package.

After some fiddling and a healthy amount of colourful swearing, she managed to remove the string and brown paper to reveal a sturdy cardboard box. She lifted the lid and there, wrapped in tissue paper, was a leather driving helmet and a pair of expensive-looking goggles. She took out the note that had been lying on top of the strange gift.

'Dear Sis,' she read aloud. 'How the devil are you, old girl? Sorry I've not been down to see you, but how about we put that right? I hear by the clothes-line telegraph that you've recently taken up driving. It just so happens that my old chum Fishy Codrington is a bit of a devotee of the automotive arts himself. Guess what! He's built himself a racing circuit. You've heard of Brooklands? Well, it's nothing quite so grand as that, but it gave him the idea, and he's paved over half the family estate in Rutland to make a course for him and his chums. He's invited me along for a few days and he said I could bring a guest. Do you fancy it? Obviously you can bring whatshername and we can all have a jolly time together. You might need the enclosed – I told Fishy you were both excellent drivers. Reply soonest. All my love, Harry.'

She held up the helmet and goggles.

'Good old Harry,' I said. 'Do you fancy it? I'd been hoping we might get to the seaside, but this certainly sounds like fun.'

'Just the sort of fun we need,' she said, the glint of competition in her eye. 'I'll write back at once. And after that, cards. We haven't played cards for simply ever.'

'Right you are, my lady.'

'And more brandy. We can't possibly play cards without brandy.'

I laughed. 'Is there anything we can do without brandy?'

'Very little, I find, very little.'

About the Author

T E Kinsey grew up in London and read history at Bristol University. He worked for a number of years as a magazine features writer before falling into the glamorous world of the Internet, where he edited content for a very famous entertainment website for quite a few years more. After helping to raise three children, learning to scuba dive and to play the drums and the mandolin (though never, disappointingly, all at the same time), he decided the time was right to get back to writing. *In the Market for Murder* is the second in a series of mysteries starring Lady Hardcastle.

You can follow him on Twitter – @tekinsey – and also find him on Facebook: www.facebook.com/tekinsey.